Dear Readers,

One of the nicest things about the Bouquet line is the burgeoning of a multitude of brand-new blossoms we're cultivating in our newly seeded garden of love. Four of them have burst into bloom this month, just in time for a fabulous fall flowering.

Take a woman hiding, under an assumed name, in a small Maine town, and a man hiding from life itself; add the rescue of a couple of cute kids, and you have Wendy Morgan's debut romance, **Loving Max.**

Grab a bikini and head for the tropics. Roast beef meets tofu when flower child Tasha and button-down salesman Andrew Powell III meet at a singles resort in Maddie James's rollicking romance, **Crazy For You.** Then, in Michaila Callan's **Love Me Tender**, travel to small-town Texas, where Eden Karr employs a handsome carpenter to redesign her boutique . . . and gets a new design for living and loving as well! Finally, fly to faraway, fantastical Caldonia, where New York magazine editor Nicole is hired to find a queen for handsome Prince Rand—before the end of the year—in **The Prince's Bride** by Tracy Cozzens. Will his coach turn into a pumpkin before her mission is accomplished . . . or will love find a way?

Speaking of pumpkins, we'll be back next month with four splendid new Bouquet romances—in brilliant fall colors. Look for us!

The Editors

## "DO YOU EVER STOP THINKING, NICOLE?"

"Uh-uh." She shook her head. "Too much to do." Her eyes fluttered and drifted closed. She mumbled and he had to strain to hear. "Thank you for helping me, Rand. It means a lot to me."

"And to me," he whispered, settling his hand on hers. She didn't reply. He watched the even rise and fall of her chest and knew she'd fallen asleep. Still, he couldn't bring himself to leave her. He had blocked out this time, until five, for the picnic. For once he had nowhere else to be.

As he gazed at her face, so innocent in repose, an amazing sense of wonder filled him. He could hardly remember what life had been like before she'd arrived at the palace.

The tempting situation defeated his noble intentions. He would never have another chance. Praying he wouldn't wake Sleeping Beauty, the prince leaned close and gave her a gentle kiss on the mouth.

# THE PRINCE'S BRIDE

## TRACY COZZENS

Zebra Books
Kensington Publishing Corp.

http://www.zebrabooks.com

For my critique partner Nicole, the heroine who helped me get there; for my husband Steve, my own prince; and for my son Kellen—my inspiration.

ZEBRA BOOKS are published by

Kensington Publishing Corp.
850 Third Avenue
New York, NY 10022

First Printing: October, 1999
10 9 8 7 6 5 4 3 2 1

Printed in the United States of America

# ONE

*New York*

"You want me to do *what* for Prince Rand?" Nicole Aldridge's smile froze as she stared in astonishment at her uncle.

Now that he'd voiced his outlandish proposal, Uncle Phillip relaxed in the chair across the desk from her. He settled his cane against the wall behind him and repositioned his old-fashioned bowler on his lap. "Dear Nicole, you are the perfect person to help the prince find a suitable bride. You will be serving your homeland in a time of great need."

He made it sound as if he wanted her to take up arms for Caldonia. According to palace insiders, the king and queen were frustrated enough to declare war. Their only heir, now thirty-six, still hadn't married.

Lord Phillip Aldridge gazed pointedly around Nicole's cluttered Tenth Avenue office. Framed covers of past magazine issues adorned the walls, each illustrating a major feature she had written for *Aristocrats*. More than one showed Prince Rand.

Nicole knew Uncle Phillip did not respect her decision to pursue a career. Caldonians took pride in their old-fashioned values, in staying one step behind the rest of the world. No doubt her uncle believed she should have married and settled down in Caldonia—and become a happy homemaker.

Instead, she had not only abandoned her homeland, she lived in loud, bustling New York City. Worse, she worked for a magazine that profited from sharing the private lives of royals like the Hollingsworths of Caldonia.

Uncle Phillip waved his pudgy hand. "Surely, during this time of emergency, you can see your way to leave this—this—"

"It's called a magazine, Uncle," Nicole said dryly. *"Aristocrats* is a well-respected publication, not a sleazy tabloid. I've even won a few writing awards."

Uncle Phillip stroked the brim of his bowler. "Yes, your dedication to work is one reason I suggested you for the position, dear. And you are familiar with the ways of the rich and titled. You know many of them personally, including eligible ladies, don't you?"

Nicole picked up a pencil from her desk and began fiddling with it. "Well, yes, I've interviewed dozens over the years for features I've written. But you're asking me to be a matchmaker! I don't have any experience in that area. I've never even *been* married, so how you can expect that I'd—"

Uncle Phillip raised his thick gray eyebrows. "I'm not asking you to act as a traditional matchmaker, dear. Merely as a—what's that word so popular here in America—a consultant. Yes, a consultant—that's what the prince said. Your task will be to find Prince Randall Hollingsworth the ideal wife. That accomplished, you may return to your little job."

Nicole bristled inwardly at Uncle Phillip's narrow view of her life. It wasn't that pointless. After all, she *did* help satisfy people's curiosity about how the royals lived.

Besides, to try to find Prince Rand the *ideal wife* . . . Such a woman didn't exist. Everyone with any inside knowledge *knew* that Prince Rand loved his freedom—especially where women were concerned. Almost every month, *Aristocrats* ran a photo of him parading some high-toned beauty on his arm—and never the same woman twice.

"So how does the prince feel about this plan?" Nicole asked, tapping her pencil rhythmically on the desk.

"Quite simply, it was his idea."

"*His* idea?" This was a scoop of massive proportions. Nicole could already envision the cover headline:

### PRINCE RAND SHOPS FOR WIFE
#### RANDY PRINCE MAKES PLANS
#### TO SETTLE DOWN

Rather than writing the story this time, however, she'd be on the inside, helping to make it. Helping to determine her country's future. The thought stirred up memories and feelings she'd long forced to the background.

Distracted, she allowed the pencil to slide from her fingers. It began rolling toward the edge of the desk. She caught it and dropped it in the desk drawer, then forced herself to clasp her hands neatly on her blotter.

"When he suggested hiring a consultant to help him find his princess," Phillip said, "I immediately thought of you. It's an excellent opportunity for you to return home, dear. After I mentioned you to him, it was agreed you should be interviewed for the post."

Nicole arched her eyebrows. "Oh, and I had no say in this decision?" The royal family was known for its decrees.

Uncle Phillip cocked his head and stared at her. "Dear, it's for the good of Caldonia."

She could almost hear the Caldonian National Anthem playing grandly in the background.

Uncle Phillip continued. "Royals from other countries have endured scandal, as I'm sure you're aware. All those divorces and affairs." He waved his hand in disgust. "A miserable business, simply miserable. Not like the old days, when people respected the throne."

Nicole chose not to comment on that generalization.

"Prince Randall has determined not to make the same mistake, despite being pressured by King Edbert to marry with all expedience. With the proper forethought, we can locate the perfect wife for our prince, I'm certain of it. And you're the perfect girl for the job."

She shook her head. All of this was too sudden. How was *she* supposed to find the prince a wife? "But how—"

"You will figure that out, dear. Of that, I have no doubt." He rose, apparently satisfied that their interview was at an end. He held out his hand.

Nicole couldn't deny a tingle of excitement at the prospect. To be on the inside of a royal family, for once; to see how one worked, instead of merely interviewing them . . . Maybe someday she would even get permission to write a book about her experience.

But to be employed by the Randy Prince, of all people . . . Everything inside her reacted negatively to such an idea. She shook her head, regretting that she had to disappoint Uncle Phillip. "I—I can't, Uncle."

"What?" Phillip retracted his hand and returned to the leather chair across from her desk. "How can you say no, Nicole, when your country needs you so desperately? You were always such a good girl, so bright and full of promise—"

"He's not the kind of man I want to work with," she blurted out.

Not surprisingly, Uncle Phillip looked appalled at such a disloyal statement. "How can you say that about your prince? Regardless of what kind of man he is, he *is* your prince, Nicole. Someday he will be your king." He waved his hand in the general direction of Manhattan. "You haven't been completely absorbed by this—this frantic American culture, have you? Please tell me it isn't so. You *do* still consider yourself a Caldonian citizen."

"Of course, Uncle. But Prince Rand—he's so, so—" She faltered, knowing if she elaborated she would be digging herself an even deeper hole with Uncle Phillip, who was a hereditary member of the House of Lords and the torchbearer for all that was Caldonian.

Phillip waited expectantly for her to finish her sentence. She had to say something. She sucked in a breath and forged ahead. "Prince Rand has a reputation, Uncle. He's frivolous, superficial, and far too handsome for his own good. As far as I can tell, he's done nothing for his country except enjoy his wealth and privilege. I don't think he relates to the common people at all."

Uncle Phillip gazed at her speculatively. "Most people in Caldonia believe the prince is doing as he should, carrying on the traditions of our country."

"Traditions?" Nicole almost laughed out loud. Caldonia was mired in traditions, many of which were completely useless. If that's all the prince cared about, she had even less respect for him than before. "The royal family stays so far removed from the people that they have no idea what the country wants or needs. I don't find that very impressive."

Despite her disrespectful words, Uncle Phillip's mouth turned up in a wry smile. "I'm offering you an opportunity to influence a man in a high position—a man you seem to believe needs to be shown the error of his ways. Yet you would turn it down." He shook his head dolefully. "This doesn't seem to be the same scrappy girl who told off the King's Chamberlain because the ladies' restroom was in the basement of the House of Lords. Remember that, Nicole? It thoroughly embarrassed me, but I understood why you were so upset. You always seemed to have others' best interests at heart. That is why I expected you would serve your country someday."

*Instead of desert.* The unspoken statement hung in the air between them.

Nicole sighed, uncomfortable with the memories flowing over her. Uncle Phillip didn't have to remind her how badly her parents had wanted her to stay in Caldonia and attend college there. But she had wanted a real education. She'd had no interest in attending the finishing schools that masqueraded as women's colleges in Caldonia. The universities where the real learning took place were still only open to men.

Her father—a professor at one such university—encouraged her to stay and try to change the school admission rules. Filled with youthful fire, she'd planned to do just that—until the night her parents had driven away, heading for a faculty function, and never had come home. On one of Caldonia's many narrow, poorly marked highways, they were killed by a drunk driver. More than once, she'd blamed Caldonia itself for their deaths—for its leniency toward drunk drivers, for its lack of highway maintenance. For everything. Uncle Phillip had served as her guardian during her last year of public school, but she'd come to America as soon as she could get away.

She gazed around her office, at the comfortable, if cluttered, life she had built for herself in New York—and back at her staid, concerned Uncle Phillip, who represented the heritage she'd turned her back on.

In truth, her dream hadn't been all that sweet for a long time. For the past few years, she'd found herself wondering whether she'd made the right choices after all—spending her time and energy producing nothing more valuable than a few hours of entertainment for people fascinated by the wealthy and titled.

"A wife can have a strong influence on a man," Uncle Phillip said. "If you were to help him find a suitable woman, perhaps he would change his ways."

"I suppose that's true," Nicole said slowly, feeling her inner defenses begin to crumble. Yet to face her memories, to return to the country she both hated and loved, to work for the government she blamed—

Phillip's voice turned coaxing. "I know you still love your homeland, Nicole. You understand what seeing the prince properly wed will mean to our country."

"Yes, of course, but—"

"Your parents honored the royal family, Nicole," he said gently. "They would have been so proud."

Nicole blinked hard, trying to rein in the emotions his words stirred. Yes, if her parents were still alive, they would have been thrilled to see her employed by the Hollingsworths. In such a capacity, she might finally have the opportunity to influence Caldonia for the better.

Before she'd completely realized it, Nicole made her decision. She stood and extended her hand. "All right, Uncle. I'll try."

Uncle Phillip clasped her hand warmly. "Excellent, Nicole. I knew I could count on you. I told the prince you wouldn't turn down this opportunity." He smiled broadly. "I've secured us tickets on the eleven o'clock flight tomorrow."

"Tomorrow! But I have—"

"What is more important? Publishing photos of aristocrats or saving Caldonia?"

Nicole sighed and shook her head. Put like that, she had to agree. Maybe she could tell her boss it was a family emergency. Of king-size proportions.


*Fortinbleaux, Caldonia*


"Well, have you thought about what I said?" King Edbert sat in his antique, overstuffed chair and glared at his tall son, his thick brows drawn into a scowl.

"Yes, of course, I have," Prince Rand said, irritated that his father thought he even had to ask. The king had only threatened to destroy his dreams, after all.

"You only have eight months," the king said. "Your role is to carry on the line. The people expect it! You have no siblings, so you must stop wasting time and get to it."

Rand's stomach began to churn, and he thought longingly of the antacid bottle in his desk. It was on the other end of the castle, in his own wing—a world away.

Yes, he'd reconciled himself to the necessity of meeting his parents' demands. He had little choice. But to be forced to find a wife when he had yet to meet a woman he wanted to share his life with—

"I know you, Randall," the king said darkly. "You won't enjoy what I can do to you."

The king's arrogance grated on Rand. His father knew nothing of his secret work. He didn't even begin to suspect.

Rand had been far too careful. Which made his father's assumptions all the more galling.

"You won't be happy without your allowance," the king continued. "Mark my words, you'll be reduced to penury for all but the basic necessities if you don't find yourself a suitable wife before the year is out. You'll have no staff. No decision in what charities you support. No role in the government. No more expensive trips, no more sailboats, no ski vacations in the Alps. Nothing but what I give you directly."

"I understand." Rand forced the words through his tight jaw. He hadn't taken time for such expensive diversions for several years. Long before that, he'd grown bored with them. Bored and lonely and disconsolate. Fed up with his parents, with the staid, stiff way they governed their country, with his own inability to make a difference.

Until he'd struck on a solution. His allowance was enabling him to put his plans into motion. But he wasn't about to explain this to his father—a man who had never once considered his son's thoughts, or his feelings, even when the prince had been a little boy and cried in the night.

Rand had been terrified of the dark nursery, of the vast ceiling high above, of the windows that stretched tall enough to let in monsters. The king hadn't wanted Rand's nanny to comfort him; he said it would weaken the boy's character. He'd only hired nannies who toed the line, even if they didn't share his strict views.

If it hadn't been for those few kind women who had secretly shown him caring and compassion—before they were dismissed—Rand might not have learned what love could be. Certainly not through the example of his parents' marriage. Which is why having a woman forced on him in a loveless match disgusted him.

Coldness seemed to be the Hollingsworth curse. A curse Rand feared he would never escape.

He turned from where his father held court in his antique chair; then he looked through the balcony doors toward the verdant hills and the capital city sprawling below.

For the past year, he'd been attempting to lay the ground-work for his country's future—something his father didn't have the interest or the energy to do.

Now, just when the pieces were about to come together into a meaningful whole, Rand was forced to expend energy in this search for a suitable wife—and try not to lose everything he'd worked for in the process.

If only he could escape, even for a little while. Get away to some place where he could concentrate on his important tasks, break free of the restraints centuries of tradition had wrapped around him. His thoughts began to drift into the future, into his own plans to make Caldonia a prosperous player in the modern world, not a relic of a bygone era.

His mother's strident voice shattered his daydreams. "Well? Has he agreed?"

Reluctantly, Rand turned back around. Queen Eurydice walked rapidly across the polished parquet floor in her sensible shoes and stood before the king—her husband, if one could call theirs a marriage. They were rarely seen in the same room, except on state occasions. They had maintained separate apartments from the day they had wed. Few Caldonians found this odd, for the queen had fulfilled her main purpose years ago by giving birth to Rand. The fact his parents were together now only showed how critical they both thought it was for him to carry on the line.

"You must make him agree," the queen said, her tight-lipped expression and old-fashioned chignon making a once beautiful face appear old before its time.

"I have agreed," Rand said coolly, feeling as if he'd just signed his life away.

The queen nodded. "Excellent. I knew you would see sense. Since not a single one of the ladies I have suggested to you over the years has met with your approval, you are free to find your own bride, as long as she is titled, well bred, and of noble stock, as the law demands. You should thank me that I didn't arrange a marriage for you before now."

"I'm arranging my own," he said dryly. "You've left me little choice."

"What do you mean?" the queen asked.

"I'm hiring help," he announced, "a consultant to assist me in finding the right wife."

"A consultant!" the king said. "Is this more of your nonsense, boy? I won't have it."

"You *will* have it." Rand tamped down a flare of anger, his temper straining the tenuous bonds of his self-control. In the past year, he had learned that strong emotion had no place in negotiating business—which was exactly what was taking place. "She's going to help me do precisely what you want me to do, so I suggest you not try to fight me on this."

*"She?"* the queen asked, her lips tightening. "Who is this woman?"

Rand's stomach churned and he longed for an antacid. He turned toward the windows again, his gaze not on the expansive view, but on his muddy future. He hoped this woman would be as promised—as energetic and resourceful as Lord Phillip had led him to believe.

If not, he would have precious few options left.

"Well, son?" the king demanded. "Answer your queen. Who is she?"

When he finally answered, he spoke more to himself than to his parents. "The one who will save me."

# TWO

"Remember when I brought you here as a girl, Nicole?" Uncle Phillip asked as the limousine drew closer and the royal palace appeared through the trees.

"I could never forget that," Nicole said, unable to tear her eyes from the sand-colored edifice. "You wanted me to absorb the great events of Caldonian history, and I just wanted to run through the halls, annoying the guards."

"I expect this time you'll show a tad more respect," Uncle Phillip said, chuckling.

Nicole smiled at him. She had been unprepared for the magnitude of emotion that welled inside her the moment she'd stepped from the plane onto Caldonian soil. In that confusing instant, she'd wanted to kiss the ground in joy at once again seeing her country's vineyard-covered hills, crystal-clear lakes, and distant mountain peaks.

And she'd wanted to cry because almost nothing had changed. The twisting roads were as ill maintained as before, the signs still inaccurate or missing. As if Caldonia wanted to keep strangers from feeling too comfortable.

Their chauffeur turned the limousine into the private drive. The Caldonian Royal Palace was nestled in rolling foothills ten miles from town in its own thousand-acre park. It had been built as a castle in the eleventh century, and improvements and additions had continued over the years until the twentieth century, when national policy had first begun to favor the old over the new. Nicole knew that modern plumbing had only been installed forty years ago, and it was restricted to the living and business sections.

As she gazed at the palace, her chest constricted with emotion—why, she couldn't say. True, the three-story, turreted monument to Caldonia's love of the antiquated represented the heart of Caldonia and its spirit. Its beauty could easily distract a person, she reminded herself sternly. Make her forget there were serious problems with this country and its government, problems that affected real people.

Problems that Prince Rand ignored.

She had received approval to take a leave of absence from the magazine in case the prince hired her. She was beginning to hope he would, so she could finally do her part to help her country. Once that was accomplished, she'd be on the next plane back to New York.

She accepted the chauffeur's hand as she stepped out of the car and onto the curving drive. She smoothed her suit skirt and gazed up, unsure where to look first because there was so much to take in. So much to remember.

As always, four uniformed guards stood in pairs on either side of the entrance portico's immense quadruple doors. A dozen flags fluttered in the crisp mountain air along the portico's roof. The center and largest flag bore the familiar golden lion on a green field.

"Exquisite, isn't it?" Uncle Phillip came around the car and joined her in gazing at the palace. "I truly should come here more often. It gives one a sense of belonging that's easy to forget in all the hustle and bustle."

Nicole smiled at his pointed remark, knowing he was referring to her own cosmopolitan life. Phillip, Baron of Duprenia, didn't even live in Fortinbleaux, the capital city. He kept to his country estate, except when called by tradition to take part in the formalities of the House of Lords, where he held a hereditary seat hundreds of years old.

Though his younger brother, Nicole's father, had been nothing more than a college professor, she hadn't minded her family's lack of title. Until her parents' deaths, she had been blessed with a wonderful childhood.

Once inside, she and Phillip followed a green-uniformed palace butler down the ornate hallway toward the prince's private apartments. On the way, Nicole gazed in awe at the majesty around her, seeing it for the first time through an appreciative adult's eyes. True, Caldonia could barely be seen on a map of Europe. But it didn't lack for pride.

National treasures were displayed with great care throughout the white-marbled entry hall. Paintings of the tranquil Caldonian countryside hung on the ornately painted, papered, and molding-embellished walls. Glass cases held swords, urns, dishes and other artifacts from throughout the centuries of Caldonian history.

They took a left turn, then a right into the huge Hall of Ancestors. Nicole wished she had more time to examine the paintings. As a ten year old on tour, she hadn't paid much attention to the details. Now she saw the past kings and queens in a new light. If she actually found the prince his wife, she would be helping to decide the future of the kingdom—and the face of the queen whose portrait would hang in the empty space beside his.

She paused before the last painting, one of Rand himself. The portrait artist had placed him in polo clothes, beside a proud chestnut mount.

"He does enjoy a rousing game of polo," Phillip said beside her. "However, I do not believe playing polo will be a requirement of his future mate."

"No," Nicole murmured, her gaze absorbing the familiar features of the man in question. His face bore the audacious attractiveness which made him a gold mine for *Aristocrats*—high cheekbones, ebony hair, and dark, expressive eyes. And that arrogant expression—as if he ruled the world. To find such a man a wife . . . Thousands of women around the world would jump at the chance to marry Prince Rand, but Nicole had a strong feeling he would not be easy to live with.

And he might be just as hard to work with.

"You're here! Welcome to Caldonia, miss." A jovial gentleman who appeared to be in his fifties approached them from a pair of gilded white doors to the right.

"Nicole, this is Gerald Simpson, Prince Rand's personal secretary."

She stepped forward and clasped his hand. "I recognize your name. I'm very pleased to meet you."

"Excellent of you to come all this way, to help us with our little . . . shall we say, challenge?" Gerald chuckled, his eyes crinkling attractively. Nicole couldn't help but smile back. He seemed a very likable fellow.

After small talk about their trip, and Phillip's success in bringing Nicole back with him, Phillip begged another appointment. "I shall leave you in Gerald's most capable hands."

"Thank you, Uncle," Nicole said. "I'll call you as soon as I know."

"Know?" Phillip asked.

"Whether I have the post."

"Ah, of course. Well, good-bye, Nicole, Gerald." Phillip squeezed her hand. "You'll do fine, dear. Relax and be yourself." He turned and began retracing his steps through the palace with the butler.

"This way, Miss Aldridge." Gerald crossed to the tall doors he'd entered through and opened the one on the left. He gestured her through, and Nicole found herself in yet another hallway.

After several minutes of walking, they approached a massive pair of doors, above which hung the royal crest. A green-coated guard swung the door wide for them, then clicked his heels together smartly.

Beyond lay a luxurious sitting room. Heavy antique sofas fronted a fire crackling cheerily against one wall, probably to supplement the drafty palace's antiquated heating system. Broad windows overlooked a garden filled with spring blooms.

"You must wait here, miss," Gerald said, "until you're

summoned. I am hopeful the wait won't be long, however. I keep Prince Rand on a fairly tight schedule."

"I don't mind waiting. This room is beautiful."

Gerald smiled. "That's the spirit, miss." He crossed to the far wall and disappeared through another set of double doors, but didn't latch the door behind him.

Nicole pondered Gerald's puzzling statement as she took a seat near the fireplace and stared at the huge grandfather clock near the door.

Nearly two hours later, she knew exactly what Gerald had meant. Seven times she'd heard the damned thing chime, and still she sat waiting, fiddling with her purse, rechecking her makeup in her compact, peering through the crack in the door into the inner sanctum beyond. Almost two hours waiting for the prince to summon her.

Nicole wondered what sort of appointment kept him. Knowing his reputation as well as she did, she realized it couldn't be anything serious, which only made her wait all the more aggravating.

This morning, she'd taken great care with her appearance, selecting a conservative taupe suit even the prince's mother, the stodgy Queen Eurydice, would approve of. Nicole had styled her shoulder-length brunette hair into a sensible French roll. She'd also decided on her large glasses rather than contacts, since she thought they made her look intelligent.

She wanted the prince to know she intended to work hard at this job, if he gave it to her, despite the unique nature of the assignment.

She sighed. The way the prince was treating her didn't give her much hope of being taken seriously. Caldonia was notorious for its backward view of a woman's place in the world. The idea of a woman working outside the home was still frowned upon by most of the citizenry—or at least by the men, who held the reins of power.

Which made her wonder why the prince would consider hiring her at all.

She heard a door slam in the inner room. She sat up straighter and smoothed her skirt.

Gerald's voice floated through the door, sounding slightly distressed. "Your Highness, you're running behind schedule by almost two hours. Miss Nicole Aldridge is waiting for you. After that, you must get ready for tonight's reception with the diplomats from England and Austria."

"Who?"

"The diplomats—"

"Not *them.*"

Nicole recognized the prince's voice from news shows—strong and imperious. He was actually in the other room, only a few feet away. Despite his reputation—or perhaps because of it—the other women at the magazine would kill to be in her shoes right now.

As a loyal Caldonian, she respected the prince's position. But she had more sense than to get absurdly excited at the prospect of meeting him. She sucked in a breath and tried valiantly to steady her nerves. Cool and professional. That was how she wanted to appear.

"This woman. Who is she?" she heard him ask.

"The consultant from America," Gerald patiently explained. "The one who might help you find your bride, Your Highness."

"Ah! That one. She's here now? I'd completely forgotten she was coming today. My racquet snapped, of all things. Held up the match for some time."

His *racquet?* Nicole frowned. Apparently, while she'd been cooling her heels waiting for him, he'd been playing a few relaxing games!

"A shame, Your Highness. Wasn't that racquet your favorite?"

"Yes, and it took forever to find a decent graphite replacement. They tried to give me an old-style wooden one. Well, don't keep the girl waiting," Prince Rand said. "Send her in."

"But—"

"Gerald, you just said we don't have all day. Let's get this business under way, if we're going to do it at all."

"Yes, Your Highness."

Gerald reappeared through the door. "This way, miss. I apologize for the wait. The prince was . . . delayed."

Nicole rose. She couldn't keep the irony from her voice. "I'm sure."

She met Gerald's gaze, but he appeared impassive. She wondered if the prince's irresponsible behavior had irritated him as well.

He led her into the prince's office, a mahogany-lined, very male domain. Still, the tall windows let in considerable light, and the suite's decor appeared quite modern compared to the strict traditionalism she'd noticed in other parts of the palace.

A sitting area with an emerald brocade sofa and chairs fronted another fireplace, also lit. Its marble mantel held sailing and polo trophies. An eighteenth-century architectural drawing of the Parthenon hung on the wall above.

"Your Highness, this is Miss Nicole Elizabeth Aldridge of New York," Gerald intoned.

Nicole turned toward the prince. She'd seen his image a thousand times, in a thousand different settings, a thousand outfits. Now, he was real, and photos didn't do him justice.

Despite the dispassionate expression on his aristocratic features, his dark eyes shone with intensity as he silently examined her from head to toe. The angles of his face were even more pronounced than she realized, his features almost severe—and definitely compelling.

His presence seemed to fill the room, commanding attention. Whether this came naturally to him, or had been trained into him, the effect was the same—more powerful than she had ever imagined.

Her gaze slid over his muscular bare legs and arms. She couldn't help noticing how well his dark coloring contrasted with his white shirt and shorts. Despite having seen photos of him engaged in almost every sport imaginable, she had *not* pictured him wearing tennis whites when they met.

She had to remind herself how irritated she was with him for making her wait. Still, she knew better than to let him see her true feelings. She curtsied as well as she could in her suit skirt. "Your Highness, it's an honor to be called on to serve you."

Prince Rand dismissed her practiced gesture with a wave of his hand. "Yes, well, that's entirely unnecessary. Now make yourself comfortable so we can get on with this affair."

He gestured to the green-and-gold wingback chair before his desk, and Nicole slipped into it. His casual demeanor stunned her. Where was the protocol, the ten minutes' worth of obsequious posturing that should have been expected of her as a lowly citizen?

She couldn't shake the feeling she'd walked into the wrong office and stumbled on a Prince Rand look-alike. Still, she carefully crossed her ankles and tucked them under the chair in the ladylike posture her mother had taught her.

Rand didn't seem to notice either her manners or her confusion. He moved behind his desk and sat in his black leather chair, then propped a foot on an open desk drawer. He leaned way back in his chair, his fingers entwined in his lap. "Gerald, I can take it from here."

"Yes, Your Highness. If you need anything—"

"Right."

Gerald crossed to another door and disappeared through it, shutting it behind him.

Nicole barely noticed Gerald's departure. Rand's cool gaze had fastened on her. She stared back, knowing etiquette demanded that she wait for him to speak first. Not that this man seemed concerned with etiquette, she thought as her gaze swept over his casual posture.

"So you're the one Phillip has been going on about—his niece who lives in America. I admit I'm glad you came, though it's unfortunate it has come to this. Do you think you can do it?"

"Certainly," Nicole began, starting to pitch her skills. "In fact, I—"

"Wait. There's one thing . . ." He swung his chair upright with a bang. He slid open the top desk drawer and glanced inside, then shoved it closed and moved on to the next drawer.

"I promise to do my best, Your Highness, but I admit I have never done this before," Nicole continued, nonplussed by his behavior.

The prince didn't reply. Nicole wondered if he'd even heard her since he looked so distracted. He slammed the second drawer and opened the third. "Damn, where did I put that thing?" He hit the intercom button. "Gerald, where's that thing—"

"On the bookcase to your left, Your Highness."

The prince turned his chair and glanced over his shoulder. "Ah! He's right. He's always right." He rolled over and lifted a magazine from the stack, then began flipping through it.

Nicole stared at his broad back, trying to figure out what was going on. She would never in a thousand years have pictured Prince Rand as absentminded. Perhaps international terrorists had stolen the real prince and supplanted him with this one? She shifted in her chair and recrossed her ankles.

"Here it is!" He swung around with a copy of *Aristocrats*. Opening the magazine, he showed her a spread with a two-page photo of Rand at a charity function, with Lady Joanna of England on his arm. The headline screamed:

## PRINCE RAND STILL SOWING WILD OATS

"You wrote this, didn't you?" he asked.

Nicole's chest tightened and she felt a blush coming on. Her byline stood out from the page in eighteen-point type. Yes, she'd written it, and he knew damned well she had.

In the whirlwind of Uncle Phillip's visit and his unexpected offer of a job, she had completely forgotten the year-old article. An opinion column about Prince Rand's social life.

"Yes, Your Highness, but it was so long ago, I don't think—"

"Let me refresh your memory." Prince Rand turned the magazine back around and began to read. " 'Throughout vast changes wrought by the centuries, Caldonia stands as a shining example of stagnation, of a country unable to face the challenges of the new millennium. Take, for example, her royal family, which proudly traces its bloodline back to the fifth century. . . .' and so on and so on." Rand waved his hand in the air.

He began scanning the article while Nicole fidgeted, remembering now what she'd written, knowing he was about to come across it.

"Ah! Here's the passage," Rand continued. "I should have marked it. 'Prince Rand, heir to the throne, is bucking tradition. Of all the heirs, he is the only one who did not marry before age thirty. Perhaps he is too enamored of his playboy lifestyle to settle down? Meanwhile, Caldonians wait and worry. Will the line die out with the Randy Prince?' "

Rand closed the magazine and stared at her. "Randy Prince. Clever turn of phrase."

Nicole felt her blush deepen, yet she lifted her chin. She had coined that phrase, and it had stuck like glue to Prince Rand in every bit of copy published about him since. Is this why she'd been brought here, for a personal tongue-lashing? "Excuse me, Your Highness, but I didn't mean any—"

"Do you have any idea of the furor those words caused?"

Nicole sat stiffly, ready to defend herself "I only wrote the truth," she replied coolly.

Rand arched an eyebrow. "Ah. The truth. You journalists always say that, but you don't know the first thing about it. When my father was so blatantly reminded that he and all his predecessors were married before age thirty, whereas

I've had the good sense to wait, my God, the roof could have caved in on the palace and he wouldn't have been any more furious."

That was what this was about—not the "Randy Prince" phrase? Nicole gradually sucked in a breath, amazed and hopeful that it was so.

"That's why you're here." He flipped through the magazine. "You know all these—these women you feature in here. Titled women from countries around the globe. Your job is to find me one that I can live with in a reasonable state of happiness."

"Excuse me, but" —she knew she was risking royal wrath in questioning his decision—"if I've angered you, why would you hire me?"

His gaze whipped up to meet hers, his eyes widening in surprise. For a long moment, he gazed at her, his dark eyes assessing, his expression contemplative. Slowly, he closed the magazine, set it aside, and stood up. Moving in front of his desk, he stared down at her.

Only then did she realize she'd taken the impertinent liberty of forgoing the proper address. "I mean, Your Highness," she quickly added. Her stomach fluttered, and she wondered if she were about to be dismissed.

To her relief, she saw a trace of amusement in his eyes. His well-shaped lips turned up crookedly, and Nicole felt the warmth of his gaze travel every inch of her body. She grew undeniably aware of how his tennis shirt stretched over his broad chest, and how strong and well-toned his legs were. He crossed his arms, and her gaze went right to his biceps.

The realization that she was even a little susceptible to his sexual magnetism rubbed her raw. She preferred men with character—even if she had yet to establish a meaningful relationship with one.

"Since you are so bold as to ask, I'll explain," he finally said. "I didn't realize the connection when Lord Phillip first suggested you for this job. I don't generally pay attention to journalists' names. Later, when I realized which journalist you were, my instinctive reaction was to tell Phillip there was no way in—" He stopped himself, propped his palms on the desktop behind him, and looked toward the ceiling distractedly. "No way I wanted you. But the more I thought about it, the more logical it seemed."

His potent gaze zeroed in on her, and she froze.

"In my book, if a person helps cause a problem, he—or she—can damned well help fix it."

Nicole ached to respond, to point out that it wasn't her fault he had yet to marry. But Rand didn't give her a chance. "You *are* a Caldonian citizen. It's time you showed it."

"I've always been loyal," Nicole said, fighting down a surge of guilt at his insinuations. She longed to tell him off, to tell him exactly what she thought of his behavior, of his own lack of loyalty to their country.

She couldn't, not without embarrassing Uncle Phillip, who had recommended her for this assignment. Yet she was beginning to think she should never have come. This interview seemed to be going from bad to worse.

"I'm glad to hear that, Miss . . ."

"Aldridge," she said proudly.

"Yes, Miss Aldridge. The situation is this. My father has given me an ultimatum. He wants me engaged before the year is out."

"And if you aren't engaged by then?"

He crossed his arms. "That isn't your concern. Your job is to help me solve my little problem so that it doesn't distract me."

Little problem? And a distraction? This was how he defined the tremendously important task of finding his life-mate?

Dismay swept through Nicole at discovering the true prince after all. He might be more informal than she'd expected, and he might be somewhat endearingly absent-minded, but he was definitely the irresponsible and shallow Randy Prince.

He was oblivious to her feelings. His gaze focused on the

distance. "Now I've spent a little time thinking of the kind of match I ought to make," he said.

He shoved off from the desk and approached the French doors, which led to a terrace decorated with plants and flowers in heavy Grecian urns. Beyond that lay a broad swath of lawn backed by a natural forest.

Rand clasped his hands behind his back and stared out, as if seeing something other than the pleasant view. "I'm not seeking a love match or even the appearance of one. Just an appropriate companion who will understand and embrace her role. Her country of origin isn't of great concern as long as she's of noble blood and able to adapt to Caldonia. I want a woman who is compatible with me—one who will barely make a ripple in my lifestyle."

Nicole scrambled for her purse. Pulling out a palm-size notebook and pen, she flipped open the cover and began scribbling down his requirements as fast as she could.

He continued without pause. "A wife who will understand when I'm angry, agree with me on important matters, not argue or fill my life with inconsequential details. She must be able to handle those."

Nicole arched an eyebrow at his egocentric requirements. In person, he demonstrated even more arrogance than she had expected.

"She must be strong willed, not weak in her mental capacities," Rand said. "Able to take the strain of a royal spouse, yet not domineering or aggressive. A companion, not an enemy. I don't want to have two armed camps in the palace."

As she jotted down his words, Nicole wondered where that sentiment stemmed from.

"She should be a perfect mother for my future children. Warm and caring. A perfect hostess for social occasions." His feet spread, Rand gazed toward the ceiling as if imagining this paragon of womanhood. "Perfect bloodlines, of noble stock, and no colored past. In short, the perfect wife for a prince."

Nicole's hand ached trying to keep up. She scribbled one final note and glanced up at him. "Is that all?"

Rand ignored her ironic tone. He crossed behind his desk and planted his palms firmly on the surface, leaning toward her. "I expect you to work diligently on this project, Miss Aldridge. It will mean late hours and little free time. Now and then, barring my other duties, I will advise you. After all, it does bear some importance to the future of the realm—and to my future. Are you up to the task?"

"Of course I am. Your Highness," she added belatedly. "I've already begun compiling data on the most likely candidates on my laptop."

"Excuse me?" His gaze landed on her lap.

Despite knowing how backward Caldonia was, his confusion took her completely by surprise. She didn't care to have his potent gaze on that part of her anatomy, so she rushed to correct him. "My—my portable computer. I brought one with me."

His eyes snapped up from her lap to meet her eyes. "Oh, a laptop *computer!* Of course. You have one of those small computers here? I've been meaning to acquire one myself. You will have to show it to me. We have yet to introduce computers to the palace," he added dryly. "Perhaps in another fifty years or so."

No computers in the palace in this day and age? Nicole prayed he was joking. Since he wasn't smiling, it was difficult to tell. "Certainly, I'll show you. Whenever you wish."

"Excellent." He came back around the desk. "I believe Gerald has arranged a room for you here in the palace."

Nicole shoved her notebook and pen in her purse. "I have the job?" she asked, standing up.

"You are willing to take it on, aren't you?"

"Yes, I—"

"Good," he said briskly. "Thank God, that's settled." He thrust out his hand and Nicole took it, pleasantly surprised to see he wasn't expecting her to curtsy. His grip was warm and firm, not crushing. He obviously knew how to touch a woman. *To shake a woman's hand,* she corrected herself.

As if reading her thoughts, he smiled warmly across their hands. The sight sent a jolt of heat through Nicole. Yet she kept her own smile cool and businesslike, unwilling for him to think she was affected by his charisma. She did *not* want to come across as another Prince Rand groupie especially since he was her new boss.

He released her hand and again pressed the intercom button. "Gerald, show Miss Aldridge to her room."

Gerald entered instantly. "Your Highness, you must begin to dress. The reception begins in an hour. This way, Miss Aldridge." He gestured toward the door.

"It's only another state reception," Rand said in that dry tone Nicole was growing familiar with. He slapped Gerald on the back. "Don't worry so much over trivial matters, Gerald. It's turning you gray."

As soon as the door had closed behind them, Gerald muttered *"He* is turning me gray, nothing else."

Now that she'd met the prince, Nicole could understand that. The man seemed to take lightly things others felt were serious—such as choosing a wife.

Yet Nicole found herself wondering if he really was as superficial as it appeared. There was something about him, an intensity she'd sensed just below the surface. She wondered if his absentmindedness, his occasionally distracted demeanor, hinted at depths few people could see.

Perhaps he wasn't completely irredeemable. Nicole took heart. In finding the future queen, perhaps she *could* influence the future king in ways that would help her country. She could make all the difference for Caldonia while proving her loyalty to everyone—including herself.

She pulled in a breath, feeling more challenged and excited than she had in years.

There was only one tiny hitch: her annoyingly female reaction to Prince Rand. She resolved to do her best to think of him only as her employer—and not as an incredibly attractive man.

# THREE

*Journal entry, April 9: Prince Rand is both more hand-*
*some and more arrogant than I expected. His ideas about*
*marriage are positively medieval. Still, I'm excited about*
*this opportunity to serve my country in such an intimate*
*way.*

Nicole stopped typing, her gaze frozen on the word *intimate.* She would be helping to find some woman who
would be sharing the prince's bed. A warm flush suffused
her as an image of the prince, naked from the waist up,
lying against pillows in a massive bed formed in her mind.

Exasperated, she shook her head to force the thoughts
away. Perhaps he was rather good-looking. That didn't
make him any better of a prince, and with his randy behavior, he left a lot to be desired as far as serving his country
went. Satisfied that she'd regained full control of her wayward hormones, she hunched over her keyboard again.

Before she could type another word, a knock came at
the door. Nicole answered it to discover a grim man standing outside her suite clasping a heavy briefcase. Nicole studied him—short, balding, and intense, his face as gray as
his outdated suit.

He glanced her over, his eyes narrowed assessingly. Nicole had the feeling he found her wanting.

"Edgar Burbinder, solicitor to the prince, ma'am. I handle all legal affairs for His Highness, Prince Rand."

"Please come in." She let him into the sitting portion

of the well-appointed rooms. Her suite was even more comfortable than Prince Rand's anteroom, with decidedly feminine touches. Tiffany lamps, floral table coverings, and a
chaise longue draped in velvet burgundy beside the fireplace.

Mr. Burbinder took a seat in one of two floral-cushioned
love seats and set his briefcase carefully on the coffee table.
"We must take care of important matters before this association goes any further."

Nicole nodded as she sat across from him. "I see." But
she didn't, not yet.

He popped the latches on the case and the lid sprang
up. Retrieving a sheaf of papers, he spread them on the
table facing her. He withdrew a pen from his inside jacket
pocket and used it as a pointer. "Sign here, here, and
here."

"Would you mind explaining what these are?" she asked,
picking up the paper and scanning the fine print.

"Very well. Agreement not to discuss with the press, not
to publish a single word, not to tell a soul about what goes
on here inside the palace walls, particularly, but not limited
to, facts and speculation on the royal family, its activities,
its plans, its involvements, and above all, its personal affairs."

"Oh." So much for an inside scoop. She really wasn't
surprised. During her stay here, she would have to stop
thinking like a journalist and start thinking like a palace
employee. She only hoped she wouldn't lose herself in the
process.

As she signed the papers, her gaze slid to her laptop
computer on the white-gilt desk in the corner. On its screen
was her newly created journal about her experience with
Prince Rand. Certainly she could still maintain a private
journal. No one could require her not to. And maybe someday . . . She finished signing her name with a flourish.
"There."

"Thank you, ma'am." Mr. Burbinder gathered the papers and closed his briefcase. He stood. "That is all. Good

evening." He let himself out before she could show him
the door.

Nicole sighed and turned to take a closer look at her
new home. She wondered how long she'd be living here.
The goal was to see Prince Rand engaged before the year
was out, and it was already April. That gave her a little more
than eight months.

She entered the bedroom portion of her suite. A set of
French doors let out on a balcony. Dusty rose-and-silver
carpeting matched chintz throw pillows and the velvet
cushion on the vanity seat, the same subtle print appearing
in all three. Queen Anne antique furniture decorated both
rooms.

A gauze canopy sheltered the king-size brass bed, which
was covered in a white spread dripping with Spanish lace.
The bed seemed fit for a princess—or at least a noble.

From the expansive view, Nicole realized she'd been
placed in the west wing, on the second floor. She remembered from her research on the palace that Prince Rand's
private apartments were also in this wing, probably just
down the hall.

Was this elegant, feminine suite where Prince Rand's
dates stayed when he brought them to the palace? Nicole
ran her hand along the pure white bedspread. His beautiful
women may have slept right here in this bed. Or did his
lovers simply sleep in his suite and share his bed? Nicole
doubted the conservative Queen Eurydice would approve
of that.

Nor did she really need the answer to such a question.
The knowledge wouldn't help her find him a suitable wife.
But while Rand had employed her, she felt some responsibility to the woman she might find to marry him. She
certainly hoped he'd be a good husband to her. As far as
she was concerned, that meant putting an end to his randy
ways.

Through another door lay a private bath. At least she'd
been placed in the wing equipped with indoor plumbing.
Still, the fixtures appeared unchanged since the original

installation, an old-fashioned—if charming—claw-foot tub and a sink with a skirt.

Nicole could appreciate the beauty of the traditional—as long as it embraced the efficiency of the new. She looked under the skirt and saw the exposed plumbing.

"Do the pipes pass inspection?"

The deep voice startled Nicole and she jerked upright. Prince Rand's face stared at her from the mirror above the sink. He was standing just inside her open bedroom door.

She spun to face him, irritation outpacing her deference. "Your Highness! Excuse me, but do you usually barge into people's rooms without knocking?"

He shrugged nonchalantly. "The flag is posted outside your door, and your door was unlocked. That usually means my servants are ready and willing to be available to me. It's an old-fashioned system, but we find that it works. Is that a problem for you, Miss Aldridge?" He gave her a pointed stare.

Nicole's cheeks grew hot. She had seen the foot-long green flag in a bracket beside the lintel, but hadn't realized what it meant. And Gerald hadn't explained. He'd been called away to another task right after showing her to her suite.

She pulled in a steadying breath and slipped into the bedroom, trying to appear poised. "Once I learn the proper protocol around here, no, it won't be a problem." She lifted her chin. "In the future, when I need privacy I'll remove the flag *and* lock my doors."

Nicole thought she detected a flicker of embarrassment in his dark eyes. He was, after all, standing in her bedroom.

Prince Rand in her bedroom . . . Her office mates would love to hear about this. Of course, he was fully dressed, which did nothing to detract from his appeal, she realized in dismay. He had changed for the reception into a tailor-made tuxedo that clung to his athletic frame. His black jacket was cut to display a green-and-gold satin sash across his white shirt, leaving no doubt he was a royal prince.

Nicole realized that, while she'd been looking him over,

he'd been returning the favor. No doubt she compared poorly to the elegant women he usually spent his free time with.

She could tell nothing from his expression, which was no doubt for the best. She was slender to a fault, her figure nothing to brag about, her hair an average brown, her face reasonably pretty at best. Besides, she didn't care what he thought of her looks!

She still couldn't believe he'd just dropped in on her like this, as if it meant nothing. Then again, to him, why should it mean anything? She was a servant—an employee just like Gerald—and he was one of the most powerful people in the country. Maybe eventually she could bring a little more equality to the palace. Until then, she had better get used to being around the man, despite how incredible he looked in a tux.

He seemed to realize that neither of them had said a word for a solid minute. He took a step backward, toward the bedroom door. "Very well. I'll wait out here for you. In the sitting room. Join me when you're through inspecting the plumbing," he added with a wry twist to his lips. "It's antiquated and very noisy, but it still works. Therefore, it won't be replaced. That's the Hollingsworth way."

He turned and left the bedroom. Nicole was just breathing a sigh of relief when she heard him call out, "I came to see your computer. I believe I saw it on your desk? Ah, there."

Nicole's heart stopped beating as she remembered the personal observations about him that she'd left on the screen. She ran after him.

She reached the desk at the same instant he did.

The screen was black, the screen saver engaged. Nicole sighed, thankful for the reprieve. She spun the laptop toward her and tapped a few keys, sending her private journal into the land of stored data bits and away from prying royal eyes.

From the other side of the desk, Rand leaned over the

computer to watch what she was doing. Yet Nicole had worked fast. She was positive he hadn't seen a thing.

Her eyes skidded up to find his face inches away, and her breath caught in her throat. She fought not to notice his tantalizing, spicy cologne.

"Is it turned on?" he asked softly, his gaze intent on hers.

*Turned on? Oh, my.* "It—it's on, yes," Nicole said, glancing away in an effort to regain her equilibrium. "That was a screen saver. See? This is the usual interface." She swung the computer to face him.

Without waiting for further instruction, he sat down, turned the computer toward him, and began tapping keys. "How much memory does it have? How many gigabytes of storage space?"

So the man knew his computers, did he? Then why had he asked her if it was turned on? Rubbing at her crossed arms, she scowled down at his bent head.

"What programs do you prefer?" He glanced up at her. "A word processor, perhaps?"

"Why would you ask that?" she asked, conscious again of her previously exposed journal. She was positive she'd been fast enough to hide it.

He shrugged. "Because you're a writer. And I expect you to draft reports on the princess candidates. Or were you planning to communicate with cave paintings?"

Nicole's throat clogged as she found herself irritated by the man.

Then an incredible thing happened. He smiled at her.

The smile transformed his face, revealed his irritating remarks for the teasing comments he'd intended them to be. As Nicole met his warm gaze, she didn't see a prince for the first time, but a man with a wicked and subtle sense of humor. A man with an entirely unexpected personality, independent of his title. Suddenly, she no longer felt so intimidated by him.

A surprising sense of yearning swept through Nicole, and she fought it down. Rand looked far too attractive in that tuxedo, and that smile could melt any lady's heart.

"What exactly did you need to know about my computer?" she asked quietly.

He turned back to the screen and clicked a few buttons. "I always enjoy a good game of solitaire," he said casually, bringing up the card game.

Why had he come here? Just to play cards or for some other reason? "You mentioned there are no computers in the palace."

"Mmm, no. I've arranged for salesmen to come by, but Father thinks it's a frivolous expenditure that has no place in our agrarian economy. Of course, he has neglected to consider that technology *does* play a role for our competitors."

Nicole shook her head in disbelief. Still, from all she knew of King Edbert, his attitude was hardly a surprise. "What do you think?"

"I think I want one of these. It's a slick device, very fast. Perfect, an ace!" He swept the ace to the pile on top of the tableau. "One could get rather addicted to this, I fear."

Solitaire was such a minor feature of what the computer could do. "Try surfing the Net sometime," she answered with a smile.

"I have. But not from here. Have you ever tried—"

A loud knock interrupted him. Nicole found Gerald at the door, his face creased in worry. "I know this is highly unlikely, but I was wondering, miss, if you might have seen Prince Rand about. He has disappeared from his room, and his car is waiting. Perhaps you noticed him passing in the hall or—"

Nicole stepped back and swung the door wide. "Join the party."

Gerald's gaze landed on Rand, still engrossed in his card game. His eyes grew wide. "Your Highness!"

"Not now, Gerald. I'm doing vital research."

There was that dry sense of humor again. Nicole bit back a smile.

Gerald didn't find the prince quite so amusing. "But, Your Highness, your car is ready."

Rand ignored him. "Ah, another ace! I think I'm going to win this one. You've brought me luck, Miss Aldridge. A sign of things to come, I hope."

He flashed her a smile filled with warmth and intimacy. To Nicole's chagrin, a swift shaft of feminine awareness raced through her, followed by an even stronger bolt of panic. What had she gotten herself into?

Such a reaction didn't belong in the workplace—certainly not with this particular employer. It had to be a short-lived infatuation, if she could even call it that. Once the Randy Prince showed his true colors, these wayward feelings would vanish. Definitely.

"It takes at least forty minutes to reach the hotel," Gerald said, appearing increasingly worried. "We mustn't keep the visiting dignitaries waiting. They cannot start without you."

Rand's intense eyes searched Nicole's face. "It seems we'll have to try this again another time."

Before she could gather her sense enough to respond, Gerald cried, "Your Highness!"

The prince finally tore his gaze from her and rose from the desk. "Very *well*, Gerald. You needn't yell. I'm not exactly deaf." He crossed to the door, then clapped Gerald on the back. "We must get *you* a computer, don't you think? You can use it for your correspondence."

Gerald didn't look too keen on the idea. "Certainly, sir. Whatever you say."

Gerald opened the door wide, but Rand stopped and turned back to Nicole. "Miss Aldridge, I expect you to show me a list of prospects at our next meeting."

"Which is . . ." she prompted.

Rand turned to his secretary. "Gerald?"

"Ten o'clock tomorrow, Your Highness, ma'am." He nodded at each of them.

"Ten o'clock!" Nicole said. "That doesn't give me much time."

"I'm sure you can handle it," Rand said with an imperious wave of his hand. "I imagine you have most of the information at the top of your head."

"Some, Your Highness," Nicole said, trying to absorb the tossed-off compliment. No doubt it meant nothing to a man who was used to servants jumping to please him. Yet, she realized suddenly, she didn't want to disappoint her new employer either. How had he done it? How had he motivated her just like that? "I'll pull as much information together as I can."

As soon as the men left, Nicole grabbed the phone, knowing she had a long night ahead of her. Instantly, a voice said, "What number, Miss Aldridge?" She heard crackling on the line. Another antiquated system. She prayed the phone lines were up to the task.

"I'd like to place a call to New York."

A half hour later, her laptop, plugged into the phone line, was accepting a download of a good portion of the database from the *Aristocrats* offices.


At 10 A.M. the next morning, Nicole again found herself passing time in the anteroom of the prince's office. She watched the minutes tick by on the grandfather clock. 10:10. 10:30. Gerald had told her to wait to be summoned, so she did.

"This is ridiculous," she said to the empty room. She stood and crossed the carpet to the firmly shut door that led to the prince's inner office. If he were in there, who knows who he could be meeting with? A foreign ambassador, a head of state, even the king. Still . . . Tentatively, she knocked.

"Come in," came Rand's voice.

Nicole hesitated. She'd half expected he wouldn't really be in there. What if he grew irritated at her intrusion? Still, they had been scheduled for ten, and she'd spent all night on her assignment.

She pushed open the door.

"Ah, there you are. You're late, Miss Aldridge."

Rand was leaning against the front of his desk, wearing a polo outfit—green shirt with the Caldonian crest, tan riding breeches, and shiny brown knee-high boots. His brow furrowed in thought, he absently toyed with a long-handled polo mallet. Clearly he planned on spending the day playing while his staff worked.

"I've been waiting out there for your *summons*, Your Highness."

Rand arched his eyebrow at her cool tone, but didn't appear the least apologetic. "Oh. Did Gerald tell me you were here? Perhaps he did. Next time, feel free to knock to make certain I know you're there."

She couldn't resist. "Perhaps you should put out a flag."

His brows shot up, and she felt his gaze assessing her. "You do manage to make a point, don't you?" he said dryly. "Such a practice would, of course, upset protocol set by centuries of palace tradition and place the royals on the same level as the servants." Again he scrutinized her as if trying to figure her out.

Nicole tightened her hands on her thick folder, knowing she had stepped over the line with her flip remark. She wondered if she'd pushed him just a little too far.

To her surprise, he smiled. "I'll have to consider it." He glanced at his watch. "Now, let's get to it, or Gerald will have my hide. I have a lot to do today, once we conclude this business."

*I'll bet,* Nicole thought, eyeing his leisure clothes.

"So." He smiled. "What do you have for me?"

There was that smile again, all charm. To her consternation, Nicole found her irritation evaporating.

He leaned the mallet against the bookcase and settled in his desk chair. Nicole sat before him and opened her folder on her lap. Within was a thick stack of papers—two hundred and fifty of the finest marriageable young women on the planet. "I did my best to begin a list, Your Highness, but—"

He snapped forward and lifted his hand. "Hold it right there."

Nicole jerked back at his imperious tone. "What?" What had she done?

He frowned at her, his dark looks giving his expression an ominous cast. "Don't say those words to me again. Except in public."

Nicole swallowed. Was he mad? "What words?"

He threw up his hands in disgust. *"Your Highness!* I'm already quite sick of them in general, but coming from you, I find them especially aggravating." He leaned back in his chair and grinned sardonically. "Maybe because I wonder if you truly mean them."

His honesty completely surprised her. "I . . . uh . . . say them because that's what's expected, Your—I mean— Well, what *am* I supposed to call you?" she demanded. "Randy?" *Oh God, had she really said that?*

He stared at her a moment, his dark eyes penetrating so deep Nicole had to force herself not to fidget. Then he began to laugh. "This is good. You're losing your fear of me."

"I never feared you."

He waved his hand dismissively in what Nicole was coming to see as a characteristic gesture. "Of course you feared me."

"Intimidated by you, perhaps," she conceded, trying to get used to the idea that she was having a normal conversation with the man. She decided she liked the feeling.

He laughed. "Call me Rand. And in case you hesitate to do so, I make it an order."

She gave him a tentative smile. "Yes, Your—I mean, yes, Rand."

"Excellent. Now what's that pile of papers you have there? Some surprises, I hope?"

"Perhaps." She rifled the edges. "As you can see, there are quite a few eligible young ladies among the peerage. I needed to ask you . . ." She lifted her gaze from her papers and met his intense expression. Her words faltered. She found herself wondering how many Caldonian citizens would kill to have such undivided attention from their future ruler.

"Yes?" he prompted.

It took her a moment to recall what she'd needed to ask him. The way he kept gazing at her made her feel like the absentminded one. "My task would be much easier if you gave me a few more details about the sort of woman you're looking for."

"Go on."

"It might help to start with you."

He cocked an eyebrow. "Me."

"Yes." She opened her notebook. "Your interests, your goals . . ."

"How in God's name does that make a difference?"

"If this woman is to live with you, you ought to share a few interests in common. Trust me, it's wise."

"And you know this from your wealth of experience with men?"

She didn't miss the ironic curl to his lips. Was he teasing, fishing for personal details, or merely enjoying annoying her? She hesitated to guess. "I don't have . . . Never mind about me. Common interests make sense. Besides, we have to start somewhere."

"Very well." Rand leaned back and placed his booted feet on the desktop, then pulled in a breath. "I plan to stabilize the economy in the next few years, broaden our economic base. We're too dependent on the wine industry. I'm particularly interested in high-technology fields, as you may have guessed from my reaction to your portable computer. You have to get me one, by the way. I don't trust Gerald to know what to buy."

"About your goals—" she prodded, wanting to keep him on track.

"Yes. I want to improve the national health. We don't always get high marks in that area because we're a wine-growing nation, and unfortunately, we have a higher than average level of alcoholism. The citizenry is not well educated in regard to health matters. It's . . . unacceptable."

Nicole couldn't help thinking about her parents and the irresponsible drunk who had killed them—and walked away from the accident. To most Caldonians, he wasn't a criminal. He'd just imbibed a little too heavily of the family label, which was to be expected during the spring barrel-tasting season.

She found herself studying Rand, absorbing the thoughtful frown that had gathered on his striking face. Her chest filled with warmth. For the first time, a leader of the country was actually acknowledging the situation. He knew it was a problem. That was half the battle. Then they could move on to a solution. . . .

As if uncomfortable under her scrutiny, Rand ran his hand through his hair and glanced away. He slid open a drawer and pulled out a cigar. Grabbing a gold lighter from the desktop, he lit the smoke and dragged in a deep puff.

Nicole stared at him, nonplussed by his contradictory action. This was a man she expected to lead the charge to improve the country's health? Irritation swelled inside her. She'd clearly jumped to conclusions. She had forgotten Prince Rand enjoyed the pleasure of a good cigar—and a good drink, for that matter. Among a hundred other pleasures. Hardly the type to set a positive example.

She forced her attention back to her list of questions. "What about your interests? I recall you enjoy horseback riding and sports. You were a captain in the Royal Navy, and you still love sailing. You have a home in the country that you often retreat to, yet you enjoy city life as well. You collect antiquities, particularly from the Grecian and Mycenaean cultures. Also, you love pets, and as a consequence, one of your favorite charities is Humanity to Animals. You studied law at the university, and you oversee the House of Lords when it is in session." Her gaze flicked up. "Anything else?"

His expression was unreadable. "You've done your research well, Miss Aldridge."

She hesitated, unsure whether she'd scored any points by reciting so many facts about him. It was time to move on to the next topic, difficult as it might be. "There's another area we ought to discuss."

He waved the cigar at her and the smoke curled toward the ceiling in a narrow gray stream. "Go on."

"I know you're aware that sometimes royal marriages fail because of a lack of common interests."

"We've already discussed that," he said, frowning impatiently.

"Right. There can be, however, another factor, which I think is relevant to consider in your situation as well."

He smiled sardonically. "Only one?"

"I'm talking about a more personal factor—for the man usually," she said, fiddling with her papers and wishing she were anywhere else on the planet but right here, right now. "A previously existing . . . situation."

His eyebrows rose slowly. He lowered his feet from the table and leaned his elbows on the desk, his eyes boring into hers. "You may get to the point anytime, Miss Aldridge." He slid an ashtray in front of him and tapped the cigar into it.

Nicole's heart began beating double time. Couldn't he help her out here, just a little? She drew in a deep breath. "Is there, perhaps, another ongoing circumstance, another . . . personal relationship that should be taken into account?"

"Miss Aldridge," he drawled, a corner of his mouth turned up, "are you asking me if I have a mistress?"

"Yes!" she cried in exasperation.

He sat back and began chuckling, but his laughter soon grew, filling the room. Nicole felt like melting into the floor. She sat there, stony faced, waiting for him to get over his paroxysm of mirth long enough to answer the question. The issue was hardly irrelevant, and it should certainly not be treated so lightly.

He choked and caught his breath. "Isn't the issue rather one of love?"

*Love?* The man hadn't mentioned that word until now in all this talk of a wife. Perhaps there was yet hope for the woman in question. "I'm not sure I understand the context—"

"I don't *love* another woman. I'm not in love, I have never been in love, and it's far too late to expect I'll ever *be* in love. Therefore, whether or not I have a mistress is completely immaterial."

Nicole tightened her hands around her notebook, trying to control her instant negative reaction. While she, in her modern way of thinking, would never settle for less than love and total commitment from a husband, other women would be quite content to marry Rand for convenience's sake—and all the trappings of being a royal spouse.

She was savvy enough to know when to move on to another topic. "Very well. What about your future wife's appearance? What are your preferences in that area?"

He took another drag on his cigar. "You mean, should she be pretty?"

"Well, yes. Are you considering only attractive women? And do you have, perhaps, a preference for coloring? Blond, redhead, brunette—"

He shrugged. "Coloring is immaterial to me. I don't care what she looks like, as long as she fulfills her duties properly. Except she must be presentable, of course. No obvious defects. I have the family line to think about, you know."

"Of course," Nicole said wryly. She had a hunch he cared more about his future wife's looks than he let on. "No preference for hair coloring then," she said, making a note.

Rand scratched his brow, his look one of concentration. "Actually, I do prefer a woman of definite contrasts to a washed-out appearance. I tend toward brunettes, though that is not a firm requirement and by no means should be used to weed the women out."

"Very well." Nicole had to stop herself from touching her own brown hair, done up again in a French roll. He was scrutinizing her again, and she wondered what he saw. Not that it made any difference.

The conversation took an even more uncomfortable

turn. "As for her figure," Rand began slowly, "since we are getting down to brass tacks here." His eyes had an undeniable sparkle as they flicked over her own body. "I also don't have strict requirements there. However, I would like a nice figure, as any man would. Properly rounded, but not in an obvious way. For instance, you, Miss Aldridge, are neither skinny nor fat. I would like her not to be a stick, and preferably not obese, for that shows a regrettable lack of self-control." He took another drag on his cigar.

Nicole coughed into her fist, glad for the opportunity to put him on the spot in return. "Excuse me, Rand, but the same could be said of your smoking habit."

His eyebrows shot up. He glanced at his cigar, then met her gaze. "It bothers you when I smoke?"

She lifted her chin. If they were going to work together . . . "Yes."

He considered her words for a moment. "Blunt, aren't you?" he said wryly.

"I see no reason not to be, sir. I mean, Rand."

"Very well. I can be reasonable." He squashed the cigar out in the ashtray. "I only smoke on occasion, Miss Aldridge. I'm not addicted, you realize. But while you're here, I won't indulge."

Not addicted. She wondered about that claim. "Thank you, Rand. And by the way, please call me Nicole, since we're on a first-name basis."

"Nicole. Wonderful name. I'd forgotten it." His sensuous lips turned up in a smile that threatened to destroy her concentration. Nicole forced herself to focus on the papers in her lap. She wondered if he were flirting with her or if he always tried to win women over by charming them senseless. He'd probably been using his charisma on the female gender since grade school.

She leaned closer and set the thick file on the desk, again noticing his subtle, spicy scent. Inside on individual sheets were a few paragraphs summarizing each candidate's background and traits and, on some sheets, a digitized image.

"This is just a start, but in here are short profiles of all of the eligible titled women who meet your requirements. On first glance, that is. Once we narrow the choices down, I can provide more in-depth profiles."

He leaned back, pulled the folder onto his lap, and opened it. "Excellent. You don't take much time, do you?"

Nicole glowed at the compliment. She felt a yawn coming on and clenched her jaw muscles to keep him from seeing it. "You asked me for a list—"

She could see the amusement in his eyes. "I wasn't expecting you to spend all night on this. We have slightly more time than that."

"Do we? I thought King Edbert wanted you engaged by the end of the year."

He shook his head dolefully. "My God, you're worse than he is! Every minute counts, according to him. You'd think I had a biological clock like you women do. And my mother has her own methods of pressure. Tries to foist women on me when my defenses are down. That's exactly what you're going to help me avoid—the pressure. The feeling of being on display for these—these *women*. This time, I'm going to be the one in control, the one doing the hunting." He sighed, focusing on the file. He flipped open the cover and pulled out the first sheet. "So what have we got here?"

As he glanced at the paper, Nicole began writing down what he'd said. A real coup, to capture such a personal sentiment from the world's most eligible bachelor. She couldn't tell anyone about it now, but she would put it in her journal.

"Lady Isobelle Young of Northumbria," Rand muttered. "I hardly think so." He tossed the sheet away and it floated to the floor. "Far too aggravating to be around for more than ten minutes at a stretch."

"May I ask why?" Nicole reached down and grabbed the paper.

Rand shrugged. "Certainly. She prattles endlessly about absolutely nothing. A most annoying habit. One, thank God, you do not possess."

Nicole set the paper facedown on the desk, intending to start a rejects pile.

After one glance at the next candidate, Rand tossed that paper aside as well. "Met her at a charity ball two years ago. Excruciatingly dull."

The third candidate met the same fate. "She's extremely loose with her favors. And while her charms are considerable, that makes her completely unacceptable."

Nicole couldn't help wondering if Rand himself had enjoyed her favors. She watched the papers fly as he went through them, and she gave up trying to keep them off the floor. It began to look like a snowstorm had hit as Rand reviewed and rejected almost every carefully prepared sheet. All that work . . .

It occurred to her then that she should have followed his instructions instead of being so intent on impressing him. He had asked for a list, not a dossier on each woman. Which would have taken a fraction of the time. And she could have gotten a decent night's sleep. She tried to hide another yawn behind her hand.

When he finally got to the bottom, only thirty prospects remained. He closed the folder and handed it back. "Now we have somewhere to start."

Nicole flipped through the princess prospects. Most were from European countries. Three were from Caldonia, and two were Middle Eastern princesses—her "surprises." Apparently, they were women he didn't know enough about to reject outright.

"I'll give you profiles on each of these women, which you can consider at your leisure," she said. "May I suggest the next logical step?"

He waved for her to continue.

"We should invite the candidates to various social functions, one at a time, so that you can spend time with each one. I can work with Gerald to coordinate that."

He frowned thoughtfully for a moment, then nodded. "Very well. Come up with some sort of sheet I can use after meeting each one."

"A sheet?"

"Yes, you know, some kind of evaluation form. So I can remember how each one struck me. If they remain in the running, I can refer to it later."

Nicole bit the inside of her cheek, forcing herself not to reveal how appalled she was. Women weren't horses, for God's sake. "So you intend to grade them."

He arched his thick eyebrows. "Grade them? You make it sound so—cold. I merely need a sheet to jog my memory."

Nicole continued to stare at him skeptically.

He stood with slow deliberateness. Rounding the desk, he planted himself in front of her. Nicole gazed up at his towering frame, feeling decidedly at a disadvantage.

"It may sound cold to you, Miss Aldridge—Nicole," he said, his voice carrying a decided chill. "But don't forget: Romance has nothing to do with my selection of a wife. You're suggesting I meet and spend time with possibly thirty women."

"Unless we weed some out beforehand," Nicole said, equally cool. *Unless you fall for one of them and end your search. The way matches ought to be made.*

He strode away, retrieved his polo mallet, and began hitting an imaginary ball across the carpet. "Naturally, I may forget some of the finer points of each candidate," he said over his shoulder. "An evaluation sheet will help me remember." He glanced up and caught her gaze. "I'll even let you help me fill them out after I meet them."

Nicole sighed. He was the boss, after all. At least the sheets would help *her* keep the women straight since she probably wouldn't meet them herself. "Very well. I'll prepare a sheet right away. Perhaps you can help me with the scale you intend to use?" she asked, unable to mask her annoyance.

"Scale?"

She no longer wanted to stay seated while he roamed around the room. She rose and walked over to him. "How various qualities should be weighted. For instance, looks. You yourself said looks were of less importance than character. Perhaps looks would be given, say, a five. And character a seven."

Despite her ironic tone, he tapped a tanned finger on his chin, as if seriously considering her outlandish proposal. "Yes, a very good idea. Very good. Write one up, and I'll tell you if you're on the money."

"I'll do my best," she said, unable to keep from adding, "Perhaps through a few mathematical computations we'll be able to determine which woman should be your wife. That would make things easier, wouldn't it?"

Without saying a word, Rand stiffened and turned his back on her, poising the mallet for another imaginary slam. Nicole stood uncomfortably nearby, knowing she'd angered him. She wondered if she should leave or wait to be dismissed. No doubt she'd just stepped way out of line—and Rand was too egocentric to deal with someone disagreeing with him.

Still, something in the set of his shoulders disturbed her, a tenseness she hadn't seen before. She began to regret her flip remarks. "Rand—"

"You may go, Nicole," he said briskly, without looking up.

"Thank you," she murmured. Feeling uneasy and unable to pinpoint why, Nicole gathered up her folder and notebook and slipped through the door.

The moment Nicole was gone, Rand tossed the mallet aside and stared at the closed door. His stomach was already reacting to the stress with its usual slow, agonizing burn.

The woman had definitely been a contributing factor, with her poorly concealed disdain. He recalled exactly what she'd written, words he'd seen on her computer screen in her apartment before he'd found her inspecting the plumbing. She'd labeled his ideas about marriage medieval.

*Medieval!* "Damn."

Rand crossed to the desk and toyed with a crystal paperweight bearing the Caldonian crest. No doubt she believed matchmaking belonged in the Dark Ages. If she only knew how difficult it could be trying to find the right wife with the clock ticking and the weight of a country on one's shoulders.

He slammed down the paperweight. "Bloody Americanized woman."

Frustrated, he rubbed the back of his neck, trying to ease some of the tension there. He couldn't fathom why he cared what she thought. He seldom worried how his employees viewed him.

Nor should he spend so much time worrying about his marriage or the methods he should use to find the female in question. Let this brash American woman, this Nicole, handle it. He had much weightier matters to deal with.

He crossed to the bar and downed two antacid tablets with a glass of water, hoping the fire in his gut would stop long enough for him to focus on something other than his marital decision—and the impending deadline forcing him to it.

He sat behind his desk and yanked out a report on the country's gross national product from a corner stack. He opened it before him.

For the past decade, every quarter showed a decline. Caldonia was going nowhere fast. Unemployment was on the rise, and crime had started to follow. What had once been a contented, placid country was taking on all the problems of the modern world—with none of the solutions.

Something had to be done, but his father refused to listen. According to the king, winemaking had supported the country for centuries, so why should it be any different now? After all, people still drank wine, and they always would, his father reasoned.

"We're entering the damned twenty-first century," Rand said to himself. He dragged a hand through his hair and leaned back, massaging his neck.

He felt so tired. There were never enough hours in the day. That charity tennis exhibition had thrown yesterday's schedule completely off, and he hadn't had a moment to work on his secret economic strategy. This morning's fund-raising polo match for the Historic Preservation Guild would be yet another drain on his time.

His father insisted he take part in such events, for the good of Caldonia. The king no longer understood that leading a country meant more than attending social functions. Charity was all well and good, but supporting a charity here and there would do nothing for the country as a whole. Major change—that was what was needed. A new vision.

With any luck, he'd find a wife who understood that, who could support him in his attempt to revitalize the country.

He sighed, his gaze falling on the papers scattered across the carpet. Unsuitable women, every one of them. In all his parents' talk of his marriage, of finding a woman of proper breeding and quality bloodlines, little was ever said about whether his future wife would contribute to the country.

Or whether she would make him happy.

He certainly had no illusions about romance. He lacked the luxury to even consider falling in love. But he hoped at the least to find a suitable woman he could also care for as a friend. God knows, his parents had spent years in a cold, loveless marriage. He had no intention of raising his own children in such a chilly household.

That was why he'd hired a consultant: to find just such a woman.

Nicole Aldridge might think him a walking anachronism, but she certainly seemed enthusiastic enough about her task. He smiled to himself as he recalled her trying to hide her yawns. He'd merely needed a list. He knew most of these women already. But she had gone way overboard. She was ambitious and enterprising, just as her uncle had said.

He closed the report and leaned back, gazing into space. She was such a pretty thing, with her creamy complexion and oval-shaped face. Why she hid her face behind those ridiculous owl-framed glasses, he couldn't fathom. And that hair. A nice color, sort of a coffee brown. He wondered how long it was when she let it hang loose.

He couldn't deny that, aggravating as she could be, he wouldn't mind spending time in her company. As long as she kept her American ideas about romance to herself. Such as in that journal of hers.

She'd written other things, he now remembered, about how arrogant she found him. And how handsome. How had she put it? Oh, yes. He was more handsome than she'd expected. . . .

With a start, he realized he was grinning to himself like an idiot. Instantly, he frowned. Where was his concentration? He had to get through this report before the polo match. He forced his thoughts off of Nicole Aldridge and back on the document before him.

# FOUR

"Start with these, in this order."

Prince Rand handed Nicole five of the dossiers she had prepared on the thirty women. He sat across the breakfast table from her on the palace terrace, looking cool and handsome in a tan sports coat and black slacks, which clung to his athletic legs. If she didn't know better, she might forget he was the prince since he appeared so relaxed.

She wished she didn't enjoy the sight of him so much. She'd never been one to pant after a man, regardless of how handsome his face—or how well built his body was. Her reaction made her feel appallingly unprofessional.

A week had gone by, and this was the first she'd seen of Rand in that time. She'd been occupied compiling detailed dossiers on the princess candidates, complete with eight-by-ten glossy photos sent express mail from the *Aristocrats* offices.

Her task completed, she'd sought an opportunity to present her work to Prince Rand. She'd had to wait over the weekend since he'd left town on personal business, according to Gerald.

Nicole could certainly imagine what that meant. Sailing on the Mediterranean, perhaps, or visiting his remote country estate—no doubt to luxuriate in the charms of one of his mistresses, whoever she might be this month. Typical behavior for the Randy Prince.

Breakfast today was the only time Gerald could squeeze her in to see him.

She could think of worse settings. As she looked over the gardens and broad swath of lawn, she admired the fountain and the profusion of flowers surrounding it. Here in southern Europe, spring had already come. On the lawn, peacocks strutted, fanning their tail feathers.

Nicole turned her gaze from the birds' brilliant azure-and-emerald plumage and examined Rand's top five selections. A quick glance confirmed her suspicion—Rand had a preference for a pretty face, despite his claim to the contrary. Perhaps she shouldn't have gone to the trouble to write up profiles when the photos would have been sufficient, she thought, unable to stifle her irritation or her disappointment in Rand.

The five women he'd selected would all be considered attractive, even stunning. The icy blonde on top bore a striking resemblance to Grace Kelly. "Lady Colette DuPrix of France?" Nicole asked, unable to keep the hesitation from her voice.

Rand sipped his coffee. "Is that a problem?"

"Could you tell me what made you select her first?"

He shrugged. "Simple. It says in her profile that she loves pets. I love pets." He gestured to his golden retriever, asleep on the terrace steps. "A common base from which to start. You're the one who said common interests were important."

"Mmm." Nicole set the papers aside and resettled her glasses on her nose.

Rand set his coffee cup down with a clatter, drawing her attention. "What's that noise you just made?" he asked with a frown. "Something's on your mind."

"Nothing. I . . . Nothing." It amazed her that he could read her so well. She had a suspicion she wouldn't be able to hide much from this man. She gripped her cup, determined to remain composed, or he might suspect he'd gotten under her skin. She couldn't stand the embarrassment if her new boss discovered she had succumbed to his potent male charms.

"Nonsense," he said, his strong voice compelling a response from her. "What is it? I made my choices based on the profiles *you* provided, Nicole, so if you have a concern, out with it."

"Have you met Lady Colette?" she said slowly.

"No. However, her profile is so complete, I feel I already know her." His compliment was accompanied by an indulgent smile. "In fact, the search might end tomorrow if things go well."

His words stunned Nicole. "Tomorrow?" She would be going back to her day-to-day life in New York that soon?

A niggle of dissatisfaction wound through her. Would she really feel she'd done her part if this was all she did for Caldonia? Would she have done anything positive to help her country? Lady Colette didn't strike her as the type to take an interest in national reform—even if she and Rand would make a stunning couple. But the final decision wasn't hers to make.

"The queen has invited Lady Colette to a soiree," Rand explained, toying with a teaspoon. "I believe she has accepted. It's a perfect opportunity to spirit her off for a private dinner. I know my mother will welcome the suggestion even though it robs her of a guest."

Nicole blinked at him in amazement. For a man who had dragged his heels over marriage this long, he seemed remarkably determined to move ahead. "I'm impressed. You work fast."

His glittering eyes met hers. "I do if it suits me. Right now, it suits me."

Nicole dropped her attention from his potent gaze back to Lady Colette's lovely face. Her heart tightened. She found it impossible to remain dispassionately professional.

Since returning to Caldonia, she had started to discover a different prince from the Randy playboy portrayed in the press. The real prince. A man with a sense of values despite his reportedly hedonistic ways.

He had certainly seemed concerned for Caldonia, with his talk about economic plans and the national health. Yet now, where her own project was concerned, he had decided to take the shallow route to selecting a wife.

No doubt he had been entranced by the woman's goddesslike countenance. Apparently, he knew nothing about her personality, which Nicole had only hinted at—in a diplomatic way—in her profile. She'd used words like *spirited, ebullient, loving*. And Lady Colette was all those things, after a fashion.

People saw other people in different lights, Nicole reasoned. It wasn't her place to poison Rand's perceptions of a woman he had yet to meet. For all she knew, magic could happen between them, and Rand could discover his soul mate, despite his claims that romance played no part in his search for a wife.

"You have yet to share your concern with me, Nicole," he said softly, entreatingly, his gaze exploring her face.

Nicole glanced at her half-eaten omelette. Her stomach was so tense, she knew she couldn't swallow another bite. She shoved the plate away and forced herself to face him, her chin high, her professional demeanor in place. "My concern is irrelevant. Have a wonderful time tomorrow. I hope you enjoy her company. And here—" She pulled a blank evaluation form from her folder on the table. "Don't forget to fill this out afterward. I'll begin working with Gerald to set up social occasions where you can meet the next few ladies as well."

Rand nodded. "Excellent." He leaned back and stretched out his long legs. "I believe this is turning out to be quite fun. Don't you agree, Nicole?"

*Fun?* Nicole could think of a few other words to describe it. Sending Rand off to enjoy himself with other women was her job, she told herself sternly. She needn't get her feelings bent simply because he had poor taste in women—beautiful, stunning women at that.

"I'm happy to serve you in this capacity," she said, careful to keep her voice evenly modulated. "I've enjoyed the opportunity to serve my country."

She could feel Rand staring at her, and she sensed his

puzzlement at her formal demeanor. She kept her gaze on a peacock strutting by twenty feet away.

Rand pounded on Nicole's door. The sound echoed up and down the marble hall. He didn't care if he woke half the palace. He would have it out with her—right now. The brass bracket beside the lintel was empty, her flag removed to indicate she was on her own time. Probably because it was almost one in the morning. But he was not in the mood to wait until daylight to call Nicole on the carpet about the evening's debacle.

He allowed a few seconds to pass, but heard nothing through the thick wooden door. Unused to waiting, he raised his fist to pound on the door again. Then she opened it, just a crack, her sleepy brown eyes peering out.

Rand planted his palm on the door and shoved it open the rest of the way. Nicole stumbled back. He watched her eyes grow wide behind her glasses as she took in his appearance—his unbuttoned jacket, his undone tie, his untidy hair. Good. He'd let her see the havoc she had wreaked in his life this evening.

He strode into the center of the room and Nicole quickly closed the door behind him. His gaze fastened on her back, and with a start he saw that she was wearing her nightclothes—a pale blue floor-length gown and robe. She had a surprisingly svelte figure—modellike, graceful, and small boned. But not skinny. His gaze slid along the slope of her back to her nicely rounded hips. Definitely not skinny.

A sudden, unwarranted flare of desire swept through him, irritating him all the more. He wasn't supposed to want *this* woman, for God's sake. He had imagined seducing Lady Colette tonight. Lady Colette. He shuddered. It was definitely all Nicole's fault.

Facing him, Nicole pulled the front of her robe closed, as if she could read his illicit thoughts. Guilt surged in Rand's blood, adding fuel to his fury.

"Um . . . my flag was removed, in case you didn't notice." Her remark made him scowl. "Well, then, how did dinner go tonight?" she asked calmly, as if trying to deflect the storm she knew was about to erupt. "What did you think of Lady Colette?"

Rand didn't even want to hear that name. He had the urge to take Nicole by her slender shoulders and shake her. Hard.

At the thought of such a passionate display, his blood pounded into every part of his body. Suddenly, his throat felt incredibly dry. A drink. He needed the distraction of a drink. Glancing about, he located the bar behind the desk but saw no bottles on the shelves.

"Don't you have anything to drink around here? I have an intense craving for a whiskey." He collapsed on the nearest love seat. He stretched out his legs and leaned his head back on the cushions.

To his surprise, his tensions began to ease for the first time since the disastrous evening had begun four hours earlier. He didn't understand why. It made no sense. He'd come in here eager to dress her down. Except she wasn't wearing a dress.

Nicole slowly lowered herself onto the burgundy chaise longue beside the fireplace. "No, I haven't asked for the bar to be stocked. I'm sorry."

He stared at her face, framed by the firelight. She'd let her hair loose from the tight French roll she usually wore, the thick locks hanging to her shoulders in gentle waves. One mystery solved. Another immediately took its place as Rand imagined weaving his fingers through her hair, discovering whether it felt as silky as it looked.

Damned if he couldn't take his eyes from her. Nor did he have the energy to try. Her face appeared different when framed by her hair. Not prettier, for she was an attractive woman anytime. But having her hair down softened her features, giving her an innocent look that was making it difficult to stay angry at her.

Fiercely he reminded himself that she might look innocent, but she certainly wasn't. Not this time. His gaze dropped to the swell of her breasts under her satin robe, and heat pooled in his stomach. Where in the hell was a whiskey? Where in the hell was his sense? "Where are your clothes?" He asked the third question out loud in a rough tone, not giving a damn if he sounded unreasonable. "You're not dressed properly."

"I'm—I'm ready for bed," she began to explain. "I was about to go to bed. What—"

Her intimate bedtime routine was the last thing he wanted to hear about. He leaned over and yanked on the frayed cuff of his slacks. "Look what that bitch did to me!"

Nicole stared at him in shock. "Lady Colette?"

"Her Pomeranian!" he explained. "One of *three*. The little beast chewed right through my pant leg. I've got dog hair all over me." He batted at his jacket sleeves, and fine white hairs drifted up.

"She brought her dogs?" Nicole asked, sounding adequately shocked. "I know how fond she is of them, but to take them on a date with—"

"You tell me she likes animals. You write that she loves pets!" Rand said, irritation surging through him anew. "Don't get me wrong—pets are *fine*. But not crawling all over me during dinner. Yapping in my face! Biting at me! Damned obnoxious little beasties. And the way she *coddled* them—she even let them eat off her plate." He gave a humorless laugh. "That would go over sensationally at a state dinner."

"So it didn't go well," Nicole said. For some reason, her posture seemed to relax, just when her guilt ought to be getting the best of her.

And he was finding it damned hard to stay angry with her. Did she have to look so pretty sitting there, with that amazed look on her face? He refused to lose the edge to his temper simply because she looked good enough to eat.

She covered her mouth with her hand, her eyes sparkling in the firelight. No. That wasn't amazement—it was amusement. "So you find the situation humorous, do you?"

"Well, you have to admit, it's sort of . . . funny?" She bit her lip, obviously trying to hold back a laugh. "Your hair. It's sticking straight up."

That did it. Rand's anger came back in full force. He shoved his hand through his hair in a attempt to smooth it back in place. He hated to look the fool in front of this woman of all people. She carried no illusions about him as it was.

Jumping to his feet, he pointed an accusing finger at her. "You caused this, Nicole. You said she was a loving woman. Those were your exact words."

She threw out her hands. "She loves her pets."

He crossed to stand before her. His hands on his hips, he glowered down at her. "Where's the paperwork on her?"

Apparently, Nicole knew better than to argue with an angry prince. She rose and crossed to the desk. Adjusting those ridiculous glasses on her nose, she glanced over the desk and located Lady Colette's folder. "Here."

Rand snatched it out of her hand. Before turning his attention to the file, he gave her one more pointed glare. He intended to intimidate her. Instead, he found his vision filled with Nicole's charming face as she tried not to laugh—the amusement bringing out a wonderfully relaxed and approachable aspect to her he'd never seen before. An aspect he wanted to see more of.

Irritated at his reaction, he flipped through the file and found the betraying passage. He jabbed at it. "Right here. You wrote, 'Lady Colette is known for her ebullient disposition, her charm and her—' " He halted, the words springing out from the page. His anger couldn't stand the strain. It dissolved like snow tossed into a fire. He sighed and continued reading more slowly. " 'Her attentiveness to her pets.' It appears I overlooked that part."

Admittedly, he hadn't read Nicole's report that thoroughly. He'd selected the woman because of that stunning face. He'd imagined her to be another Grace Kelly, perhaps even seen her beauty as a sign that he'd found his princess, as Prince Rainier of Monaco had.

And he'd just wanted to get the damned business over with. He'd jumped to conclusions. That didn't excuse Nicole's part. He snapped the folder closed. "I'm paying you for an *honest* assessment of these women. You *knew* what she was like."

Rubbing at her satin-clad arms, she glanced away, a trace of guilt finally appearing on her face. "Well . . ." she began.

"Didn't you?" He shook the offending folder at her.

Her gaze whipped up to meet his. "Yes! I knew she was eccentric with her pets. And . . . self-absorbed and oblivious to other people's feelings. But I didn't want to sway your opinion or color it with my own perceptions. After all, you're a man. Men often think certain traits that women find irritating are charming. I was afraid that if I'd told you what I *really* think of Lady Colette, you might not have wanted to meet her."

Her admission struck him harder than he would have predicted. He didn't need this from her of all people. He received far too much filtered information from obsequious politicians, hidebound bureaucrats, and well-trained palace servants.

From Nicole, he wanted honesty. Needed honesty. He slammed the folder back on the desk and turned to face her. "Damn it, woman. I *value* your opinion. You make the most sense of anyone I've run across in a long time. Don't pull anything like this again. Tell me *exactly* what you think from now on. I can't stand the thought—"

He couldn't allow himself to finish. His gut told him to leave right then before he voiced any more of these ill-placed feelings, risked blurring the line between employer and servant, noble and commoner. "Take it as an order," he said coldly. "Review everything you've written about these women and revise as necessary. Tomorrow, we start over." He strode to the door.

"Yes, Your Highness."

Rand paused with his hand on the knob, hearing the hesitancy in her voice, the sudden return to formality. He had jarred her with his manner or his demands. Or with his presence here so late at night.

What was he doing? He didn't want her to begin fearing him. God, no. Not now. The barriers were finally coming down, and he was discovering someone he could be honest with, someone he could be himself with. A friend. It was so ill advised, yet so right.

Turning around, he gazed at her standing by the fireplace in her nightgown. He'd gotten her out of bed to rant and rave at her, and she'd only been trying to please him.

His emotions tangled inside him, and he had a hard time knowing what to say. He wasn't used to feeling at a loss with women, certainly not with ones wearing big owl-framed glasses and staring at him apprehensively.

Looking at her only made his conflicting emotions worse. Above all, he needed to remind himself that she was his employee, nothing more.

"You . . . do good work, Nicole," he finally said, feeling unusually awkward. "If I ever forget to say it, remember I've said it this time," he added gruffly. Without waiting for a response, he strode out the door and shut it firmly behind him.

# FIVE

"Who's next on the list? Certainly some woman among all of those you've profiled will be worthy to be my wife."

Three women, three disappointments. Nicole closed the file on tonight's candidate, knowing she would probably never open it again. She slid the file to the bottom of the stack on the desk in her suite. The delicately pretty Lady Joyce DeWinter, nineteen and fresh from finishing school, had turned out to have a decidedly specific preference when it came to matters of the heart, and it did not include persons of the male gender.

Nicole handed him the next folder. Candidate number four. Rand pulled it from her and opened it. "Lady Patricia of our own Caldonia. Indeed. I should have selected her first. I've met her briefly, and she seemed congenial enough. Certainly a fine-looking woman. Well educated, talented, and according to your own assessment, she's well liked and agreeable, a spirited conversationalist. Excellent. She even likes the out-of-doors." He looked toward the French doors and the starry night beyond. "Plan a picnic for us, Nicole. With the good weather we've been having, an outing would be ideal. I can show her the estate, and take her horseback riding. According to you, she's a superb horsewoman. We seem to have many things in common."

"Yes, Rand," Nicole said, scrambling for the notebook on top of her desk. She began writing down his requirements.

Certainly the date should be a successful one. Lady Pat

had no black marks against her that Nicole could think of. She'd make a fine wife for a prince.

Nicole realized the prospect didn't please her as it should. It irritated her that she was allowing her own attraction to Prince Rand to surface, even in the privacy of her thoughts. She would never do or say anything to indicate how she felt or allow her personal feelings to flow over into her professional responsibilities. But it would make her job much more difficult if she failed to put her own confused feelings for him out of her mind—and her heart.

Besides, she had never been successful where men were concerned. Oh, she'd dated off and on over the years, but whenever a man demanded more, she'd broken it off. Those casual relationships had never felt right enough for more intimacy. She'd begun to think one never would. And deep down she was too old-fashioned, she'd discovered to her dismay, to allow intimacy without it meaning something. Or everything.

Her gaze fell on Rand, and she quietly set the notebook on the desk. Since he wasn't looking at her, she felt safe in studying him. The fire cast highlights and shadows across Rand's aristocratic profile, making his features appear strangely enigmatic as, lost in thought, he gazed toward the night sky. He'd kicked his shoes off and unfastened his top shirt buttons, and he was sipping on a whiskey from her newly stocked bar.

Nicole knew that, as the years passed and she remembered this time in her life, she would always picture Prince Rand like this. Not speaking to a crowd, not appearing before the populace, but relaxing in the intimacy of her apartment. A man comfortable enough in her presence to completely be himself. Pride suffused her that he felt so at ease with her, that she had made him feel that way.

A niggle of guilt tugged at her then, and she wondered whether she should suggest he leave, since it was growing late. That was probably the well-bred thing to do. But she had no desire to see him leave. He seemed to fill the room with his presence and make her world come alive, whether he was pleased or angry, or silent and contemplative, as he was now.

"Nicole."

Her heart beat harder at the intimate tone of his voice. She forced her own voice to remain steady. "Yes, Rand?"

He turned his head and looked at her, a playful smile on his lips. "Could I, ah, finish that game now?" He gestured toward the laptop computer on her desk.

Nicole smiled at the uncharacteristic hesitancy in his voice. Perhaps he didn't have as may opportunities for mindless recreation as she'd assumed, or a simple computer game wouldn't mean so much to him. "Of course. Help yourself."

He sat down at the desk, and she helped him pull up his saved game. "Your own computers will be here in a week by the way."

He glanced up. "So soon? You're always so efficient. How many did you order?"

"Three. A desktop and a laptop computer for you, and a desktop for Gerald."

"Excellent. After we convert him, we'll start to work on my father."

The king? Nicole hadn't even seen the royal couple yet. She wasn't looking forward to meeting the rigid, tradition-bound pair. In some ways, she was amazed Rand hadn't turned out even more domineering and traditional than he was. Compared to them, he was woefully modern. Yet it bothered her that he didn't do more to modernize his country if this was how he felt. Perhaps he'd be willing to listen to suggestions.

Right here at the palace she'd seen numerous areas for improvement, some small, some far more complicated. As a working woman, one area in particular had been bothering her since her arrival a month ago. "Um, Prince Rand, I've noticed that your employees—"

He didn't lift his eyes from the screen. "Hmm? Ah, I believe I have won this game. Do you have any others?"

"How about blackjack?"

He leaned back. Lifting his arms, he stretched deeply, straining his shirt over his broad chest. He most definitely felt comfortable around her, Nicole thought with secret pleasure.

He waved the hand toward the screen. "Put it on, or pull it up, or push the button—whatever you say."

Nicole bent over his shoulder and pulled up the game. He leaned close to watch how she did it. Her hair brushed his cheek briefly. She forced herself not to jerk away, not to make more of the casual physical contact than it warranted. She stepped back. "There."

"Your hair looks nice down like that," he murmured. He gestured toward her hair, but stopped short of touching it. "It's very . . . nice," he repeated awkwardly. His gaze flicked back to the computer screen. "Now what about my employees?"

Nicole didn't think he'd heard her, but she was still trying to digest this unwarranted interest in her appearance. Fiercely she reminded herself he was only casually interested. As a prince, he was no doubt used to saying whatever trivial thing crossed his mind. "It's just that I notice your employees are all men. Except for me."

He leaned back, his jaw muscles tensing and a dark cast clouding his features. "You're the only one I hired without their involvement," he finally said.

"The king and queen, you mean."

He nodded curtly, his body growing stiff. Conflict within the royal family had long been rumored. Rand was not a pushover—that was obvious. Yet he was in his mid-thirties. How often had he clashed with his parents over the years? "You don't get along with them."

He considered her statement for several seconds. "It's complicated," he finally said, which told her little, yet acknowledged she was right. "You don't need to worry about it."

His reticence frustrated her. She longed for him to share something more of his life, of the problems that caused the tension she noticed so often in his shoulders, in the way he carried himself. Something a friend would share. "Rand, if you want to talk—"

"You were saying something about male employees," he said rapidly, cutting her off. "I take it you believe we should hire more professional women, such as yourself?"

Nicole sighed. At least he was willing to discuss this subject. "It would help set an example, yes. I know a lot of Caldonian women are frustrated by the lack of tolerance for them in the workplace. That's one reason I left here, for opportunity."

Frowning, he pushed up from the desk and paced about the room. "You believe we have a problem supporting women?"

"Yes, I do." She waited anxiously for his reaction, expected rationalizations, arguments about women's lack of abilities—perhaps even laughter.

She got none of those. Instead, Rand appeared distressed. He shoved his hand through his thick hair and sighed deeply. "Actually, we're losing many of our young men and women both," he said wearily. "That's why my high-tech strategy is so important, despite what my father says. If we can build in enough incentives to make Caldonia an attractive location for clean industry, we would not only be providing jobs, but the right kind of jobs for young people."

"Yes!" Nicole nodded enthusiastically. She had longed to hear someone in power in Caldonia speak like this. That it was Rand filled her with pride and a sense of surprise.

For years, she had believed Prince Rand a playboy with little interest in serious matters. Perhaps he did play hard, but his heart was in the right place. She'd never expected to discover that.

"After all," she said, "Not every young person wants to make wine. Besides, there are only so many old family wineries. A lot of the young people can't find jobs, but the population just keeps growing."

"Exactly." He slapped his palm on the desktop and

grinned up at her. "Exactly. I knew a modern woman like you would understand."

His warmth filled her with an amazing sense of rightness. She finally had the ear of someone who understood, who cared. "That's why I left, Rand—for opportunities I couldn't find here—even though I missed it here. More than I realized until I came back."

He leaned against the desk and crossed his arms, his eyes never leaving her. "Nicole, you shouldn't have left. You should have stayed and tried to make a difference."

The fact he'd voiced the same thought she'd tortured herself with over the years made it no easier to hear. Nicole stiffened and turned away from him, a coil of anxiety and anger mingling in her stomach. How dared he judge her? He didn't know what it was like to lose his parents. Having parents she clashed with would be far better than having none.

"Nicole?" Rand asked.

The concern in his voice only made it harder for her to shove her pain back in the past where it belonged. "I'm here now. Isn't that good enough for you?" she finally said, unable to keep the stress from her voice.

A tense silence hung in the air. Defiantly, she kept her eyes glued to the starry night outside. She heard a sigh, then a low-voiced admission. "Your coming back is more than good enough, Nicole."

The words danced over her body like cleansing water, washing away a good portion of her old guilt. She squeezed her eyes shut, savoring the feeling.

A moment later, his large, warm hand slid up her upper arm and rested on her shoulder. She couldn't contain a soft, barely audible gasp. She hadn't expected him to come to her, to touch her with such a gesture of concern.

An intimate warmth filled her. Rand's touch was gentle, yet she felt his underlying determination not to allow her to withdraw. Hardly daring to breathe, she stood completely still, afraid any movement would cause him to remove his hand, to leave her side.

He dropped his hand long before she was ready. "I wasn't being fair. Hell, I'm the goddamned heir to the throne, and what have I managed to accomplish?"

The agony in his voice pulled at Nicole. She turned around, and found herself gazing up into his tension-filled countenance. "It's not too late," she said softly.

"I'm beginning to believe that I can't do it alone. Perhaps this is an opportunity staring me in the face. Perhaps—" He glanced down.

*Don't withdraw now,* Nicole silently begged. *Say what you're feeling.* "Rand?"

"Perhaps you'll help me," he finally said, his eyes connecting with hers.

The prince of her country thought she could help? Nicole felt overwhelmed, astounded by his faith in her abilities. He had an entire country's worth of resources at his disposal, yet he was asking her for help. "I'd love to do whatever I can."

A slow smile began to form on his lips. "Perhaps you have time to help me develop a proposal on how computers could be used to improve efficiency in our government," he said carefully. "It's an idea I've been toying with. . . ."

"I can do that," Nicole said instantly, hoping she was up to the task. The thought of another assignment thrilled her. While selecting the princess candidates had been time consuming, she now found her days much more free. Rand had the lion's share of the work.

Besides, if she became useful to the prince in another capacity, perhaps he would offer her a permanent job. To her surprise, she realized she would relish such a prospect, even though it would mean returning to life in backward Caldonia. She'd be playing a role in changing her country for the better—something she'd once dreamed of, something she'd been too angry and afraid to try before. "It's a wonderful idea, Rand. I'll start right away."

He cleared his throat and stepped away, looking past her. "Yes, well. I'm hoping my new wife will have the same enthusiasm toward her country that you do. I don't believe I mentioned that as a preferred trait, but perhaps I should have."

"That would be good," Nicole said slowly. She should be pleased he agreed with her on this point. But she felt almost jealous of this woman.

Worse, she felt chastened, even though she knew he hadn't meant to remind her of her place in his life. Thank goodness he had no idea of her attraction to him. He believed she was just as enthusiastic as he about finding him the perfect wife. As she should be.

"Tomorrow we'll start work on the computer proposal." He frowned. "No. Tomorrow's Saturday. I have an . . . appointment. I won't be back until late—if then."

No doubt another visit to his mistress. Nicole battled back a tightening in her stomach at the image of him enjoying himself in the arms of some beautiful woman. It was none of her business.

Rand continued. "We'll have to do it Monday. I'll make certain Gerald schedules us time." His eyes glowed. She found it hard to look away.

But look away she did, resolve building in her chest to fulfill *all* her duties equally well. "And we'll set up your date with Lady Patricia."

His smile faded, a shadow of tension sliding over his features. She barely heard his words as he turned away. "Good. That task can't be neglected, at any cost."

# SIX

*Journal entry, Monday, May 20: The palace seems incredibly quiet with Prince Rand away. If I hadn't received this exciting new assignment from him, I would definitely be going stir-crazy. I've found so much information that I believe will be useful to us, but I'm frustrated that I can't share it with him because he's off playing. Gerald says he should return sometime today—from where, I'm not certain. I've dropped a few hints, but he's the ever loyal servant and won't spill the beans. He's protecting his employer's privacy—which I suspect means that Rand is having a torrid affair. Who is she and what does she mean to him?*

Nicole yawned. Last night, she'd hardly slept. She kept listening for Rand's footsteps outside her apartment, half hoping he'd stop by before retiring. But he hadn't returned to the palace as his schedule indicated he would. Nicole longed to believe that her feelings about him were true, that there was more to him than she had suspected back in New York. Certainly, he seemed interested in modernizing his country. But why hadn't he done something about it?

When he disappeared like this and stayed away, forgoing his commitments, what else could she think except that he really was a frivolous playboy, a man she shouldn't respect?

On the one hand, she longed to know where Rand kept disappearing to. Yet if she actually knew who the prince was with and what they were doing—

*No.* She didn't want to know.

She rested her hand on her chin and gazed at her love seat in which Rand relaxed when he visited her. How would he treat his lover? Before meeting him, she would have expected he'd be callow, spoiled, and demanding. Perhaps he was. But now, she couldn't help thinking from his consideration toward her that he would be attentive to his lover's needs.

His lover—no doubt a sensuous beauty who knew how to satisfy him. They were probably spending their hours together skiing, sailing, dining by candlelight. Making love.

*Stop it,* she chastised herself. *Just stop it.* Pacing onto the balcony, she looked over the broad lawn bordered by colorful flower beds, but their serene beauty barely registered. Why should she care that he spent time with women, probably even had a mistress? He would hardly be the first royal to take a mistress. Nor could she completely blame him for wanting to escape the demands of palace life for a private indulgence.

*Indulgence.* At that word, she squeezed her eyes tight. It sounded so sensual, so untamed. It burned deep inside her, searing her where no one else could see. She had no right to judge Prince Rand and certainly no right to be feeling this raw, painful longing, which had nothing whatsoever to do with her work for him.

Certainly, he was handsome. Yes, she enjoyed his company. They got along well. But in all the time they had spent together, he had never once stopped being a prince.

She sucked in a deep breath of clean spring air. At least Rand didn't suspect her feelings. He was as off-limits as a man could get, and she would be wise to remember that. She couldn't allow herself to play with fire even in the privacy of her own thoughts.

And definitely not in reality. She would have to keep her emotional distance from him. No more laughing or joking. No more casual addresses. No more allowing him into her apartment late at night—something he didn't seem to expect from his other servants.

Her apartment telephone rang shrilly. Glad for the interruption, Nicole went back inside and picked up the receiver by her bed.

"Miss Aldridge?" Gerald said. "Prince Rand has just returned, and he is anxious to speak with you."

Nicole fought down her excitement at Gerald's words. The prince had been expected to return sometime today and get back to work.

*Yes, but he wants to see you now. He doesn't want to wait,* a little voice reminded her.

Because of her new project, no doubt. That was all it was. She told Gerald she would be right there, then gathered up her thick research files.

When she reached the prince's office, she found Gerald standing beside Rand's desk, a distressed expression on his genial face. Rand was glancing over a document on his desk.

"You were expected this morning, at the breakfast for the Architectural Preservation League, Your Highness," Gerald said. "I had thought you were returning last evening, or I would have notified the queen's secretary."

"My mother appeared, didn't she?" Rand asked uninterestedly.

"You know they want to see *you,* sir."

*No surprise there,* Nicole thought. The queen of Caldonia had never been popular. Not like her playboy son.

"Don't fret over it, Gerald," Rand said jovially, flipping another page and scanning it. "I'm sure they were happy to have the queen there." He began patting his shirt pockets, and Nicole noticed he was wearing snug jeans and a casual button-down shirt with the top two buttons undone. The outfit definitely suited him.

No doubt his mistress thought so too—enough to keep him so occupied he'd ignored his appointments. Nicole clung to her irritation at his lack of responsibility as defense against his charm and the warmth she felt as she silently watched him.

"Now I know I put that list somewhere," Rand said, talking as much to himself as to Gerald. "I just had it."

"Try your top drawer, Your Highness," Gerald said.

Rand opened the drawer and pulled out a legal pad. "Aha! I want to share this with her when she—" He glanced up and saw Nicole waiting by the door. A broad smile broke out on his face and he called out cheerfully, "Ah, the woman of the hour."

Nicole bit back her answering smile. She had just resolved to keep her distance. She shouldn't encourage him.

Yet he gazed at her as if she held the secret key to the kingdom. He rose and crossed toward her, gesturing to the pile of files in her arms. "Don't tell me all of this—"

"It's our project, yes," she said, feeling a thrill of satisfaction that she'd impressed him. Yet she kept her face impassive.

"My God, you've been busy, haven't you? Here, let me." He took the heavy stack of files from her arms, placed them on the coffee table, and sat down on the sofa before them. "Let's see what you have here."

"Sir, may I remind you that you don't have much time," Gerald said.

Rand ignored him and began flipping through the first of Nicole's files. "Oh, here." He handed her the legal pad he'd pulled from his desk. "Some thoughts I had on our project. I thought if you had time . . ."

"I'll look them over as soon as I can," she finished for him.

"Thank you, Nicole."

The warmth of his gaze flooded every one of Nicole's senses. She forced her own gaze away in an effort to maintain her equilibrium.

"Your afternoon is set aside for your picnic with Lady Patricia," Gerald interrupted from the other side of the coffee table. "And while I've endeavored to move your morning appointments around, you are still scheduled to be interviewed by the reporter from *Caldonian World* magazine in nineteen minutes."

"You're meeting with the press?" Nicole asked.

"It would seem so," Rand said dryly. "The quarterly has-the-prince-found-his-princess-yet interview."

"I wish you had something to report," Nicole said in all honesty. His inability to answer such questions reflected poorly on her own work.

Another man came into the room from the back door—a door Nicole had learned led up a staircase directly to Rand's private apartments. She never went through it.

She recognized Armand— a small, wiry man who sported a narrow, waxed mustache that would have been in fashion if the man had lived a hundred years ago. She usually saw Rand's valet on the upper floor, but today he had brought Rand's clothes to him. He carried a black suit, a white shirt, and a Caldonian green tie on gold hangers.

"Your change of clothes is ready, Your Highness," he said.

Rand glanced up uninterestedly, then back to the file. "He's always wanting to dress me," he murmured to Nicole conspiratorially. "Like I'm some kind of giant toy doll."

She couldn't help smiling at that remark. She could think of worse ways to spend her time than clothing Rand. Her gaze roved over his casual shirt tucked into those skin-tight jeans. Back in New York, she had rarely seen photos of Rand dressed so casually, except perhaps for fuzzy, out-of-focus paparazzi photos that *Aristocrats* refused to purchase.

Since moving into the palace, she had noticed that Rand wore such clothes when he had no scheduled appearances. She wished the world could see this other side of him, as she could. The casual look certainly fit him. It gave him a rugged aspect that contrasted with his usual sophisticated image. "Why do you have to change at all?" she asked softly.

"Appearances, what else?" he replied as if bored by the subject. "These are amazing numbers, Nicole. Are you saying here that productivity increased by this much because of information systems put into place?"

Nicole had to admit she was impressed by how badly

Rand seemed to want to work. The man was full of contra-
dictions. "Yes, I found—"

"Your Highness," Gerald interrupted, glancing at his
watch in agitation. "We now have only fifteen minutes. You
still must change. Only twenty-five minutes are allotted for
the interview, and following that, you have a meeting with
the Agricultural Affairs Committee. I strongly recommend
you not be late, sir. The members are still distressed over
your remarks last fall about grape growing not being sufficient industry for Caldonia."

Rand sighed and flipped the folder closed. "All right."
He stood and reached for the suit the valet held out to
him.

"Don't," Nicole said impulsively.

Rand accepted the hanger and glanced over at her.
"Don't what?"

"Don't change. Here." She crossed to him and took the
suit hanger from his hand. She peeled off the coat and
held it open. "Put this on over your shirt. But don't change
the rest of your clothes."

"That's unacceptable," Armand said, crossing his arms
decisively. He looked toward Rand as if awaiting confirma-
tion.

Rand ignored him. He cocked an eyebrow at Nicole.
"And the reason would be . . . ?"

She held up the jacket encouragingly. "Try it."

Rand shrugged and slipped the jacket on. He tugged it
into place, then looked down at his outfit, trying to see
without benefit of a mirror.

"Yes," Nicole said, her chest expanding with pleasure.
He looked both sophisticated and relaxed, polished and
playful. He was, to put it simply, gorgeous. "That's perfect."
Without thinking, she stepped in front of him and began
adjusting his shirt collar. Glancing up, she caught him gazing at her, his eyes crinkling with amusement.

Nicole stepped back, shame filling her at her weakness.
This was no way to keep her distance. She turned to the

other men. "He looks much more approachable this way, don't you think? More human. Armand, Gerald?"

"He isn't supposed to look human, Miss Aldridge," Armand said. "He's the prince!"

"The people will be able to relate to him better if they know he's one of them," she said, turning her gaze back on Rand. With a trace of guilt, she reveled in this excuse to look at him thoroughly, up close.

"They aren't meant to relate to him," Armand insisted. "They're the masses!"

"Nicole is one of the masses, Armand," Rand said coldly. He looked at Nicole. "So you think this works. Does it make me look more modern?" He smoothed the jacket front.

"Definitely."

"Fine. I'll wear it. Now let's get back to work."

"But, Your Highness—" Armand began, his face turning red.

Rand silenced him with a look. "Thank you, Armand, but the matter is settled. You may go." Armand left, followed by Gerald, who tapped his watch significantly before leaving.

Finally alone, Rand lost no time in focusing his full attention on Nicole's research. "What's this?" he asked, pulling out the second folder.

She sat across from him. "Articles that discuss computer use in businesses and government, both small and large. Many of them have systems that could work for us."

"Excellent work, Nicole." He flipped rapidly through the file, but to her delight, he stopped briefly on sections she had hoped he'd find especially helpful. "And so complete."

"Thank you, Your Highness," she said carefully, uncomfortably warm from his praise. Why couldn't he find fault with her as he did with so many other things?

At her formality, a frown gathered on his forehead. Yet he said nothing, but merely gazed at her speculatively.

She smoothed her skirt. "I had the time this weekend since you were . . . occupied."

She longed to hear he hadn't been with a woman, but he appeared not to notice her hesitancy, her subtle hint for information. He smiled. "You never take a break, do you?"

She couldn't look into that appreciative gaze and keep from smiling back. So she kept her gaze from meeting his. She passed an even thicker file to him. "Articles in this file discuss the economic implications of computerized countries versus noncomputerized countries. It might give you some ammunition to use with the king, Your Highness."

"Thank you, *Nicole,*" he said pointedly. As he flipped through this new folder, his eyes widened. "How did you gather so much data? We only discussed this Friday!"

"I made a trip to the library in town. There was very little information there, so I pulled a lot of it off the Internet," she explained.

"Ah." He nodded sagely. "The Information Superhighway. You can do that from here at the palace? I thought our phone lines might be too archaic for that."

"It took me forever, but the palace operator found me a more modern link, and I managed. Perhaps we can find a way for Caldonia to use the Internet to expand its business base—to find proposals to submit bids on, attract investors, that sort of thing."

He closed the file, his penetrating gaze searching her face. "So, in other words, you worked all weekend on this."

"Not *all* weekend." She cleared her throat, fighting a tremendous awareness of how alone they were and how she longed to be herself with him, to openly share his enthusiasm. But she couldn't do it. The risk was far too great. She raised her chin and said carefully, "Don't you think the idea has merit, Your Highness?"

His exuberance seemed to dim. "Of course I do, but you need to relax and take a break now and then." He dropped the files back on the table. "Nicole."

*Enjoy myself like you do, Rand?* she longed to say. *Ignoring your responsibilities to dally with a lover?* Keeping her back stiff, she looked past him toward the broad swath of lawn backed by forests outside the window. It was a lovely day for a ride with Lady Pat. While Rand had missed other responsibilities, he'd made sure not to forgo his most enjoyable appointment. That ought to please her since she had arranged it. Yet it didn't.

"Every time I see you, you're working," he said, his voice low, prodding at her protective inner wall. "You need your rest, your recreation. You need to enjoy yourself."

"I enjoy working, Your Highness," she said coolly, wanting desperately for him to abandon this subject. She didn't know how much longer she could resist looking directly at him without him suspecting something. And she feared what he would read in her eyes.

He leaned forward, resting his elbows on his spread knees. "I know I can be demanding," he said softly, his gaze attempting to search hers. "I can forget other people have lives that don't involve me and our work. I want you to tell me, Nicole, if I go overboard."

*If only he would stop this,* Nicole cried silently. *Stop trying to dig deeper past my defenses. Stop being so damned understanding and warm and considerate!* "I don't—" she said harshly, then caught herself and moderated her tone. "I don't feel that way."

"I keep you up past your bedtime as it is, popping in late at night like I do."

It was the opening she needed to start redefining their relationship. Nicole hated the idea of forgoing his evening visits, but they had to end. "Perhaps it would be best—"

"Excuse me." Gerald's cultured voice cut through their conversation. He stood at the side door. "Your Highness, Miss Aldridge, I have regrettable news regarding Lady Patricia."

"Lady Pat?" Nicole asked, coming to her feet.

Rand cocked an eyebrow. "Out with it, man."

"She has eloped, Your Highness. As of yesterday, she is no longer Lady Patricia of Caldonia, but Mrs. Steven Abbot of Fort Lauderdale, Florida."

Nicole gasped. The *Aristocrats* staff must be going crazy over this news.

"What?" Rand echoed.

"That's all the information I have," Gerald said. "The man is an American businessman—a contributor to one of her favorite causes or so I'm told by her household staff. I expect her parents—the earl and countess—are in need of, shall we say, our condolences?"

Nicole met Rand's equally shocked gaze.

"Damn, they're dropping like flies," he said, sagging back on the sofa. "Soon I'll have to choose between the laundry maid and the washerwoman."

He seemed to be taking the news fairly well, considering he'd just lost his hottest prospect for a wife. "On to the next one," she said resolutely. "This *does* present us with an opportunity, however."

"In what way?"

"You wanted more time on our project. Now that the picnic's canceled—"

"No." Rising, Rand came around the coffee table and stopped before her. "I have a better idea. Why don't you take Patricia's place?"

Nicole froze, unsure she had heard him right. "Me?"

"It's a shame to waste the picnic after Gerald went to all that trouble setting it up."

"Actually, Your Highness, it was not very—"

Rand talked over his protest. "See? Gerald's heart will be broken. All that work for nothing. Don't do it to him, woman," he said with mock sternness.

"This is so, Your Highness," Gerald said, finally playing along. His eyes crinkled warmly. "I worked frightfully hard on the arrangements. Deciding on the composition of the sandwiches—turkey or roast beef? Ordering the basket packed . . ."

Rand grinned and rubbed his hands together. "Then it's settled. Perhaps now we can teach you how to relax."

Nicole felt the energy from his enthusiasm through every part of her body. He wanted to spend time with her. *On the computer project, Nicole. It's nothing more than that. Don't lose sight of your number one purpose: finding him a wife—a suitable noble wife. And you're not in the running.* "Maybe we should stay inside and use the time to work—"

Rand's intercom buzzed, cutting her off. Gerald strode to the desk and pressed the button. "Prince Randall's office."

"Gerald, the reporter and photographer from *Caldonian World* have arrived," came a male voice, which Nicole guessed belonged to a member of the palace butler staff.

Rand sighed. "They're early. Gerald, go tell the press officer I'm on my way."

"Yes, Your Highness." Gerald turned and headed for the main office door.

Rand glanced at his watch again. "Damn, there's never enough time. But this afternoon, we're making time." He lifted his warm gaze to Nicole. Nicole couldn't look away. She was so rattled by his suggestion, she didn't have a chance to put up her defenses.

"Found time is even better than found money in my book, and one should spend it on something enjoyable," he said. "You, my dear, will meet me at the south terrace promptly at noon."

She had to stop him. Now. "But, Your Highness, I don't think—"

He strode from the room before the protest had left her lips.

"Do you find the food unsatisfactory, miss?"

Rand watched as Nicole smiled at the white-gloved servant who hovered over the picnic blanket. Her plate of food, virtually untouched, rested on a foot-high portable table that had been placed between them.

"Not at all. It's delicious," she said. "Truly exceptional, thank you. It's just that I ate a large breakfast."

The servant smiled at her tactful response.

While Nicole had responded with her natural grace,

Rand noticed, she continued to hold herself aloof, at least from him. It rubbed him raw. He was determined to get to the bottom of it. He wasn't at all sure why it was so damned important to him, but it was.

For their picnic, she'd changed into jeans and a cotton shirt, and she'd tied her hair back with a colorful scarf. She'd also tied a cardigan sweater over her shoulders to ward off a possible early May chill, though they now enjoyed sunny, cloud-free skies. Despite being away for a decade, she obviously remembered how changeable the weather could be at this time of year. Which meant that the country of her birth was still in her blood.

He studied her profile as she gazed at the magnificent view of Fortinbleaux in the distance. Its red roofs, pinnacles, parks and neat, clean streets appeared like a picture postcard. Her posture conveyed stiff formality despite the fact she was sitting on the ground, her legs neatly tucked under her, her back straight. She seemed as bright and cold as a jewel that had finally been returned to its proper setting.

The capital of Fortinbleaux, which Nicole was studying so intently, captured the country's essence: the Old World blended with the New, albeit sometimes uncomfortably.

He sighed. Caldonia meant everything to him. The country he would rule someday had been a European melting pot over the centuries, influenced by the heritage of the French, the Swiss, and the English, among others. Since it was so small, it had fought fiercely to preserve its identity despite the encroachment of its more powerful neighbors. Yet the time had come for Caldonia to work with the outside world, instead of hide from it. He had felt that Nicole understood this and shared his feelings. Correction: She *used* to share her feelings.

In defiance of her formality, he sprawled full length on the blanket and propped his head on his hand.

"More wine, Your Highness?"

The servant standing behind Rand held out the bottle

of chardonnay, gesturing toward his half-empty crystal wineglass.

Rand reached up and took the bottle from him. "Thank you. You may go. Take the carriage."

The servant bowed and, with his companion, began walking toward the waiting horse-drawn carriage that had delivered Rand and Nicole to this idyllic spot on the thousand-acre estate. Still, they weren't alone. Rand caught flashes of the palace guards' uniforms through the trees. Two were positioned not faraway, but out of sight, to maintain privacy yet provide protection on the vast estate, which was easily accessible by the public.

Rand knew anyone else would think it foolish that he wanted to be alone with his employee. If Lady Patricia had been sitting beside him, he wouldn't have dismissed the servants. But he meant to do more than converse casually with Nicole, as he would have with Lady Pat. He meant to undermine the barriers she had thrown between them. He had an overwhelming fear that if he didn't immediately challenge her new attitude, didn't succeed in regaining her as a friend, he never would. He refused to allow her to slip away. She had answered a need in him he had scarcely acknowledged, for he had found in her someone to share his vision for Caldonia, someone whose passion burned as strongly as his own.

Nicole pushed back her almost full plate. "I know you probably didn't have a chance to review the computer information since you've been tied up all morning, but I can try to answer any questions you have."

Her cool tone grated on him. "I have plenty of questions, Nicole. But we can discuss the computer project later." He sat up and refilled her wineglass where it rested on the small folding table between them.

The clink of the wine bottle's neck against her almost full glass caused her to jerk. "No more for me please. I'm not used to drinking during the day."

"You have nothing important planned for later, do you?"

"No, but—"

"You like the label, right? You said so."

"Yes, very much. But—"

"Enjoy it, Nicole," he teased with mock seriousness. "That's an order."

She shot him an exasperated look before accepting his challenge and sweeping the wineglass into her hand. "All *right* then. I will."

He grinned as he watched her take a swallow. Good. He was getting past her barriers already.

Or so he thought—until she set the wineglass down and extracted her datebook from her satchel. She opened it on her bent knees. "I've asked Gerald about your schedule for the next two weeks. We can try to schedule Lady Montpelier to be your companion at the May eleventh polo match at Harvest Gardens. Since she lives here in Fortin-bleaux, it will be easy for her to attend. However, the next few candidates are from other countries, and we'll have to give them adequate time to arrange their schedules to mesh with yours. Perhaps—"

Rand snatched the book from her hands and snapped it closed right in front of her shocked face. He dropped it back in her satchel. "I did not intend that we talk shop when I asked you along. I'm not a slave driver, Nicole."

"No, Your Highness. I didn't mean to imply you were." She gave him a careful, guarded look. "It's a lovely day, isn't it?" Despite her words, she rubbed her arms.

Rand had no interest in discussing the weather either. "Tell me what's on your mind."

"Nothing." She straightened up and folded her napkin neatly, as if indicating the picnic was over as far as she was concerned. But there was no way back to the palace without him. "We should be returning. It's getting late."

"Nonsense. It's barely past one o'clock." He shifted the small table off the blanket, plates and all. Then he slid closer to her. "Have I done something I shouldn't have?"

"No, of course not, Your Highness."

"If I have, you merely need to tell me and I'll—" Without

being consciously aware of his actions, he settled his hand on her knee.

It was as if he'd shocked her with an electric current. She jerked away, then scrambled to her feet. She stepped a few feet closer to the vista spread out below, her back ramrod straight, her arms crossed. "Isn't this a wonderful view?" she chirped brightly. "I've never seen the city looking so perfect."

Rand cursed himself. Why hadn't he kept his hands to himself? With that rainbow-colored scarf in her hair, she reminded him of a hummingbird, flitting away before he could grasp her. He would need to find a net. A very large net.

A new theory occurred to him, not an entirely comfortable one. He hesitated, not sure he wanted to hear the answer, yet wanting more than anything to know. He cleared his throat and took the plunge. "Are you homesick, Nicole? Are you . . . missing a boyfriend?"

She shrugged her shoulders. "Homesick?" she repeated as if intentionally ignoring the second half of his question. "No," she said with some surprise. "Not at all. I miss my friends, yes. But I'm not homesick."

"Perhaps because you *are* home," he suggested.

"Yes, perhaps."

He couldn't let it go. "And . . . you don't miss him?"

"Him?"

The breath caught in his lungs and he had to force the words out. "Your lover."

"I don't have—" she began. Then she turned to face him. "I really don't think we should be discussing this," she said. "It's not relevant to my work here, is it?"

Who the hell cared whether it was relevant? "Are the men in New York blind or insane or both?" he burst out.

She avoided his gaze, but her cheeks turned the color of a fine rosé. "It—it's me, not them. They never felt right. *We* never felt right. For that." As if concerned she'd said too much, she turned her back on him.

His gaze roved over her neat, slender body, and he immediately understood. Despite how hard it was to believe, she had never slept with a man. Never been carried away by passion. No man had stripped off her clothes, baring her completely to his touch, his taste. Felt the heat of her flushed skin against his. Felt the hungry embrace of her legs wrapped tight around his waist—

Heat rushed straight to his groin, and his body reacted with fierce intensity, making his jeans feel far too snug. Thank God, she was looking away toward the city, he thought ruefully. It had been a long time since he'd slept with a woman, but it wouldn't pay to think of Nicole—his Nicole—in such lustful terms. He needed her for far more than a tumble in bed.

Nor would he ever touch her. He hadn't slept with a woman in more than a year, and now, with this new pressure from his father, he had decided to wait until he found the woman he would marry. Perhaps it was a silly idea, considering sex had meant little to him in the past. But he wanted his marriage to mean something.

Waiting was probably Nicole's plan, as well. He smiled at the odd coincidence, and a soft laugh sprang from his chest. "You're an old-fashioned girl at heart, aren't you? Waiting for the marriage ring or at least true love. You may live in New York, but you're Caldonian through and through."

Nicole turned on him, her hands on her hips. "Sure, laugh all you want. No doubt a playboy like you thinks I'm ridiculously old-fashioned. It would take a *book* to record all of *your* past relationships."

Her anger filled him with satisfaction. She hadn't called him Your Highness once throughout their latest exchange. "Why do I get the feeling you're overly concerned about my relationships with the ladies?"

"I'm not," she replied, crossing her arms defensively. "I have a purely professional interest. When we *do* find a serious candidate, she could quite likely decide against *you* as a suitable match, because of your . . . women."

Now they were getting somewhere. "My *women,*" he mimicked her dry tone. "Who exactly are you referring to?"

"Lady Irene Killian, for instance. The Earl of Southesby's wife. We ran a photo of the two of you dancing at a charity ball."

Rand tensed. Lady Irene's name had been the latest to be linked with his, about four months before his princess search began in earnest.

Nicole continued. "The rumors were that she and you—"

"Lady Killian happens to be a very beautiful woman," he said tightly, rising to his feet and moving slowly toward her. "She also happens to be the chairwoman of the Committee Against Child Abuse. At that particular event, she was seeking my financial and official support before their annual convention—both of which I willingly gave her." He stopped before her and stared down into her wide-eyed face. "As for my personal relationship with Lady Irene, while she is a delightful woman, she's quite happily married. I have never had carnal relations with her. That *is* what you're most curious about, isn't it?"

Nicole lifted her chin slightly. "Whom you choose to sleep with is not my affair, Your Highness. I am merely concerned with the effect of your reputation on your future wife."

His reputation. Did she honestly believe he had a new woman every week? Did she think he was that shallow, that self-centered? His stomach twisted at the thought, and he realized that he hadn't taken a single antacid all day. He needed one now.

He didn't want to fight with her. Returning to the table, he scooped up their wineglasses and a small box of chocolates, which had been left for them. He returned to Nicole's side and lowered himself to the ground. "Sit."

After a slight hesitation, she complied, then accepted her wineglass from him. He broke open the box of chocolates and held it out to her. "Caldonian wine chocolates. One of Caldonia's many quirks."

"Part of her unique heritage," she countered, selecting one. She examined it thoughtfully before taking a nibble. "I haven't thought of these in ages," she said, her surprise blending with a trace of melancholy. "Or any of the good times. Pretty sad of me really."

She glanced at him, and he waited patiently, knowing she was remembering her childhood here in Caldonia. A soft smile danced over her lips. "My parents used to give me these in my Christmas stocking. Teased me about getting drunk on them. Which isn't really possible since they're made to go with wine, not made from wine."

"Your parents. They sound nice," he said awkwardly. How did one discuss normal parents?

"They were." She hesitated, then added, "Thank you, Your Highness." Stiffening, she looked toward Fortinbleaux, effectively throwing up a wall once more.

The tension between them increased as the seconds ticked by. In uncomfortable silence, he stared at the cityscape below while Nicole studied the chocolate she was nibbling.

Their turn in conversation couldn't erase the previous discussion, and Rand could think of nothing else but what she must really think of him. He still had no idea why she'd become so formal toward him, but damned if he was going to play along. He supposed if he wanted her to be open with him, he had to do the same. It was a liberating realization.

He looped his arms over his bent knees. "My love life isn't as interesting as you seem to think," he began carefully, voicing thoughts he'd never spoken aloud before.

Her eyes widened, and he forged ahead. "Many citizens would prefer I remain celibate until I wed. I happen to think that's not exactly healthy. So, yes, I've had lovers, but nowhere near the quantity you seem to believe. I used to think it a grand joke, what the press writes about me. Maybe I'm getting old," he added wearily. "I don't find it that funny anymore."

"Because it reflects on your character, you mean."

"Precisely. I'm going to be these people's king someday. With my father's health getting poorer every year, it might be sooner rather than later. I'm not too keen on going down in history as King Randall, the Randy."

His words came out more harshly than he intended. He lifted his gaze to hers and she cast him a tentative smile, her eyes bright with understanding. The sight filled his heart with warmth and he laughed.

In response, her smile broadened and became the natural expression he had grown fond of. "I'm glad," she said simply.

They were the most eloquent words he'd ever heard. They reinforced all his dreams and longings, expressed a world of support. Being open with her had worked so well to bring her closer, he couldn't stop. "Don't get me wrong. I enjoy women. I wish . . ." He shook his head. "I've managed to get away for brief periods over the years. I've engaged in a few casual relationships with carefully screened women, whose discretion I could trust. I would like nothing better than to meet an attractive woman, ask her to coffee, maybe to a flick. Date a few times . . . It sounds so simple, but it isn't." His voice grew dark. "So to think I have the freedom to seduce women wherever and whenever I want, to refer to me as a playboy—" He laughed harshly. "I should be so lucky. The wrong choice on my part could ruin the family."

Rand could scarcely believe he was telling her all this. He never shared himself like this—not with his family, not with his staff. With no one. Except her.

"I admit," she said slowly, "I haven't seen you with any women since I've been here. I've—I've kind of wondered about it. I apologize, Your Highness. I'm aware I didn't make things better with my articles."

He smiled at her. He had the overwhelming urge to pat her knee or her shoulder or some part of her to reassure her that he wasn't angry with her. Just the opposite. She delighted him.

She finished off her chocolate and began licking her

fingers clean. Rand's stomach tightened at the innocent gesture. Patting her knee would hardly be sufficient, he realized in dismay. As she pulled the last finger from between her lush lips, he had a sudden vision of running his tongue along their fullness, licking *them* clean. Perhaps it had been a mistake to remain celibate for so long, he thought ruefully. Every gesture of hers set his blood racing.

"Your Highness," she said suddenly, as if afraid she would lose the nerve. "When you go away for the weekend, where do you go?"

At her confused expression, he knew she had been imagining him dallying with some woman. He hated her to think he'd been spending his precious time that way. He couldn't answer her without lying—unless, of course, he shared his secret.

*He would do it.* He didn't question his trust in her, didn't spare a thought for the risk, as he would with anyone else. Even his own parents.

He scooted closer, as close as he dared, until only a foot of space separated them. Nicole stayed very still. Her feminine presence filled his senses, but he forced his thoughts on his words. "Nicole." Carefully, afraid she'd bolt, he laid a hand on her arm. This time, she didn't pull away. The simple contact burned like fire through his palm, and he felt her trembling. "I haven't risked explaining to anyone, except Gerald, of course. But you—"

Movement in a stand of trees to the right caught his eye, accompanied by a flash of reflected light. He gritted his teeth as a wave of fury engulfed him. "My God!"

# SEVEN

Prince Rand leaped to his feet so suddenly, Nicole almost fell over. He began sprinting toward a row of trees across the meadow.

Nicole caught sight of a man darting away through the bushes. She saw the familiar shape of a camera with a long lens bouncing on a cord against his hip. Two green-uniformed palace guards raced in pursuit. A chill raced down her spine as she realized a photographer had been seeking a scoop on the Playboy Prince's personal life.

An odd feeling twined through her, and her heart filled with fresh compassion for the prince. Though *Aristocrats* magazine only bought from reputable sources, she'd seen a wealth of candid photos of the prince over the years. Though they'd only been having lunch, she felt uncomfortable and angry at having their privacy violated. This had been *her* time with Rand, no one else's.

Rand slowed, stopping by the edge of trees. A few minutes passed. Then one of the guards reappeared through the trees and spoke to Rand. She saw the guard gesturing in the direction of the pursuit, then shaking his head.

Rand swept a hand through his hair and massaged the back of his neck, no doubt frustrated at being unable to catch the man. Any photos he'd gotten wouldn't be worth much, Nicole thought with relief. The prince had merely been lunching with one of his employees.

And showing her no mercy.

His openness had stunned her. He was making it harder

and harder for her to keep her emotional distance. He'd sat close beside her and shared his heart, his secrets, his dreams. For one brief, wild moment, she'd had the urge to crawl into his lap, bury her face in his neck, and forget about everything but her crazy longing to hold him.

She shook herself, irritated at her idiotic infatuation. After several moments conversing with the guard, Rand nodded, apparently dismissing him, then strode toward her.

She braced herself, determined not to let him get past her barriers, no matter what he did. She rose to meet him. "That was a photographer, wasn't it, Your Highness?"

"Don't worry about it. Now would be an excellent time for our ride. Gerald left Apollo and Athena for us, saddled and ready to go." He clapped his hands and rubbed them together. "What do you say? You *do* know how to ride, don't you?"

His false joviality didn't fool her. "Well, yes, a ride would be nice. But the photographer—what if—"

He took her elbow and began leading her in the opposite direction, down a short path through the trees, toward a pair of saddled horses tied under a pine.

He stopped beside a strong brown mare. Nicole had forgotten how big horses were.

"Up you go." After sliding his hands around her waist, he lifted her onto the horse's back. "You suit Athena," he said. "Wise, courageous. Stubborn as hell."

"I haven't ridden in ages—" Nicole began, but he'd already turned away and swung up onto the back of the most powerful-looking steed she'd ever seen—black with white socks, sleek, and muscular. Apollo. No doubt, the perfect mount for a prince.

Rand glanced back at her once, probably to make sure she hadn't fallen off. Then, with a shout, he kicked his horse and began trotting toward a riding path leading into the trees.

Nicole tentatively kicked Athena's sleek sides, but managed only to turn her in a complete circle. Frustrated, she tightened her grip on the reins. Athena neighed and pranced backward.

Nicole stiffened and sucked in her breath. She could do this. She'd ridden before. About fifteen years before while visiting a friend. She'd spent three glorious weeks on Cecily's family estate. Cecily had been wealthy. As the daughter of a college professor, Nicole had not.

She bounced up and down on the horse's back. "Come on, horsey. Go! Come on, Athena, old girl! Fetch the prince! Now!" Frustrated at how foolish she would look to anyone watching, at how Rand was already disappearing through the trees, Nicole slammed her heels into the horse's flanks.

The horse took off like a shot. Nicole clutched at the reins, then leaned forward and hung on as the mare leaped into a strong gallop. *You're doing okay,* she told herself as the wind whistled past her ears. *Doing just fine. You can do this!*

She entered the trees behind Rand, still balanced on the thundering horse. Feeling more confident, she straightened in the saddle. The feeling of riding, of *controlling,* the powerful beast exhilarated her. Together, horse and rider broke through the trees into a clearing that dipped down into a green valley. Brisk air poured into her lungs; sunshine flowed over her like the caress of satin. And the sight of the prince alongside her, in perfect command of his powerful horse Apollo, filled her with pleasure. "Yes!" she cried.

Rand glanced over and grinned at her—just as Nicole leaned back a hair too far. Before she understood what was happening, the horse disappeared out from under her. She plummeted to the ground with all the grace of a rock. Sharp pain lanced up her leg and she cried out at the red-hot agony. Lying flat on the grass, her foot twisted beneath her, she tried to catch her breath. The blue sky spun wildly above her and nausea twisted her stomach.

She blinked and tried to focus, tried to still the insane whirl of the world and put things back in their proper place. Her glasses had vanished, and everything around had turned fuzzy. Then Rand's face appeared above her, close enough for her to focus on almost frightened eyes.

"Nicole! My God, are you all right?" He must have knelt beside her, because now he was lifting her up, helping her sit in his arms.

"My ankle—it hurts," she gasped out. "God, Rand, it hurts so bad."

"This one?" He touched her foot and sharp pain shot up her body. She howled. The worry in his eyes blended with sudden anger. "Damn, this is awful. It could be broken. I thought you said you could ride!"

"If you hadn't been going so fast—" Nicole tried to wriggle out of his arms.

He let her go and sat back on his heels. "We weren't even galloping." He threw out his arms, clearly exasperated.

"I tried to tell you I haven't ridden since I was a teenager," she shot back. "I'm not an experienced horsewoman like—like Lady Patricia!"

"But you wanted to ride, didn't you?"

The pain obliterated all her caution, and she didn't have the strength to care. "Damn it, Rand. Why did you assume I'm an expert at it?"

He stared at her, his eyes reflecting confusion, frustration, and some other emotion she couldn't determine. "Maybe because you're so blasted good at everything else?"

She didn't know how to take that remark. No doubt she'd disappointed him, but she was proud of who she was—and wasn't. She lifted her chin a notch higher. "I'm just a commoner, Rand. I didn't grow up with stables and riding lessons and all that. My glasses—" She stretched out her hands to search the nearby ground. "Where are they?"

Randall settled them on her face. They perched there crookedly and she tried to straighten the bent frames without success.

Nicole found herself focusing on Rand's clenched jaw.

He sat back, his hands balled up on his thighs. "Damn it, Nicole. If you'd bothered to tell me you were a beginner—"

"I tried to tell you, but you wouldn't let me. You just threw me on the horse and rode off! You have a very bad habit of ignoring people when it suits you."

Disbelief crossed his features. "Me? I never—"

"Yes, you do." Irritable and in pain, she had no desire to guard her words. "You aren't a very good listener at all."

His eyes narrowed. "I see. Do you have any other opinions about me?"

Nicole swallowed in a dry mouth. Battling back the roiling in her stomach, she finally forced it under control. Since she'd gone this far, she might as well continue. What did she have to lose except a job she'd failed at miserably so far? "Well, you are kind of . . ."

"Kind of . . . ?" His eyes bored into hers. "What, Nicole? Don't you dare pull back now."

"Arrogant."

His lips twitched. "Am I?"

She nodded fiercely. "Really arrogant. Exceedingly arrogant. Excessively—"

He raised a hand. "Stop! I get the picture. But I prefer to think of it as self-confident." He grinned. "Now let's get you back and have the doctor check you out." He moved closer and lifted her in his arms. Pulling her tight against his chest, he stood, cradling her securely.

Nicole closed her eyes, not only against the pain, but against the tremendously delicious feeling of being so close to him. She couldn't do it anymore: She couldn't keep the barriers in place against him. Not when all she wanted was to give herself up to his strength. The accident had stripped her pretense away, and she knew she could never go back.

He carried her over to Apollo and set her on the steed so she sat sidesaddle. Taking both her hands, he wrapped the reins around them. "Hold on tight—you hear me? Don't move."

Nicole nodded, bemused by his concern. Now he no

doubt saw her as a liability, not an asset. And a terrible picnic date.

He gathered the reins of her mount, which had wandered a few yards away, and tied them to the back of Apollo's saddle. Then he mounted behind her. Reins in hand, an arm locked around her waist, he began an easy walk back toward the palace.

The ride back was a blend of pain and pleasure for Nicole. To keep from thinking of the shooting pain in her ankle, she concentrated on the masculine hardness of Rand's body behind hers, the strength of his arm holding her waist, the tickle of his breath on her neck. Being held by him was more perfect than she'd imagined. She sighed and wiggled backward, settling deeper into his embrace. His hand clenched on her stomach, then gradually loosened, as if he was forcing himself to relax. No doubt he was furious with her.

As they entered the trees, he said in her ear, "You're also kind of arrogant, Nicole."

"Me? How can you—"

"You have a polite, diplomatic way about you—most of the time. But you manage to get your points across just the same because you're so certain you're right."

Nicole found herself smiling. He understood her too well. She was definitely outspoken, and she didn't hesitate to share her opinions, even with the rulers of her country. Perhaps that was the American in her—a belief that everyone was equal, every voice should be heard, even a commoner's like hers. "I suppose, maybe, I do sometimes—"

"Most of the time, you *are* right," he said ruefully. "It would terrify most men."

She couldn't resist. She took the bait. "But not you?"

"I'm too damned arrogant to let you intimidate me, Nicole." She heard the smile in his voice and couldn't fight the warmth that filled her at his teasing.

After a while, Rand left the road and entered the well-tended grounds behind the palace. They rode through the hedgerows, down the gravel garden path, and over the neatly kept lawn. The gardener looked up as they passed, staring after them in amazement.

"I take it horses aren't allowed in the garden?" Nicole asked.

"I'm making an exception." He rode straight to the vast west wing, then pulled up right by the terrace outside his office. "Gerald!"

Immediately, Gerald appeared through the French doors.

"Get Dr. Chapelle. Nicole has been hurt."

"Hurt! That's terrible," Gerald said, frowning. "How——?"

"Athena became skittish and threw her off," Rand explained hurriedly as he dismounted. Nicole gazed down at him in surprise. That wasn't precisely how it had happened.

Gerald seemed to find it odd as well. "Our well-trained Athena? I've never——"

Rand scowled at him. "The doctor, Gerald," he barked.

"Yes, Your Highness. I'll summon him right away." He turned to leave.

"Wait," Rand said. "Help me first. Open the door."

Gerald swung open the French doors and Rand lifted Nicole off the horse, then carried her inside. He set her carefully on the sofa and placed a pillow on the coffee table to support her injured ankle, which had swelled to twice its size.

After Gerald disappeared, Rand stripped off her tennis shoe and sock and rolled up her jeans leg. He ran his fingers over her tender skin. "Nice colors. Blue, purple, crimson——"

"Just don't touch it," she said, gritting her teeth.

He smoothed the tousled hair out of her eyes. His tender touch seemed to take the edge off the agony. "Take it easy. Dr. Chapelle will have something magic to take away the pain. Just hold on. I'll get some ice to take the swelling down."

He crossed to the wet bar against the wall. Nicole hated even this brief separation. She heard him open the small refrigerator. A disorienting red haze colored all her perceptions. She only wanted to close her eyes and block everything out, especially the pain.

A moment later, Rand returned with ice wrapped in a dishcloth. He crouched at her feet and laid it against her ankle. Nicole flinched at the sudden chill, but it also felt good.

She absorbed the sight of him: his tousled ebony hair, the way his shirt pulled across his shoulders, the gentle way his hands held the ice against her injury. No one at the magazine would believe that Prince Rand was kneeling at her feet, serving her like a nurse.

"Better?" he asked.

She nodded. "Thank you."

"For what?" His expression darkened and a muscle flexed in his jaw. He looked almost angry. "This is the least I can do after causing this."

With a pang of disappointment that warred with her painful injury, Nicole realized the truth. No wonder Rand was being so solicitous. She'd made him feel guilty. The way he'd carried her and held her against him on his horse . . . Of course he needed to get her back here some way. That was the only reason he'd held her in his arms. The only reason he would ever hold her. Only a starry-eyed fool would try to make something more of it.

Rand paced from one wall of the doctor's office to the other, desperate to work off the guilt gnawing at him. Inside a small examining room, he could see Dr. Chapelle securing a wrap around Nicole's ankle. The doctor had ordered Nicole wheeled to his palace office, where he X-rayed her ankle on an ancient-looking machine. The doctor determined her injury to be a sprain only, not a break. Still, she would have to stay off the foot for six weeks.

Rand kept reminding himself she would live. It was only a sprain. She should have spoken up when he placed her on Athena. Gotten his attention somehow. Yelled at him.

Yelled at him? A commoner? Ridiculous thought! He

turned at the door and paced back again as the doctor
directed Nicole to hold an ice-pack against her injury. Her
face had grown alarmingly pale, and he could tell by the
tight set of her lips that it hurt like hell.

He stopped at the door to the examining room. "Did
you give her a painkiller?" he demanded harshly.

"Yes, Your Highness," Dr. Chapelle said, sounding remarkably calm despite Rand's royal anger. He nodded toward the pill bottle in her hand. "Miss Aldridge, when the
shot wears off, take two pills every four hours for the next
few days. If it's not sufficient, call me."

Nicole nodded once. A thin sheen of perspiration had
broken out on her forehead. Rand fought the urge to
gather her into his arms and soothe her. She was his employee—an administrative assistant, nothing more. She
would survive this. It was only a sprain.

He paced toward the door again, his fists clenching. It
could have been much worse. She could have broken that
swanlike neck of hers! Damn, what a fool he was.

A new problem sprang to mind. How were they going
to continue work on their projects if she couldn't negotiate
the stairs to come down to his office? Dr. Chapelle said she
should stay in bed for several days; then perhaps she could
graduate to crutches. But the stairs were marble—dangerous should she fall again.

The doctor came over to him. "That is all I can do, Your
Highness. She will recover in time. We ought to move her
up to her room. The shot of pain medication that I gave
her will relax her quite a bit."

Before the doctor or his nurse could make a move, Rand
strode forward. "I'll take her." He carefully lifted her into
the wheelchair. Without another word to them, he wheeled
her out of the room as far as the foot of the sweeping
marble steps.

"I'm sorry, Rand," Nicole said, understanding that he
would have to carry her up.

*She* was sorry? Swearing under his breath, he carefully
lifted her and began the climb. She was marvelously light,

slender, and gently curved in all the right places. Fiercely he tried to stifle his wayward thoughts. But with her arms around his neck, her sweet face with those crooked glasses was only inches away. Her breath tickled his cheek through softly parted lips. Hell, if he turned his head just a fraction, he could taste her mouth.

He kept his neck muscles rigid and forced himself not to look at her. Her scent, however, was hard to avoid. She smelled of sunshine, fresh air, and spring flowers. Understated, elegant. Damned sexy. And she'd never been intimate with a man.

Possessiveness swelled in him. For now, she was all his.

As he passed the library on his way to her room, an idea struck him. He would move his office to the library. That way, she wouldn't have to negotiate the palace stairs.

As soon as he entered her suite, a waiting chambermaid turned down the bedsheets. He laid her on the mattress and the maid adjusted the pillows behind Nicole's head. The maid took the pills from Nicole and placed them on the nightstand. Impatient to be alone with Nicole, Rand dismissed the maid.

Nicole looked up at him from under drowsy lids. The painkiller must be taking effect. He had never seen her so relaxed, never seen such a sensuous smile on her soft pink lips.

Then her brow furrowed. "This is really dumb," she said in that uniquely American way of hers. "I can't believe I did this. Are you going to fire me now?"

"Fire you? When we have so much work to do? This is merely a bump on the road to success." He dragged a wingback chair beside her bed. He sat down, then explained about using the library. "I'll conduct my business from there until you heal," he said enthusiastically. He couldn't imagine she would think he'd get rid of her merely because of her injury. Especially when he was to blame. "When you're ready, you can hobble on in and join me."

"You really should get with the times, Rand." Nicole snuggled into the pillow.

Rand reached out to smooth her brow again, but pulled back his wayward hand. He'd touched her far too much today already. "The times?"

"Handicapped access. Make it a law. This palace needs it. You could put in an elevator, you know. Ramps, that sort of thing. Help the disabled be part of your society."

"Ah, I see." It was possible. The people might appreciate such a sign of a changing, modernizing government. "It sounds like a good idea. I hadn't given it much thought."

A frown creased her brow. "And drunks shouldn't be allowed to drive."

Rand recalled Lord Phillip saying her parents had died in a car accident caused by a man in his cups. No wonder she had given up on this backward country of theirs. He wanted badly to make it up to her. "You're right. Drunks shouldn't drive."

"And your road signs are lousy. Fix them, okay?"

"Okay." He would promise her anything, he realized with a shock. When had he grown so vulnerable to her? It was a strange feeling, not entirely comfortable.

She sighed. "And women—they should be admitted to the state universities. Those rules really suck."

"They suck, hmm?" He bit back a smile at her American vernacular. He should have drugged her weeks ago; then she would have opened up to him sooner. He had no idea she had so many ideas whirling through her mind. "Do you ever stop thinking, Nicole?"

"Uh-uh." She shook her head. "Too much to do." Her eyes fluttered and drifted closed. She mumbled and he had to strain to hear. "Thank you for letting me help, Rand. It means a lot to me."

"And to me," he whispered, settling his hand on hers. She didn't reply. He watched the even rise and fall of her chest and knew she'd fallen asleep. Still, he couldn't bring himself to leave her. He had blocked out this time, until five, for the picnic. For once he had nowhere else to be.

As he gazed at her face, so innocent in repose, an amazing sense of wonder filled him. He could hardly remember what life had been like before she'd arrived at the palace.

The tempting situation defeated his noblest intentions. He would never have another chance. Praying he wouldn't wake Sleeping Beauty, the prince leaned close and gave her a gentle kiss on the mouth.

# EIGHT

Despite the soreness of her injured ankle, Nicole couldn't remember being so happy. Every day since the accident two weeks ago, she woke up looking forward to her work. She'd never imagined Prince Rand—portrayed by everyone, even her, as an arrogant, self-absorbed playboy—could work so hard. Like a low-grade fever or a buzz of interference, her strong attraction to Prince Rand never went away. It remained in the background waiting for her to tune in—if she dared. She kept the heat at bay by throwing herself into their projects.

And each hour she put in—whether drafting a report on highway accidents or contacting leading Caldonian women for their support on changing the university admission rules—she felt the strong sense of fulfillment that only valuable work could provide. She'd spent far too many years at the magazine when there was so much important work to be done. But only because Rand had made it possible.

Only two things cast a shadow over her new career working with the prince. The first was her inability to locate a serious princess candidate for him. And it was almost June. Prince Rand never mentioned her failing in this area, but it weighed on Nicole more and more as the days slipped by. None of the candidates so far passed the most basic test. None intrigued the prince enough that he wanted Nicole to arrange a second date with her.

The second disappointment was Rand's frequent, unexplained disappearances on personal business trips to some unnamed place, for some unnamed purpose. This time, he'd been gone not just a weekend, but five long days.

Dressed casually in slacks and a blouse, Nicole hobbled to the library on crutches. To her relief, when she arrived, she discovered Rand had returned to the palace and was already at work. He was dictating into a machine more thoughts on the proposal he would soon bring before the Grand Assembly, a sweeping set of reforms designed to increase the attractiveness of Caldonia to foreign investors.

She stood at the door and watched him, pride sweeping through her. She wanted the world to know this man, who worked hard, who cared. She'd never seen a man so full of energy. Sometimes he would fade out and stare into space, his mind a million miles away. When he returned, he would have a new strategy or a plan of attack to approach a particularly nasty barrier. The harder they worked, the happier he seemed. He was an inspiration.

At the same time, her selfish side was glad she didn't have to share him—at least where his work was concerned. His mysterious mistress might have his body, but Nicole shared his hopes for Caldonia. She would be a complete fool to wish she could have both.

He looked up and their gazes connected. A thrill of excitement sizzled through her at the delighted expression in his eyes. *Five long days* . . . Valiantly, she fought to maintain her professional composure. "Good morning, Rand."

"Come in! I have wonderful news. Sit." He turned off the dictating machine and pointed to the love seat in the library's conversation area.

The room's ceiling rose two stories high, and tall windows with stained-glass insets let in muted light. Floor-to-ceiling shelves were filled with books new and old—mostly old, Nicole thought with a smile. Helping to relieve the smothering burden of tradition for her country had made the aesthetic aspects of its heritage much easier to appreciate.

Contrasting sharply with the library decor, a new desktop

computer sat atop an expensive rosewood desk. Already, files on their new projects filled its hard drive. Her own laptop sat beside it, and she had transferred the princess files to the larger computer as well.

She sank gratefully into the love seat and set her crutches aside. "What's your news?"

"An incentive program." He explained how any industry deciding to build in Caldonia would receive free utilities and a tax break for the first three years.

"That sounds workable," Nicole said.

"It's more than workable." Rand crossed to the door. He darted a glance up and down the hall, then closed the door securely and returned to her side. "It's already working."

"I don't understand." Rand had yet to present his ideas to the stodgy, conservative Grand Assembly or to get the members to buy in to his reforms. He might be the prince, but the government was still representational.

Rand sat beside her, his eyes glowing intensely. "It's time I revealed my secret."

His secret . . . about his personal weekends? Nicole shifted her position, trying not to reveal her sudden discomfort—and her awareness of his nearness. "Go on."

"You know when I leave for the odd weekend here and there on personal business?"

"Yes," she said slowly. Perhaps she didn't want to know his secret after all. He might have said his relationships were more infrequent than his playboy image indicated, but that didn't discount the possibility he'd set up some exotic mistress in a villa somewhere. He began speaking, and she shook herself from such thoughts to concentrate on his words.

His eyes shone with excitement as they met hers, pulling Nicole into the warm circle of his potent attention. "I haven't told anyone but Gerald what I'm about. I didn't want to jinx it prematurely. But, Nicole, since you're intimately involved in our project, I can't help wanting to share my news with you."

*Our project* . . . He'd gotten himself engaged. That had to be it. He'd been romancing a woman on the side, and now he was going to marry her. No wonder he hadn't been concerned about Nicole's lack of progress. A sick feeling unfurled in her stomach, and she battled the reaction. If only she could tell herself it was professional disappointment that he hadn't needed her to find his wife. If only she believed the lie.

*His engagement was the goal,* she reminded herself sternly. Her disloyalty shamed her, and she forced her unwarranted reaction into the deepest recesses of her heart. She fought to keep her voice steady. "Go on."

"I wanted to tell you before, Nicole. I almost did on our picnic, in fact. But—" He glanced at her wrapped foot. "Yes, well, we were interrupted. I was distracted after that."

"Rand?" she asked slowly, amazed to see such a usually composed man so hesitant. *He's in love. What else could explain his barely contained ebullience?* Her heart twisted in her chest, and she suddenly found it difficult to breathe.

His eyes returned to hers, searching deeply. He must have been pleased with what he saw, for he chuckled as if a great weight was finally falling from his shoulders. The sound played along her nerves like a sweet invitation. He breathed deeply and began.

"For the past year, I've been taking as much time as I could, traveling to other countries, those with strong, diverse economies—meeting with businessmen who might be willing to establish industry in Caldonia."

"Oh!" His revelation struck her at the deepest, most primal female level. His trips had nothing to do with a woman. *They never had.* All those nights he'd been away, those long endless nights when her mind had been filled with images of him in passionate embrace with a mistress well practiced in meeting his sexual needs . . . *She was a fantasy. She didn't exist.*

Relief poured through Nicole—irrational, sweeping relief. She fought to maintain her equilibrium, to hide her reaction from him, to display appropriately pleased surprise, nothing more. But she couldn't suppress an answering grin, and she knew he read the joy in her eyes. *Be happy that he's even more dedicated than you ever expected,* she told herself. *Hang your joy on that and on his astounding success.*

"It's damned exciting." He braced his arm on the back of the sofa and turned toward her, tucking one knee on the cushion between them. The scant inches between them buzzed with electricity. His energy seemed to enfold her, causing her blood to heat to an alarming degree.

Nicole battled back her instinctive female attraction. She had to maintain her composure at all costs.

"I just returned from the United States, Nicole," he said. Her name, spoken in his husky timbre, seemed to vibrate along her spine. "A top computer firm wants very much to open a plant here. A manufacturing plant for printer supplies and tiny . . . What's the term?" He waved his hand, searching for the word.

"Chips maybe? Microchips?" Nicole's relief transformed into an excitement that matched his. Microchips! Not a lover, not a wife. "What a boon for Caldonia! A chance to enter the modern world at last."

He slapped his knee enthusiastically. "Yes! Microchips. They believe our labor base is more educated and will be easier to train than in other countries. Of course, I sold them on that point." The words poured from him like water through a burst dam.

Grinning at his boyish enthusiasm, she laid her hand on his arm. "And it's true, Rand. You're right! You're absolutely right! This is wonderful news!"

She had the sudden, insane urge to embrace him, even kiss him, and for the briefest of seconds, she believed he felt the same. He leaned closer, his arm sliding behind her head along the top of the sofa. In response, she slid her hand up his arm toward his shoulder.

His expression caught hers, his eyes sparking with an unnaturally brilliant light. "Nicole—" Gradually, as if caught in a spell, he drew even closer, impossibly close. She could hardly draw breath as his gaze dropped to her lips, then slid up again to meet hers, filled with unspoken long-ing. His handsome face filled her vision, and she found herself leaning toward him as well until his sensuous lips were a mere breath away.

He couldn't—they couldn't—it was insane. "Rand—" Nicole stiffened and jerked away, facing resolutely toward the bookshelves across the large room. "Thank you for trusting me with your news," she said coolly, desperately fighting the overwhelming urge to fall into his arms, into *him*. She ran moist palms along her skirt, smoothing it.

She felt the sofa shift as Rand shot to his feet. He paced around the coffee table toward the center of the room, patting his jacket pockets with swift, desperate motions. "Damn, where are they?"

He paused at the desk and yanked open a drawer, dug around in it, then came up with a cigar. "There!" He knocked papers on the desk aside and found his solid-gold lighter. He puffed into the flame, bringing the tip to a red-hot glow. "Don't say it," he grumbled over his shoul-der. "I know I promised not to subject you, but—"

Frustrated and refusing to acknowledge why, Nicole shot back, "And you say you're not addicted?"

He faced her fully, his feet planted wide. "Damn it, woman! Must you call me on *every* weakness I have?" he said caustically. In defiance, he sucked in another large puff and exhaled it in her direction.

Nicole stiffened, unused to such a tone, confused by his sudden change of mood. She fought to keep her voice steady, but she couldn't keep from expressing her opinion. "Very well. Contaminate your lungs. They're probably black as sin by now anyway. You'll die young—that's all. Any children you have—should you ever get around to finding a princess perfect enough to be their mother—won't even remember you."

He hissed more smoke between gritted teeth. "I don't expect her to be perfect, but I expect her to have a damn sight more grace than you're exhibiting right now."

"Grace?" Nicole's blood pulsed hard in her veins at his

ridiculous insult. She crossed her arms over her chest protectively. So he thought she compared poorly to his titled girlfriends. She was past caring. "So it's graceful to let your husband pollute his body and say nothing about it? You prefer a woman to grin and bear whatever hedonistic diversions you decide to indulge in—is that it? Because you're royal, you're indestructible?" She snorted in a very unladylike fashion. "I suppose that's why you pop antacids like candy."

"You're worse than a nagging wife!" He waved his hand toward her, his eyes glittering dangerously. "I hardly need a lecture from you. You're just my—my employee!"

*Just my employee.* The words struck Nicole like a knife in the stomach, despite their truth. How could the morning—which had started out so wonderfully—fall apart so fast? Nicole reached for her crutches, hating the damn things, desperately longing to be able to stride from the room.

Before she managed to get to her feet, Rand was there, pulling the crutches from her hands. He flung them away. "I haven't given you leave to go, Nicole."

Nicole's hand was halfway to his face before she realized she was about to slap the prince. She forced her fingers into a tight ball. She shouldn't let the man get to her; she couldn't let him see how he affected her. Instead, she fell back down on the sofa, sitting primly, trying her damnedest to appear unaffected by his outburst.

"I beg your pardon, Your Royal Highness," she bit out between clenched teeth. "I didn't think you were in the mood to work."

His steely gaze pinned her where she sat. She felt like a butterfly affixed to a display board as he examined her through narrowed, dispassionate eyes, which showed no hint of his earlier warmth. "Didn't I hire you to find me a suitable wife?"

"Of course. You know we—"

"Well, damn it! Find me one!" He took another drag on his cigar and blew it out. "One that knows how to treat a royal spouse—and doesn't mind a little harmless smoke!"

Nicole couldn't keep from speaking her mind with this infuriating man any more than she could stop breathing. "Every time I've mentioned the princess project in the past two weeks or mentioned setting up more dates, you've turned the conversation in another direction," she said hotly. "It's your own fault the search has ground to a halt." She waved the smoke away from her face. "If you weren't so pigheaded, you might realize that you can use your little addiction to cigars in a positive way—a way to help your country."

"What?" He froze and stared down at her. "What in the hell are you talking about?"

She forced herself to rein in her temper, to sound reasonable despite his aggravating manner. "Didn't you say you wanted to improve the national health?"

His lips thinned. Perhaps he guessed where she was heading. He sucked in another puff and exhaled slowly. "Go on."

As Nicole also sucked in a breath, she couldn't avoid filling her lungs with the sickly sweet cigar smoke that lingered in the air like a gray halo. She coughed. His eyes narrowed at her reaction; they were as dark and hard as steel. She knew she would no doubt anger him further, but it was too late not to speak her mind. "Perhaps if you took a positive step in caring for your own health, you could serve as the focal point for a national campaign."

"A national campaign."

Nicole smoothed her hands along her thighs again. "An awareness campaign. If you gave up your cigars, asked our countrymen—and women—to give up their smokes, too . . ." Her voice trailed off as his cool, appraising eyes stared at her, unflinching. So it was a silly idea. It called for personal sacrifice, and a man raised to have everything he wanted no doubt found the idea ridiculous, distasteful in the extreme.

He shifted his gaze to the cigar he held between his fingers. Nicole braced herself. She could hear the minutes tick by on the mantel clock over the fireplace. Was he formulating his next attack? From what direction would it come?

No doubt she'd deeply offended the stubborn man. His personal habits were none of her business, after all. She was a brash, outspoken commoner who'd clearly stepped over the bounds of propriety. *Forget propriety. The bounds of common sense!*

As if in defiance, he raised his cigar slowly and deliberately, then took the longest, deepest drag she had ever seen him take.

He held the smoke in so long, Nicole feared he would pass out. Eyes closed, he exhaled in a long, slow stream. That accomplished, he leaned over the coffee table and smashed out his cigar in the ashtray resting by her injured foot.

He lifted his gaze to her as he ground the cigar into a mushy pulp. "Well, I had certainly better remember that cigar, hadn't I? Since it's my last."

Nicole caught her breath, her eyes widening. "Really?" she said softly, amazed at the joy his announcement brought her. "You mean it?"

He arched an eyebrow. "You don't believe I can give up such a hedonistic diversion?"

She bit back a smile. "No, that's not—" At his narrowed gaze, she nodded vigorously, wanting him to know she supported him completely. "I mean yes. Yes, of course, you can if you really try."

He straightened up and propped his hands on his trim hips. "I expect so. I'm not addicted, Nicole. Not to cigars, at any rate." His gaze skimmed over her face, then slowly slid down her body.

Nicole felt the heat of his gaze in every pore of her suddenly sensitized skin. He couldn't mean—

Without meeting her eyes again, he turned toward the desk and jabbed the intercom button. "Gerald, get in here. I have notes that need to be transcribed. A lot of them. Miss Aldridge is going to help me draft a new campaign."

"Using the . . . computer, sir?" Gerald asked hesitantly. Rand might have set him up with one, but Gerald still resisted using it, finding it frightfully complicated. So Nicole had done most of the transcribing and writing for their project.

"Yes!" Rand barked back.

"Usually Miss Aldridge . . ." Gerald hesitated again.

Rand slammed his palm on the desk. "Get in here. *Then* we'll decide who does what!"

Nicole had the oddest feeling he wanted Gerald around for a more personal reason—to keep from being alone with her. The thought sent an alarming curl of heat up her spine.

She talked herself down from the false high. She had to be fooling herself. He hadn't really intended to kiss her. Or if he had, it had merely been a passing whim, a result of sharing his success. After all, he was Prince Rand, lover of numerous women. Despite how he downplayed his affairs, he'd surely had plenty over the years.

She was practically a nun. They were hardly going to be so swept away by passion that they'd end up here on the delicately embroidered sofa, locked in a steamy embrace. No, if Prince Rand admired anything about her, it was her mind. Which, unfortunately, was right now taking a very strange and dangerous turn.


A summons from the queen.

Nicole stared at Gerald. He stood in the archway of the high library door, his usually good-natured brown eyes solemn. "Yes, Nicole. She demands your presence in her suite, as soon as possible."

"I see." Nicole reached for her crutches and stood up. "Did she happen to say—"

"No, I'm afraid she didn't."

"Oh." Nicole wouldn't even have a chance to formulate a strategy for dealing with the stodgy and—by all reports—cold woman before she was ushered into her presence.

With a sudden, desperate longing, Nicole missed Rand. For the last two days, he'd been tied up at the Grand Assembly in meetings with the Economic Committee. There was no telling how long the session would last, but Rand was determined to keep at the legislators until they heard his message about the future of Caldonia.

Nicole swung on her crutches toward Gerald. She wore a cambric skirt with a blue-and-rose print, much looser than her suit skirts, to enable her freer movement. As a consequence, she looked much less professional than she would have liked.

Pausing before Gerald, she adjusted her glasses on a suddenly sweaty nose. He gestured toward the door and Nicole preceded him into the hallway.

Following behind Gerald, she realized she would have to negotiate the wide marble stairway leading to the ground floor. She knew the basic layout of the palace. While Rand occupied the west wing, his parents conducted their personal and business affairs from the much larger—and older—east wing. Rand went there several times a day for meals or to visit with his family, but Nicole had never had occasion to go near the place.

At the top of the stairs, Gerald supported her upper arm and slowly, awkwardly, she made her way down. "I know Prince Rand would wring my old neck if you were to fall," he said dispassionately. Nicole shot a look at him and caught a slight twinkle in his eye before he glanced back down and helped her maneuver to another step.

She and Gerald had become comfortable coworkers, sharing the same goal of supporting the prince. "When is he coming home?" she asked offhandedly, realizing after she said it that she sounded too familiar.

Gerald didn't seem to notice. "I expect his arrival before four. I believe he is scheduled to judge a children's dog show at four-thirty on the south lawn, and so I did impress on him the importance of being punctual."

Which he usually was, if it was for an official function. Though for events such as that one—what he'd said was nice to do but completely frivolous—he had been known to arrive alarmingly close to the scheduled time.

Sooner than Nicole would have liked, she found herself before the massive wooden doors that led to the queen's office suite. The doors were bracketed by a pair of green-uniformed guards.

"Miss Nicole Aldridge is here, responding to Queen Eurydice's summons," Gerald told a suited man at a nearby desk. The man picked up a house phone and said a few words, then nodded toward the guards. The two opened the doors in perfect sync, and Nicole passed through. Too late, she realized Gerald hadn't followed. She struggled to turn around on her crutches and almost fell. He smiled encouragingly and nodded his head. Then the double doors closed in her face.

Nicole looked around and found herself in an overdecorated suite so draped with heavy, dark brocades that she felt as if she were suffocating. The sweet, heavy aroma of flowers overlaid with age made her nose twitch in discomfort.

The massive gold-leaved furniture looked ancient—probably *was* ancient—even if it had been reupholstered only a few decades ago for the hundredth time. Thinking of Rand's airy, modern office suite, she couldn't imagine anyone preferring to spend time here.

"So this is the assistant my son has been going on about."

Nicole snapped her head up at the cool remark and found herself facing the queen herself. She had expected the queen's secretary to escort her deeper into the queen's domain, rather than the queen meeting her here at the door.

Stiffly, feeling as ungainly as a giraffe, Nicole tried to display some semblance of a curtsy. She bowed her head low. "Your Majesty, it's an honor—"

"I am well aware of that. What are you, the Baron of Duprenia's niece? Yes, well, don't stand there like an awkward schoolgirl. Sit!"

Grateful for the chance to set her crutches aside, Nicole

sank into the nearest wingback chair. She waited for the queen to follow suit and take one of the sofas beside the chair, but she stood near the wall, staring at Nicole through her dark, assessing eyes. Her hair was swept into a neat chignon, brown streaked with gray. Her dowdy brown dress hung in unflattering folds from her neck to below her knees. She wore minimal makeup and jewelry.

"The way he speaks of you, I had expected someone with a little more flair," she said, her tone disparaging as her eyes swept down Nicole's simple attire.

Nicole could hardly defend herself. She didn't understand the nature of the queen's dissatisfaction, and even if she did, this was the *queen*. Nicole had no recourse but to sit still and take whatever the woman planned to dish out.

The queen picked up a folded newspaper from a nearby table. "I am going to assume that your obvious lack of sophistication is the root of the problem," she began.

Confused, Nicole asked, "Excuse me, Your Highness?"

"Don't interrupt!" Queen Eurydice stepped closer in her high-laced shoes. She stood five feet from Nicole and stared down at her. "I will assume you are not commonly so lacking in comprehension, young miss. But just to ensure there is no misunderstanding, I refer to *this!*"

Before Nicole's face, she yanked open the tabloid. Nicole gasped as understanding slammed into her. In full color, at least a foot across, was a grainy photo of her and Rand sitting under a tree, enjoying their private picnic. Or they *had* been enjoying a picnic. When this photo was taken, however, it appeared they'd been enjoying something quite different: each other. The photographer had captured on film the moment Rand had leaned close to her, intending to confide in her, his hand on her arm.

Her own face was at such an angle that her features were all but indistinguishable from those of a thousand young ladies. That's why the inch-high type proclaimed:

## RAND FANCIES
## MYSTERY WOMAN

But Rand's expression had been captured full on. Seeing again the impassioned intensity of his face, so close over hers, gave Nicole the strangest feeling of pleasure mixed with regret, for now she knew the cause of that look. He'd been about to share with her the secret of his hard work to improve the economic situation of Caldonia. It had been nothing more personal than that.

"Ah! You are blushing, Miss Aldridge," the queen said victoriously. "Which can only mean one thing. I have fairly caught you out."

"Caught me out? I never saw this before." In fact, in the past weeks, she'd noticed that the newspapers that had usually been delivered to the library had ceased arriving. She'd been too busy to miss them. Which could only mean that Rand had attempted to hide this from her. "It's—It's almost three weeks old. I—"

"Do you not have newspaper connections, Miss Aldridge? My son did not share that fact with me when he hired you. But I had my own people check you out when this—this *tawdry* item appeared! It's bad enough people like you have linked his name with every eligible female in the hemisphere. But to have his name linked with *yours*, a mere commoner with *nothing* to offer him—if it wasn't so absurd, it would be tremendously appalling."

His name linked with hers? Without asking permission, Nicole snatched the paper from the queen's hand and glanced over the article, almost as angry at being surprised as she was at being accused. "It doesn't name me. You can't even see my face! Your Highness," she added belatedly.

"Merely a matter of time before some enterprising newspaperman learns your identity, I'm sure. No doubt you'll make certain they know who you are. And to think my son hired you to find him a proper wife! The irony is absurd."

"I *am* trying to find him a wife, Your Highness," Nicole

said coldly, unable to keep from defending herself. "We're getting closer, too. In fact—"

"In fact, he spends more time with you than he does with proper women!"

Nicole opened her mouth to protest, to try to explain that men and women often worked together in the modern world without it meaning what the queen seemed to think.

But the queen cut her off. "Have you no respect for the country of your birth, girl? The country's future is at stake! Why, his head is filled with nonsense because of you! Just last week at dinner he rattled off some outlandish ideas about putting *elevators* in the palace. Elevators in *this* venerable institution of a building! The idea is absurd! Now I see precisely why he thought of such a thing. As I suspected." Her eyes raked over Nicole's tightly wrapped ankle. "Then, a few days ago, he mentioned—quite casually, mind you—that he had ceased smoking, because of a new national campaign for Caldonia."

"Yes, it's going very well," Nicole interrupted, striving to sound cool and collected despite the queen's irate manner. "Letters of support are starting to pour in—"

"Don't interrupt me, you impertinent slip of a girl!"

Nicole snapped her mouth closed, feeling undeniably intimidated. She recalled suddenly how Rand had called her a nagging wife. She had never once been accused of being a nag, but clearly it was this behavior that Rand was sensitive to—his mother's chastisement, beratement, and coldness.

The queen continued, her tone victorious. "After some skillful probing on my part, I learned the truth: He's done both these things because of *you*. Isn't that so, Miss Aldridge?"

Appalled at the way the queen's mind worked, Nicole cried, "No!"

"No?"

"I may have suggested them as ideas to consider, but I'm not the *reason*—"

"Are you not? Are you not here to worm your way into

his life, to become *important* to him as no other woman
is?"

Recalling her own pleasure that she held a special place
in his life, Nicole fought a blush at the queen's insinuating
tone. But she would never intentionally hurt him. He'd
hired her because he'd needed her help, which she gladly
provided. Her back rigid, she argued back, "Of course not!
I have Rand's best interests at heart. I—"

"Oh, *Rand,* is it? My, aren't we informal? So it's worse
than I thought," the queen said acidly. "Being so close, so
*intimate,* with the royal family must put quite a shine in
your eyes, mustn't it? You see opportunity perhaps? A
chance to entrench yourself as a regular fixture, to make
yourself important in his private life, to come between him
and his future princess."

The queen circled behind the sofa and Nicole gave up
trying to follow her movements with her eyes. Queen Eurydice had veered close to the truth, yet at the same time
she had never been farther away. Nicole's involvement with
Rand—it wasn't that way, so dark and calculating. Not that
way at all. "No, I—"

"You may have been born in Caldonia, but our country
wasn't good enough for you, was it? You ran off to get an
education, thinking you could show us the error of our
ways. It is you who need to be corrected."

The unwarranted but painfully stinging chastisement
rained down on Nicole full force. She blinked hard, forcing
her face to remain impassive, fighting an inner surge of
guilt as the queen brought her loyalty into question. "I
love Caldonia." She forced the words out through a constricted throat, but the queen spoke right over them.

"I've heard of you American women, how free you are
with your favors. No doubt your dubious Americanized
charms intrigue my wayward son." The queen rounded the
sofa to stand in front of Nicole, her diminutive form seem-
ing to stand ten feet tall, solid, immutable, and condemning.

"A girl like you—the daughter of a poor college professor, with no dowry to offer a man, with only a tenuous claim to importance as a relative of a lesser noble—"

"Mother!"

The booming voice caused the queen to start. Relief flooded through Nicole. The queen stiffened, her face a mixture of guilt and defiance as she turned to her son.

Rand strode toward her, in once glance taking in the situation, no doubt noticing Nicole's tight posture, the withdrawn way she was holding herself under the queen's assault.

"What in the hell are you saying to Nicole?"

"Do not speak to me in such a tone! And you call her by her Christian name? My, you've grown quite chummy with your employee, haven't you, Rand? Since when are you on a first-name basis with your staff?"

"I'll not stand for you berating her like this," he shot back furiously. "I hired her. She's mine to deal with. She's not out for my money or my bed. Now stay out of my affairs!" With cool purpose, despite his fiery words, he stood before Nicole and held out his hand.

She lifted her gaze to his and read the concern there.

"Come with me, Nicole," he said gently.

Nicole hesitated only a fraction of a second before sliding her palm against his and allowing him to help her to her feet. Still reeling from emotional shock, she stumbled against him, earning a wrathful, superior glance from the queen.

Rand grasped her crutches and helped her put them under her arms. Then they crossed to the door. His icy gaze on his mother, he held the door open for Nicole, and followed her out.

Nicole almost sobbed with thankfulness at being so gallantly escorted from the wrathful woman. She had been woefully unprepared for the queen's assault. Now, at least, she knew where she stood. She couldn't allow herself to forget it.

# NINE

Rand didn't say a word, even after they were past the guards at the door. Nor did he slow his pace. His firm hand on her back encouraged her to keep up with him. They reached a pair of French doors along the gallery and he swung them wide, leading her down a short flight of marble steps into an elegant parterre garden, where manicured knee-high boxwood bordered flagstone paths.

"Rand—" she said breathlessly.

He must finally have realized how fast he was pushing her, for he slowed his pace and changed direction, leading her to the nearest bench thirty feet away.

"Thank God, Gerald told me the minute I arrived that she had summoned you," he said, his face dark with fury as he dropped next to her on the bench. "What did she say to you?"

"Nothing," Nicole said softly. She tightened her hands in her lap, unable to bring herself to look at him after the queen's insinuations. Certainly she wasn't about to share with him the queen's embarrassing accusations about her designs on him.

*"Nothing?* What I heard didn't sound like nothing."

At his scalding tone, Nicole jerked her chin up and faced him, her own ire rising. "If you must know, she threw a newspaper in my face—a newspaper I'd never seen before because *someone* kept it from me!"

"Oh, that," he said mildly.

Despite his casual tone, Nicole refused to calm down.

"Perhaps if I had known about it, I would have been slightly more prepared for her reaction."

"I sincerely doubt it." The corner of his mouth turned up in a wry smile.

Nicole sighed. So maybe nothing could have prepared her for the queen. In fact, she knew instinctively that the woman was the type to make up her mind about something, *then* find evidence to support her opinion. Was the queen's dislike of her really because she was an Americanized career woman? Or did something else underlie her hostility, something more personal? In either case, the queen had already decided Nicole was bad for Rand. Nothing she did or said was going to change the queen's mind. The newspaper article had merely given the queen the fuel she needed for a full frontal assault.

"Listen, Nicole," Rand said softly, laying his hand on her arm.

Nicole instantly thought of the photo, of how such a touch between them had been displayed for all the world to see. Even now, an enterprising photographer with a powerful zoom lens might be spying on them. Glancing around, she stiffened her arm and shifted, causing Rand to drop his hand.

"I knew the photo would distress you," he said. "I know you see yourself as the consummate professional, and the implication in the article . . ."

"So what does it say?" she asked, her tone clipped. "Your mother didn't exactly give me time to read it."

His jaw tightened. "To be blunt, it says we're having a torrid affair."

Nicole felt the color rising in her cheeks. "But—But—" Words failed her.

"Precisely. You are in my employ for a specific reason, and that reason has nothing to do with . . . sex." He cleared his throat and looked away, clearly disconcerted by his own use of the word. "But you needn't be concerned. You weren't even named in the article. Nobody knows who you are. Or rather, no one knows who I'm intimate with."

*It's true. He is having an affair. Just not with you.* "Then . . . who?"

"Who what?"

"Your . . . um . . . affair."

He arched a dark eyebrow. "So we're back on that again, are we?"

"No!" she said suddenly, awkwardly smoothing her skirt. Why did she feel so young, so inexperienced? It must be the girlish skirt and the crutches that forced her to walk like an ungainly teenager. And the experience of being called on the carpet, as if she were an errant schoolgirl summoned before the headmistress. Her abraded nerves still stung from the experience; her stomach still quivered.

In retaliation, Nicole adopted her coolest, crispest tone. "I have no interest in your affairs, Your Highness, except as they relate to my work for you. *And* as they relate to me, personally." She kept her eyes pinned to a potted hydrangea across the path. "In the future, I would greatly appreciate it if you would share any such instances of public . . . speculation about my role in your life. Here at the palace, I mean, working for you. As an employee."

She'd said it every way she could, but she still felt her words inadequately expressed precisely what she *was* to Rand. She had no idea what words *would* capture the unique friendship that had sprung up between them, but simply calling them *employer* and *employee* failed miserably to express how she felt toward him.

She forced herself to face him. Just as she feared, looking in his amused eyes robbed her words of their power. Still, she plowed ahead. "It's important that we be open with each other for this . . . situation . . . to work," she said, feeling utterly lame. "For this relationship to be the most . . . productive and . . . efficient."

"Efficient." His gaze became a shade cooler. He crossed his arms and frowned at her. "That's what you value most about being here, isn't it?"

"I'm not sure . . ." Not only wasn't she sure where this

conversation was heading, but she wasn't keen on answering the question she feared he would ask.

"The working aspect. Being a professional."

Nicole forced out her answer, though it was now a complete lie. "Absolutely."

Though his expression never wavered, Nicole thought she saw a flicker of something, a closing off, within those intense eyes which were focused on her.

She pulled in a deep breath. "Since I am a professional, I need to have the facts to do my job properly," she said. "Don't try to protect me, Rand."

He arched his brow. "You would have preferred I let my mother have at you for another hour or so?"

"God, no!" She rubbed her temple. "I meant the photo—"

He sighed and nodded. "I understand. You want me to be honest with you. Very well, Nicole. I will." He smiled gently at her, the warmth back in his eyes. "The next time the press catches us in a compromising position, I'll shove the evidence right under your nose. In case you aren't quite sure what *actually* happened."

She hunched her shoulders. "Don't *say* that." Apparently, Rand was so experienced at letting such publicity roll off his shoulders, it meant nothing to him. And he had a point. Clearly, the press said what it wished, but only those actually involved knew the truth.

She flushed, feeling uncomfortable. Working for *Aristocrats,* she had accepted that some photos might not tell the whole story, but she hadn't let it bother her. She, along with the rest of the staff, had been more concerned about attracting readers. Ending up in a photo herself made her realize she should have taken more care in the past. Regret filled her for the times she had allowed the magazine to imply things—to state things—about people and their relationships that could very easily have been wrong. "I'm sorry, Rand."

His lips drew into a stiff line. "What in hell are you apologizing for now?"

"The photo!"

"It bloody hell isn't *your* fault."

"Maybe not this one, but the magazine . . ."

"Nicole, your magazine is the most tasteful product with such photos in it. And the idea a family in our position could squash all such stories is foolish. They demand access to us. It's part of the price we pay for their support."

"I don't know . . ."

"Well, I do. I have slightly more experience in this field than you do, so let it go, Nicole." His voice dropped to a tender low tone. Nicole felt a warm touch on her chin, and with gentle pressure, he lifted her face to his. "Let it go."

Her throat suddenly felt tight and she didn't trust herself to speak. She nodded briefly, pulling away just enough so he would drop his fingers.

He acted as if he hadn't noticed, but she could tell he knew he'd overstepped the bounds of professionalism. "Yes, well. Now that that's established, let's get back to some serious work. I intended to come home like a conquering hero," he said wryly, "at least in your eyes. It seems I managed to convince the Economic Committee to throw its weight behind our long-range plan for the country."

"That's wonderful, Rand." A thrill of victory filled her, and she grinned at his success. "I knew you could convince them."

He arched an eyebrow. "Like bloody hell. It was all those statistics and facts you provided that finally swayed them. Our next step is to present the package to the Assembly with the committee's backing. Which reminds me . . ." He hesitated. "I was going to wait to suggest this after your first assignment was concluded successfully."

Nicole bit her lip, her heart thudding. She wasn't comfortable being reminded how she'd so far failed to find him a wife and wondered what he meant to say to her.

"I see no reason to wait. I want you to work for me permanently."

Relief mingled with pleasure in Nicole's chest, robbing her of words.

Rand rushed ahead. "I mean even after"—he swept his hand in a broad gesture— "after you find me a wife. You've helped me envision this economic plan. I'd like you to help me see it become a reality."

"That will take years."

He shrugged. "Are you up for it?"

Nicole's mind rapidly began calculating the pluses and minuses of such a proposal. *Plus: To transform this luxurious Caldonian holiday into a permanent way of life. Minus: To live in the palace so near the royal family and the cold queen. Plus and minus: To work with Rand every day, growing closer to him, eventually watching him marry . . .*

Nicole wasn't certain she *was* up for it. "I—I'll have to think about it. I don't have to decide right now, do I?"

A confused look crossed his face. "I had thought—" He shook his head and sighed. "No, of course not. Certainly you can think about it." He stood and helped her to her feet; then he turned to begin leading the way toward the palace.

As she slipped her crutches under her arms, Nicole looked past Rand and saw the top of a white marble structure on a rise at the edge of the garden, almost hidden by tall trees. Its gently peaked roof brought to mind images of gods and goddesses, of age and learning. Of distant, exotic lands.

Rand stopped a few yards down the path. "Are you coming?"

"What is that? It looks like a Grecian temple."

His gaze followed hers. "Actually, it is."

She took a few steps toward the intriguing structure. "Will you show it to me? I've always been interested in history. It was my major in college."

"I know." She glanced back at him and caught his smile, realizing he knew her history from her application paperwork.

She turned back to the temple. "It's not off-limits to commoners or anything like that, is it? Only suitable for monarchs—or gods?"

He chuckled. "Lord, no. But I do consider it mine." He glanced at his watch. "Since I'm home early, I suppose we have time for a brief tour."

Nicole wondered if the temple served as his personal retreat. The idea made her even more anxious to see it. "I'd like that."

He grinned at her enthusiasm; then his smile faded as he glanced at her foot. "Are you sure you can make the climb?"

"How hard is it?"

"A little uphill."

"It's built on a plateau just like the Parthenon in Athens, isn't it?" Without waiting for his lead, Nicole began hobbling toward the structure. She refused to be discouraged. "I've always dreamed of going to Athens, but I haven't yet managed to get there."

"In that case—" Rand stepped quickly in front of her. "We'll have to pretend. It's this way." He gestured toward a secluded stone path, which branched to the left of the main path. Nicole had walked right by it.

Nicole found the first part of the curving, inlaid-stone path easy to navigate. Rand kept a slow, easy pace and paused to help her when the path began to rise slightly—or when her crutch got stuck between the rocks.

Nicole could just see the roof of the temple ahead when the path turned again and grew steeper. Her foot had begun to ache, her underarms were sore, and she wasn't certain she could manage without falling on her face. "I don't think—"

Before she had a chance to voice her predicament, Rand was beside her. "I had a hunch this last bit would be too difficult for you. Here." He lifted her left crutch from her hand. "I need to—" Slipping his arm around her waist, he replaced the crutch with his own strong body. "If you don't mind, this is the easiest way," he said, avoiding her eyes. "Perhaps if you put your arm . . ."

Nicole slipped her arm around his waist to help him support her. She felt the play of muscle along his back as he took the first step up the slope, and she found she had to grip his shirt tighter, causing her breast to gently graze his torso.

A wicked languidity flowed outward from her breasts, tingling across her chest and down her entire body. She concentrated on moving her uninjured foot in time with his steps and pretended it wasn't happening. If she'd known visiting the temple would require him to press his body against hers from chest to thigh, she would have demured until she was off the crutches. Or so she desperately wanted to believe.

Why did they always end up so close to each other? Riding on horseback together, having him carry her to her room, now this. Nicole resolutely stared at the path under her feet, refusing to meet his eyes, afraid he'd see evidence of her growing attraction to him. He smelled wonderful— like ocean breezes. There wasn't even a hint of tobacco on his breath, and she knew with conviction that he hadn't indulged in a smoke since the day he quit.

When she braved a glance at his profile, she found him staring straight up the path, a grim set to his jaw. She knew it was awkward for him to haul her around. He was being far too considerate in taking his precious time like this. She should have thought of that.

Once they reached the top, she realized what had seemed an eternity of torturous bliss in his arms had in reality been only a few minutes. The temple rose before them, bigger than Nicole had pictured it from below. Rand returned her crutch to her.

"Thank you," Nicole said as he stepped back several feet. She got the impression he was anxious to put distance between them, probably because she had emphasized her interest in maintaining a professional relationship. Either that or being so close to her hadn't affected him nearly as strongly as it had her.

"My pleasure," he said with a dismissive shrug. He turned and led her up the half dozen steps into the temple itself. He pointed out a smooth marble bench against a row of pillars on one side, and she slipped onto it.

He began pacing across the marble floor, deeper into the shadows cast by the pillars along the west face. He ran his hand through his hair and massaged the back of his neck in a gesture she knew reflected his uncertainty. Then he spun toward her and threw out his arms in an all-encompassing gesture. "So," he exhaled in a rush, "what do you think?"

*He cares about my opinion,* Nicole guessed, reading an almost nervous demeanor she'd never witnessed in him before. The realization fed the secret flame in Nicole's heart. She gazed up and around, understanding that what at first appeared to be a simple structure—perfect in its symmetry—was actually quite intricate. On each of the four sides, pillars rose fifteen feet to support the roof. Life-size statues of each of the twelve gods and goddesses stood at regular intervals against the pillars. "It's exquisite," she murmured.

"Not quite as big as the real Parthenon—only one-seventh the size," he said, sliding a tanned hand along a nearby pillar. "More similar to a country shrine the ancients would erect to worship a demigod, actually."

Nicole realized the entire structure was open to the cool spring air. "It's not exactly like the Parthenon, is it? There's no inner sanctum."

"I removed it from the plan. I wanted to be able to see in all directions."

"You designed this temple." Nicole stated her words as a fact, and knew that they were true. Rand didn't reply. He stood beside the pillar, his hand braced on its smooth surface, and gazed out the far side of the temple, toward the sweep of forest lying beyond.

Nicole gathered her crutches under her arms and hoisted herself awkwardly to her feet. She wanted nothing more than to walk around this exquisite structure, but she was constrained. Still, she stepped closer to him.

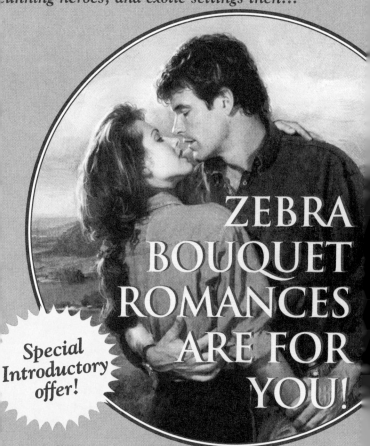

The publishers of Zebra Bouquet are making this special offer to lovers of contemporary romances to introduce this exciting new line of romance novels. Zebra's Bouquet Romances have been praised by critics and authors alike as being of the highest quality and best written romantic fiction available today.

Each full-length novel has been written by authors you know and love as well as by up-and-coming writers that you'll only find with Zebra Bouquet. We'll bring you the newest novels by world famous authors like Vanessa Grant, Judy Gill, Ann Josephson and award winning Suzanne Barrett and Leigh Greenwood to name just a few. Zebra Bouquet's editors have selected only the very best and highest quality for publication under the Bouquet banner.

You'll be treated to glamorous settings from Carnavale in Rio, the moneyed high-powered offices of New York's Wall Street, the rugged north coast of British Columbia, the mountains of North Carolina, all the way to the bull rings of Spain. Bouquet Romances use these settings to spin tales of star-crossed lovers caught in "nail biting" dilemmas that are sure to captivate you. These stories will keep you on the edge of your seat to the very happy end.

**4 FREE NOVELS** As a way to introduce you to these terrific romances, the publishers of Bouquet are offering Zebra Romance readers Four Free Bouquet novels. They are yours for the asking with no obligation to buy a single book. Read them at your leisure. We are sure that after you've read these introductory books you'll want more! (If you do not wish to receive any further Bouquet novels, simply write "cancel" on the invoice and return to us within 10 days.)

## SAVE 20% WITH HOME DELIVERY

Each month you'll receive four just published Bouquet Romances. We'll ship them to you as soon as they are printed (you may even get them before the bookstores). You'll have 10 days to preview these exciting novels for Free. If you decide to keep them, you'll be billed the special preferred home subscription price of just $3.20 per book; a total of just $12.80 — that's a savings of 20% off the publishers price. If for any reason you are not satisfied simply return the novels for full credit, no questions asked. You'll never have to purchase a minimum number of books and you may cancel your subscription at any time.

Check out our website at www.kensingtonbooks.com.

# GET STARTED TODAY –
## NO RISK AND NO OBLIGATION

To get your introductory gift of 4 Free Bouquet Romances fill out and mail the enclosed Free Book Certificate today. We'll ship your free selections as soon as we receive this information. Remember that you are under no obligation. This is a risk free offer from the publishers of Zebra Bouquet Romances.

# FREE BOOK CERTIFICATE

Yes! I would like to take you up on your offer. Please send me 4 Free Bouquet Romance Novels as my introductory gift. I understand that unless I tell you otherwise, I will then receive the 4 newest Bouquet novels to preview each month Free for 10 days. If I decide to keep them I'll pay the preferred home subscriber's price of just $3.20 each (a total of only $12.80) plus $1.50 for shipping and handling. That's a 20% savings off the publisher's price. I understand that I may return any shipment for full credit no questions asked and I may cancel this subscription at any time with no obligation. Regardless of what I decide to do, the 4 Free introductory novels are mine to keep as Bouquet's gift.

Name _____

Address _____ Apt. _____

City _____ State ____ Zip _____

Telephone ( ) _____

Signature _____ BN10B9
(If under 18, parent or guardian must sign.)

For your convenience you may charge your shipments automatically to a Visa or MasterCard so you'll never have to worry about late payments and missing shipments. If you return any shipment we'll credit your account.
Yes, charge my credit card for my "Bouquet Romance" shipments until I tell you otherwise.
☐ Visa  ☐ MasterCard
Account Number _____
Expiration Date _____
Signature _____
Orders subject to acceptance by Zebra Home Subscription Service. Terms and Prices subject to change.

If this response card is missing,
call us at 1-888-345-BOOK.

Be sure to visit our website at
www.kensingtonbooks.com

"Why haven't I heard about this talent for design you have? I mean, no one's ever written about it, have they?"

"It's just a hobby of mine, Nicole—nothing to get excited about." His unexpected modesty warmed her heart. "I rather like keeping it to myself. Though more and more I wish I'd saved the money to spend on something worthwhile, not just daydreams."

"Daydreams?" Nicole prodded, fascinated by his openness. She had often seen him drift off into his own thoughts and longed to know what world he might have entered.

"This was just a boyhood fantasy really," he said. "When I was a child, I dreamed of visiting the gods on Mount Olympus."

Nicole smiled to herself. "I think every kid who learns about the Greek myths has that fantasy, Rand. When we studied mythology in school, my girlfriends wanted to be like Aphrodite—beautiful enough to make men fall in love at first sight. I didn't want that. I wanted to be just like Athena, goddess of wisdom. Wise and beautiful, a warrior and leader . . ." Nicole could hardly believe she'd just admitted her secret childhood fantasy.

Rand leaned back against the pillar and crossed his arms, a smile drifting over his lips. "Interesting. I had a fantasy that I'd someday meet Athena and . . ." He froze, his mouth open. Then he shrugged and gave an abashed smile. "Well, you know how the gods were."

Nicole cocked an eyebrow. "Randy, you mean?"

He chuckled. "Exactly." He shook his head. "I can't believe I'm telling you this."

Nicole's smile matched his. As their conversation faded, so did his smile, but the intensity in his eyes increased. "You *are* wise and beautiful. You know that, don't you?"

Nicole stared up at him and felt a slow flush sliding over her skin, every inch from her feet to the top of her head. Not from embarrassment. From awareness. They were completely alone, and the way he was looking at her, with an almost painful longing . . .

"Your Highness!"

The out-of-breath voice made Nicole start. Gerald hurried up the steps into the temple, his face ruddy from exertion.

"Your Highness, the king is looking for you. And I warn you, he's rather out of sorts."

Rand instantly took his attention off Nicole, and she wondered once more if she had imagined that look in his eye.

"What? What does he want?" he demanded.

"He's on his way up here now. I—" Gerald looked from Rand to Nicole and back again curiously. "I thought I should warn you."

The king himself. After her run-in with the queen, Nicole could not fight a sense of trepidation. "Do you have any idea what's got him excited?" Nicole asked.

"*I* know," Rand said sourly. "Ours is a small government, Nicole. No doubt he's caught wind of the proposal I intend to present to the Assembly, and he's none too pleased."

"That's right!" The temple magnified the thunderous voice of King Edbert. Nicole stepped deeper into the shadows, not wanting to catch his royal wrath as well.

The king—looking less than kingly in casual slacks and a sweater—planted himself before his son. Nicole recognized his stern lined face, his gray-touched ebony hair. He was a half head shorter than his son. Though age softened his features, they bore the same strong cast as Rand's. "What's this I'm hearing about a newfangled plan you're touting about town?"

"If you're referring to the long-range economic plan, yes, I'm behind it."

"I figured that much. And you went behind my back!"

Rand scowled. "If I hadn't, it would never happen. And Caldonia would become an even worse joke among progressive countries than it already is."

As the argument escalated, Nicole saw Gerald slip away, and she wished to heaven she could do likewise. But she couldn't easily navigate the steep path below, not without help. She retreated to the bench and sat as still as the statues of the gods lining the temple walls.

After more accusations on the king's part, and Rand's angry defense of his proposal, Nicole heard the king say, "She's the cause, isn't she? Your mother told me how she's influenced you."

"What?" Nicole started and found two angry pairs of eyes turned her way.

"Leave her out of this. I began working on this plan—"

"Plotting against me—"

"Months ago. *Years* ago. But you refused to listen."

"She's put these modern ideas into your head! Computers even. What does our government need with computers? They can't cultivate wine grapes, for God's sake."

"Yes, I admit it!" Rand said, his exasperated voice echoing along the pillars. "Nicole *has* helped me see how backward we are in everyday things. I could only see the big picture. But change starts small. She understands that. I thank her for it every day, as should you!"

"Me? Thank *her?*" He flung his hand toward Nicole.

"Yes, her!" Rand planted his hands on his hips, as if defying his father to contradict him. "She's gotten me to see how badly we need to change and in what ways. Oh, I knew it before and tried to do what I could. But I was too uninspired to do more than take a few obvious steps and waste my time dreaming about what the future might be if we want it badly enough. Nicole is helping me define the future and make it *real*. We can't take our sweet time about it. We can't wait until I ascend the throne. By then, it'll be far too late. We have to move as fast as possible, or we'll be completely left behind. Nicole knows that. And now so do I."

Nicole felt Rand was giving her far too much credit. He'd been working hard for years to bring change to his country. She had only helped.

The king frowned thoughtfully, his eyes on Nicole. "She inspired you?"

Rand stepped closer to the king and glared down in his face. "If it's the last thing I do, I'm going to drag Caldonia

into the twenty-first century with or without you. Come on,
Nicole. We've had enough of this."

He grabbed her arm and hauled her to her healthy foot.
Nicole scrambled for her crutches, but Rand yanked them
from her and pulled her hard against him, half supporting,
half carrying her down the steps and toward the path to
the garden.

Nicole knew he wished to leave immediately to make a
point, but she was hampering him terribly, awkwardly. He
could hardly hold both her *and* the crutches and keep both
of them upright. "You could have left me there, Rand."

"Don't be ridiculous." He maneuvered quickly over a
bumpy patch. Hopping beside him, Nicole nearly lost her
balance, but he snuggled her against him and kept her
upright.

"Maybe I should quit, Rand," Nicole gasped out. "I keep
causing conflict between you and your parents."

"That is *not* an option, Nicole," he said, his expression
grim. "You're *my* employee, not theirs." As if to emphasize
his point, he locked his arm even tighter around her.

The heat of his hard body burned into her skin, searing
her in places he couldn't see, would never see. He had to
stop touching her like this, or she would not be able to
continue working for him. She would self-destruct from
the inside out.

As he maneuvered with her down the steepest part of
the path, she held her breath, but miraculously, they remained upright. She clutched his waist and tried her best
not to burden him too much.

"Don't kill the poor girl." The amused voice came from
directly behind them.

Rand froze. He turned them both around in an awkward
series of steps and faced King Edbert.

"My God, dragging her along the ground like that!" Edbert said, a small smile on his mouth. "Is that how you've
been raised to treat a lady?"

"Father?" Rand asked hesitantly. Nicole sensed that the

king's calm attitude threw the prince. Nor could she fathom the shift in his mood.

"I'll take those things." Edbert strode forward and took the crutches from Rand's hand; then he passed in front of them and proceeded down the path.

Rand's shock transmitted itself to Nicole. She had the strangest feeling that the king had decided to accept her on some level, but how or why she couldn't begin to guess.

She decided it didn't matter. She was definitely relieved not to be on the outs with the king of her country.

After a few steps, Edbert paused and turned back. "What are you waiting for?" he asked jovially. "Come, Miss Aldridge. You must be fatigued." He gestured for them to follow him.

Without a word, Rand complied, his confusion almost palpable to Nicole. She pressed her face into his shoulder to hide her smile. So much for dramatic exits.


"It was good of you to adjust your schedule on such short notice, considering how *busy* you've been," King Edbert said as he settled into his favorite chair.

Rand simmered over the veiled criticism as his father gestured to his servant, who had been standing by the wall as still and silent as a mannequin. Instantly, the man sprang to life, crossing to the bar to mix the king his usual wine cocktail.

"Sit, Randall," the king commanded. "We have something important to discuss in regard to your marriage."

Rand sighed and folded his large body into the chair across from his father. He hadn't known on which front his father would attack when he'd been summoned to his chambers a few hours after their argument at the temple. To Rand's surprise, his father was apparently going to allow the economic incentive issue to rest in favor of the marriage issue—for now.

"You're not going to tell me the facts of life, are you?" Rand asked, covering tenseness with humor. He had no doubt his father was working toward some secret agenda. As soon as he determined its nature, he would launch his defense.

"Don't be ludicrous. A drink?" He gestured to his servant, glancing at Rand with a question in his eyes.

Nicole had mentioned once in that gentle—but pointed—way of hers that hard liquor no doubt aggravated his sour stomach. Besides, he was actually thirsty for something thirst quenching. "Mineral water. On the rocks."

His father cocked his eyebrow at him. "Not your usual choice. I'm seeing a lot of changes in you lately, son."

"Not that many," he said, irritated at his father's line of discussion. What was he getting at?

The servant returned with the drinks on a tray and handed the king his, then Rand his. "You may go."

With a silent bow, the servant retreated, closing the study doors behind him.

The king took a relaxed swallow, then lowered the glass and gazed at his son. "Now to the topic at hand. I'm not certain you have a full understanding of your domestic duties. The marriage contract for us royals is not what you might think. Traditionally, once we"—he gestured to encompass both of them, the male monarchs of Caldonia—"have selected a wife, we wed and do our utmost to ensure the line will continue. Healthy children born to our queen or princess. That is where our duty ends, as far as domestic matters go."

Rand arched his eyebrow. "Meaning?"

"Shortly after, if not before, we are usually inclined to establish a confidante."

"Confidante," Rand said slowly, his nerves stretching tighter. "You mean a mistress."

A pained look crossed his father's face. "Such a vulgar term. The common working man may take a mere *mistress*. The term *confidante* carries a deeper meaning, indicating a woman who answers the need of the soul as well as of the body. A long-lasting relationship, Randall. Strong and sure. Most Hollingsworth males take their first long-term *confidante* in their twenties, around the time they marry, if not before. You have been slow in this area, dragging your feet just as you have in the matrimonial area."

"I see." He'd been slow apparently—unlike his father, who was obviously pleased to share with his son how he'd cheated on his mother. Rand knew he had, had known it for years. It was one of many areas that was silently understood but, until now, never discussed. "All right then. When did you take your first confidante?"

His father shrugged, as if the answer were obvious. "After procreation was no longer an issue and I had ensured the line would continue."

Rand couldn't keep the brittle tone from his voice. "You mean when I was born, an infant in diapers."

"I didn't feel it necessary to wait to learn the sex of the child, though I would certainly have done my duty to try again if you had disappointed me by being a daughter."

Rand glared at him, his stomach twisting with disgust. "So you had a lover when my mother was pregnant with me. Did you even try to make your marriage work?"

"Work? What do you mean by work?" The king shook his head as if Rand was speaking a foreign language. "It is working now, as it must, serving the duties and functions it must. As we must."

"That isn't the kind of marriage I want."

*"You* want? What you want isn't an issue, Randall. I had thought that was entirely clear to you by now." The momentary irritation in his voice disappeared with his next words. "Now let's get down to brass tacks, shall we?" He smiled congenially.

His convivial attitude rubbed Rand raw. He knew it was a facade. He waited, wondering which direction his father would take this ridiculous discussion. He'd already agreed he needed to marry, for God's sake. What more did his father want?

"Your Nicole," the king said. His mention of Nicole sent a quiver of apprehension down Rand's spine.

"What about Miss Aldridge?" he said stiffly.

"She is intelligent, discreet, and well bred for a commoner. Quite pretty actually. She has a delicate charm, yet I suspect a spine of iron. All the right qualities."

A sudden flare of alarm swept through Rand and his hand tightened on his glass. Did his father intend to steal Nicole and make her his latest confidante? The idea sickened him. Water sloshed on his hand and he realized he was about to break the glass. He forced his grip to relax. "What"—he could barely speak—"are you getting at?"

"Well, you do seem quite smitten with her."

*He* did? Rand raced to regroup and defend. "I'm not smitten—"

"For heaven's sake, Rand," the king said in exasperation. "Stop fighting it and make the woman your confidante."

Rand froze as his father's words sank in. The king didn't want Nicole for himself, but thought his son should take her as his royal mistress.

Nicole as his mistress? He could never take her as his mistress. He didn't think of her in such base, physical terms.

*Or did he?* A hot flush suffused his skin as he thought of Nicole, of the lust she stirred in him at the oddest moments. Laughing intimately at some joke they shared, as if no one else existed in the world. Pushing those silly glasses up on her nose while reading, completely unaware of his gaze on her. Chewing her full lower lip, making him long to run his tongue along its contours . . .

No doubt other men would wonder why his blood burned for her at those moments. On the surface, there was nothing blatantly sexual about them. Lord, he didn't understand it himself, but the hunger was always there under the surface.

With a shock of painful comprehension, he knew he'd been deluding himself. He more than desired Nicole. He burned for her. Craved her with every fiber of his being. He could take her to bed. He was almost certain he could seduce her. He had seen the answering longing in her eyes often enough though she tried to hide it.

"Establish her as your confidante now so that you may lend your energies to finding a proper wife," the king advised. "The clock is ticking, Randall. There are only six months left in the year.

"Why should you care?" he asked sharply. "What's your interest in this?"

"You're obviously wrapped up in her. Distracted. Unable to tell the important from the mundane. It's that longing, Randall, that curiosity, that quest to conquer her."

Images formed in Rand's brain faster than he could prevent them. Nicole in a satin gown, waiting for him after a day of public appearances, a secret, intimate smile on her face only for him. Her delicate hands undressing him, stroking his flesh, pulling him down onto his soft bed. Sliding her delicious, graceful body on top of his . . .

His father's cajoling words echoed his erotic thoughts, a siren song pulling him toward that which could never be. "Take her, Rand. Make her completely yours. Once you've satisfied that itch, you'll settle into a comfortable routine and return to your normal self."

The last words slammed into his consciousness, yanking him from his daydream. He didn't *want* to return to his old self. He didn't want to succumb to his father's plans. To his own weakness. An entire country's future was at stake.

"No," he muttered. Then louder as his conviction grew, he said, "No. Nicole deserves better than to be my sexual plaything. I will not do that to her."

He rose, slammed down the half-full glass of mineral water, and faced his father head-on. "I will not succumb to your ploys, father. I know what underlies this. Why you want me to settle down. You want me to stop challenging you, stop challenging the country to take the next step—a step it badly needs to take. You think to muddy my brain with the softness and comfort of a woman, to turn Nicole into a sex object when it's her mind I value the most."

"She would benefit from the association—don't fool yourself on that count, Randall," his father said, a definite edge to his voice. "She would have everything she could ever want. We Hollingsworths are very generous men when it suits us."

"Don't you dare paint me with the same brush," Rand shot back. "Have you forgotten that I'm engaged in a search for the right wife? And that Nicole is helping me to find her? Your own duplicity—that farce of a marriage you and my mother have—that is *not* the kind of marriage I will have. Not the kind of household I'll raise my children in. Because of Nicole."

"If that is truly how you feel, my son," the king said, his ice-cold voice turning the possessive term into mockery, "you are more of a fool than I had ever imagined."

Unable to stand being in his presence a moment longer, Rand turned his back on him and strode from the room.


Rand felt Nicole's presence in the library long before he looked up from his computer screen. He had stopped reading the latest draft of his proposal the moment she entered the room, but hesitated to reveal just how glad he was that she had arrived.

With each passing morning, he found himself arriving in the library earlier and earlier. He had asked Gerald to temporarily limit his obligations so he could concentrate on fine-tuning the proposal—with his ever efficient assistant, Miss Nicole Aldridge.

He ran his hand along the back of his neck and had a sudden urge for a cigar—one of many urges he'd been forced to subdue lately. Certainly, the proposal was important. But he could no longer fool himself into believing that was the only reason for his dedication to his work.

He caught sight of Nicole out of the corner of his eye as she stopped before his desk.

"Rand, I have a suggestion," she said, her tone all business.

He lifted his gaze to hers and a forbidden thrill tingled through his chest. He had told himself his passing attrac-

tion to her was all in his mind, but his body didn't seem
to care.

By God, he'd almost kissed her here in this room, and
at the temple, the urge had come over him again, even
stronger. If his father hadn't interrupted . . . Throughout
the day, he continued to torture himself by working closely
with her, enjoying her insights, her spark, her charm. As
if he were addicted to her.

He'd never felt so vulnerable to a woman before, but his
feelings were no doubt fed by their long hours working
toward a mutual goal. He had never met anyone who cared
as much about improving Caldonia as she, who seemed to
understand what he was thinking even before he did. He
valued her companionship more than anyone's. If only that
was where it ended . . .

He couldn't shake the imprint of her slender body
pressed against his. He allowed his mind to play out fanta-
sies of holding her, kissing her, learning the shape of her
with his hands, not just his eyes. At the most inappropriate
moments, his mind wandered down primitive, shockingly
carnal paths. With his own employee! An innocent lady, at
that.

If she could read his mind . . . She would undoubtedly
resign, and he would never see her again. He refused to
allow such a disheartening prospect. He would instead re-
frain from ever revealing his inner desires.

Still, though he maintained perfect decorum with her
at all times, he had the sense that on some deeper level
Nicole was perfectly aware of his unspeakably intimate
thoughts and refused to acknowledge them—for the same
reasons. Or was that only his secret fantasy?

This morning, she had donned one of her severely tailored suits instead of the flowing, feminine skirts she had
been wearing since her injury. She had even pulled on
hosiery despite her injured ankle. She was down to one
crutch now, and her ankle was supported by an ungainly
brace. Despite that, she wore a sensible pump on her uninjured foot.

His heart fell a notch as he looked at her hair, once again bound up in a tight roll. Why would she wear it up? Because she sensed his thoughts? Intended to discourage him?

The thought pricked his ire. As if he'd be foolish enough—scoundrel enough—to act on his desires! Besides, her attempt failed miserably. Certainly, combined with her glasses and the file folders clutched in her arms, she gave the impression of an unyielding schoolmistress. Yet still he imagined carrying her to the sofa and stripping her pretenses from her, along with her clothes.

"Sit down, Nicole," he said tersely.

Nicole didn't react visibly to his cool tone. She sat primly in the chair beside his desk and propped open a file on her lap. "I don't feel we're making sufficient progress on our search for your princess. Based on the priority order you established earlier, I have selected the next five women for you to consider."

Ah, so this was how she intended to play it. Just as well, since he intended the same. Still, he could not completely conquer his irritation at her cool professionalism. "You may get to the point at any time, Nicole," he said in what he hoped was an uninterested manner.

"Yes, I'm sorry. I know you're busy." She squirmed in the chair, hitched her skirt down one creamy thigh, then continued. "To speed this process along, I think it would be expedient if we invited all five of these candidates to one palace function—"

"Kill five birds with one stone?" he said dryly.

She almost smiled, but seemed to catch herself in time. "You could put it that way."

He leaned forward, fascinated at hearing her proposal, fascinated by how her mind worked. "And what function is that?"

"The Coronation Commemoration Ball."

"That overblown affair?" Ostensibly held each year to remember all the monarchs who had ruled before, the commemoration ball had devolved over the years into a high-society extravaganza. Everybody who was anybody attended the ball—a perfect backdrop for the cream of Caldonian society to strut their stuff and for the Caldonian royal family to remind its citizenry of what made them special. He hadn't thought Nicole would think such a venue suitable, considering the crowd. "Rather like bloody Prince Charming holding a ball to find his wife, wouldn't you say? Except I doubt any Cinderella will arrive in glass slippers."

Nicole jumped to defend her idea—as he knew she would. "I know it sounds kind of silly, but no one else needs to know you're shopping for a wife. The women would be delighted to attend. There will be so many people there, it won't appear as if they're trying out for anything. They'll act more natural, too, don't you think?"

He leaned back in his chair and studied her, his fingers steepled before his chest. He was barely aware as the seconds began to slip past. He couldn't decide whether to look at Nicole's face—and watch the way her large eyes darted around the room, trying to avoid his gaze—or her body, its soft curves barely visible beneath that unflattering suit.

He wished she'd open her jacket. He imagined kneeling in front of her and doing it for her. Then he'd unbutton her blouse, exposing the soft mounds of her breasts. . . . A surge of desire swept through him, potent and undeniable. God, no, unbuttoning her blouse would take too long. He'd rip it open, shove up her bra, and feast on her exposed breasts. He'd kiss her and stroke her everywhere until she was fully ready for him, begging for him. Then and only then, would he finally, deliciously enter her, drive into her softness, feel her wetness, hear her crying for him, and—

"Then you can come?"

Rand jerked as if he'd been doused with cold water. "Come?" he asked. The word came out horribly strangled. He could barely meet her gaze, but saw enough to know she was blissfully unaware of his base fantasy.

"To the ball, so that you can entertain the candidates."

"Ask Gerald. He keeps my schedule," he said roughly. "Do you expect me to have it memorized?"

"No. No, of course not." She ducked her head and he sensed his demeanor surprised her, even hurt her. He had the urge to stroke her hair, soothe her. The realization tightened his chest. His father was right. Nicole had him completely distracted. Somehow, she had so worked her way into his affections he could scarcely think of anything else.

*Get a grip, man,* Rand chastised himself. He yanked himself upright in his chair.

At his sudden movement, Nicole started, then closed her folder and curled her fingers around the edges. She appeared more nervous than he ever recalled, though she fought to hide it. Was it any wonder, the way he was staring at her?

"I always attend the bloody ball," he said briskly. "It's duty. Now tell me your plan."

"At the ball, you can look the candidates over at your leisure," she said hesitantly, "spend as much time with them as you wish."

"I see," he said slowly. He had already accepted her idea, since it made so much sense. Yet in his gut, he knew there was more to her reasoning than she'd revealed. To draw her out, he arched his eyebrows questioningly, silently prodding her to continue.

She took the bait. "Very well, Rand," she said with a sigh, the straightforward woman he'd grown so fond of finally surfacing. Their mutual attempts at cool professionalism always managed to give way to casual familiarity. "I get the feeling that you have been dragging your feet on this project, because of a few less than ideal experiences—"

"Disasters, Nicole. Plain and simple."

"All right, disasters," she said, a touch of exasperation showing. Rand reveled in it, found himself smiling at her informality. Forced himself to stop.

"I imagine anyone would detest such a series of blind

dates," Nicole said. "By trying out the women this way, you would avoid that."

"Yes, I see." Restless, he shoved to his feet and circled the desk. He leaned against the front of it and gazed down at her ingenuous face. "And you hope it will show my mother how dedicated you are to marrying me off."

She appeared only slightly abashed. She cocked her head and cast him a smile. "Actually, that was one consideration. I freely admit it."

Rand frowned, wondering how his mother would react once he explained what Nicole had arranged. Perhaps she would soften her opinion of the upstart American girl.

He hoped so. He found it difficult to speak to his mother after butting heads with her time and again in his defense of Nicole. His mother refused to believe the two of them weren't engaged in a scandalous affair, refused to believe Nicole was working hard to find him a wife. Perhaps this ball would offer a way out. "It might work, too," he mused.

"To convince your mother?"

He stiffened, irritated that he'd again been thinking of Nicole. "To find me a wife."

"Oh," she said softly, appearing almost embarrassed. "Of course."

He gazed at her speculatively and crossed his arms. An idea struck him, and he made a sudden decision. "You will attend the ball as well, naturally."

"What?" Nicole stared at him in shock.

Rand shoved away from the desk and paced across the intricately designed carpet. "I want you there to help me keep these women straight," he said, formulating his rationale as he spoke. "You can keep your eye on them, check out their reactions to me, to others. See how they fit. I find it damned hard to keep track of them all as it is."

He turned once he reached the fireplace, and he discovered that Nicole's face had taken on an alarmingly pale cast. He couldn't fathom such a reaction. It was just another royal ball, after all. "You have a problem with this, Nicole?"

She opened her mouth and seemed to force her words out. "I mean I'm not the sort—"

"The *sort?*" He was sick of the artificial walls between the nobility and commoners. "They're just people dressed in fancy clothes. Put you in a pretty dress, and you'll do just fine." He gestured toward her braced foot. "How long until that thing comes off your ankle?"

"A week. But I—"

"The ball's not for a month, so that's no excuse."

"I know, but you really don't need me there, Rand," she said rapidly, as if afraid he'd interrupt. "Not with five women occupying your time. We can discuss them afterward—"

He cut her off. "I'm to be expected to entertain five women! Three women whom I barely know, two others who are total strangers. I expect a little help!" He could not understand such strong resistance to a perfectly practical suggestion.

"What—What sort of help?"

"Remind me who in the hell I'm supposed to be evaluating, for one. Rescue me if I get tied up with someone and time begins to slip away. That sort of thing."

"But your mother!" Nicole said. "She won't want me there. And your father—"

"Hang my mother!" So *that* was her concern. At the shocked look on her face, he modified his tone. "I'll explain this little enterprise to her, Nicole, and explain exactly why you'll be there. As for my father, he's . . . modified his opinion of you." Indeed, his father had continued to push the idea that he take Nicole as his mistress, and he continued to resist. "Don't waste a moment worrying about my parents, all right?"

She didn't look convinced, but she finally nodded. "If you say so."

# TEN

"Where have you been, Nicole? The prince has been growing anxious." Gerald approached Nicole as soon as she stepped into the foyer of the grand ballroom.

She glanced past him. A sweeping staircase led down a full story into the ballroom, crowded with the glitterati—women in designer gowns, men in tuxes, the press cordoned off in one corner. Every year *Aristocrats* magazine ran a ten-page feature on the ball, showing heads of state, nobles, celebrities, and Prince Rand with a new "date."

Her stomach fluttered. "I'm sorry, Gerald. I was last in line for the palace hairdresser."

Gerald smiled, his warm eyes crinkling. "He did a marvelous job. You look like a painting I saw once in some book about Greek myths, I should say."

Nicole warmed at his compliment; at the same time, she tensed at a suggestive note in his voice, as if he knew why she'd wanted this style. The fashion editor at *Aristocrats* had found a designer willing to lend her a gown in the hope it would be photographed. By chance, he had a gown to meet her description. As she'd explained to him, though the gown exceeded her wildest expectations, no one would be taking pictures of *her.*

In the Grecian style, the gown bared her arm and draped in soft folds from a gold belt at her waist, making her waist look tinier than she ever thought it could. She wore gold highheeled sandals and her hair—what had taken the palace hairdresser so long—was swept high on her head, partly braided and wound with gold cord. Curling tendrils framed her face and brushed her neck. She wore no jewelry. Nothing she owned would do the gown justice.

As a surprise for Rand, she wore her contacts in place of her glasses. He'd never seen her without her glasses, and she wondered how he would react.

"You do realize this is quite an honor, don't you, Nicole?" Gerald said softly.

Nicole looked at him, confused by his uncharacteristically tense tone. "I'm here to work, Gerald."

Gerald raised an eyebrow. "I only hope the prince has thought this through."

Nicole had established a comfortable working relationship with Gerald, the only other person Rand trusted with his secrets. Now she began to wonder what Gerald really thought of her. She stiffened her spine. "I don't understand."

Gerald grasped her elbow and steered her to the side of the hall. He lowered his voice. "I generally back everything he does, Nicole, as you do. It's my role and my privilege to be on his staff, to help him with his goals and his agenda for the country. And I was supportive of his decision to hire someone to help him locate a suitable bride, as you know."

Nicole nodded, but the tenseness in her stomach intensified. "Out with it, Gerald."

He sighed, clearly uncomfortable with whatever he had to say. "I'm concerned that your—that his—that . . ." He glanced up, as if expecting to find words on the ceiling.

Nicole found herself shaking her head in confusion and trepidation. Gerald had never been so at a loss for words, had never been less than calm and collected.

Gerald lowered his gaze, a deep sigh issuing from his lips. "I'm just an old man, a worrier by nature, as you know. He's told me more than once that he has a handle on things, so I'll keep my nose out of it." He gave her a smile, tucked her arm in his, and patted her hand. "Enjoy yourself, tonight, Nicole, but never forget why you're here."

Nicole nodded, already mentally ready to carry out her duties. She certainly didn't need Gerald to remind her why she'd been invited.

She allowed him to escort her toward the head of the stairs, where a green-uniformed butler waited. The butler held out his hand. "Card?"

Nicole had no card, but Gerald pulled out a vellum invitation from his jacket pocket.

"This is Miss Nicole Aldridge of Caldonia, niece to Lord Phillip, the Baron of Duprenia," he intoned, as if the title actually carried weight.

At the butler's skeptical glance, Gerald added, "She's attending at the personal invitation of Prince Rand."

The butler cocked his eyebrow, but announced her name in a ringing voice to the milling crowd below, and she began descending the stairs, alone. She glanced back at Gerald, and he waved once, then vanished. Apparently, he hadn't been asked to attend.

A few people nearby glanced toward her, then returned to their conversations when they realized she was nobody special. She didn't mind. She was too excited at actually being here to concern herself with making an impression on the five hundred titled, famous, and wealthy guests.

Then she caught sight of Prince Rand, and her heart somersaulted. He separated himself from a group and approached the stairs. Her steps slowed as she looked at him. He was breathtakingly handsome in a tailored tuxedo, his princely emerald sash identifying him for anyone foolish enough not to know who he was. She saw him every day, spent hours working closely with him. But he still managed to steal her breath away.

Particularly now. He paused at the foot of the stairs and gazed up at her, his eyes glowing with unabashed appreciation—and something far more unsettling. A slow smile spread over his face. Nicole shivered with delight, deeply satisfied that her efforts to prepare for this evening met with his approval. She had told herself he would barely notice her presence, considering the number of people he had to entertain. She had tried to convince herself he'd forgotten he'd invited her. Being wrong had never given her more pleasure.

His eyes never left her as she floated down the stairs toward him. *Enjoy yourself, but never forget why you're here.* Gerald's words raced through her mind and she yanked her gaze from Rand's. She wasn't Cinderella about to be swept off her feet by the handsome prince.

She had almost reached the foot of the stairs when the prince strode quickly up the last five steps to meet her, breaking with protocol. A member of the royal family never went out of his way to meet a commoner. Apparently, Rand was willing to set aside tradition.

*Because of her.* Nicole's blood pounded and she felt his gaze in every part of her body.

He leaned close to her. "You took your own sweet time, didn't you?" he asked teasingly. "You missed the royal receiving line. Maybe that was intentional." He chuckled.

His gaze swept up her body and settled on her face. "You . . ." He paused, as if searching for words. Then his gaze seemed to cool and he spoke briskly. "You look different without those ridiculous glasses of yours. Gives me a chance to see your eyes clearly. Now come." He tucked her arm in his and turned to escort her down. "I'm trying to remember all the details on the five women we invited to this affair."

And that was that. Her lack of glasses—and her elegant Grecian gown—hardly affected him. Nicole valiantly battled back her foolish disappointment. He saw women in elegant gowns all the time, but she had expected more of a reaction. She fiercely reminded herself that impressing the prince with her looks was not what she'd been hired to do.

"I've already eliminated one lady who has a tendency to giggle at highly inappropriate times," Rand said. "I swear she was laughing at my mother's dress in the receiving line."

"Oh, no," Nicole said, unable to contain a smile. "We couldn't allow that."

Despite his mention of the queen, as Nicole glided down the steps beside the prince, she felt as if she were walking on air. When she managed to tear her eyes from Rand, she realized that, this time, people were watching.

Wherever Prince Rand went, whatever he did, they noticed. She would have to remember that, here in this public place—and treat him with all the formal courtesy his position demanded, regardless of how casually familiar they were with each other in private. She caught a bright flash out of the corner of her eye and saw that a photographer had taken a photo of the two of them. She yanked her hand from his arm.

Rand frowned and glanced toward the photographers. He shrugged. "Nothing to worry about, Nicole. They've already shot rolls and rolls of film by now—and not just of me."

"If you say so," she replied, not feeling quite as blasé as he did. Rand was obviously the most popular subject for the press at the gala.

"We're doing nothing out of the ordinary tonight," he said in a reassuring tone. "Except that you're here to help me with a special project."

She nodded, not able to meet his gaze. Her chest tightened as she guessed what he was really saying: He was treating her no differently from the way he had other arriving female guests.

Rand positioned her on the side of the ballroom near a potted palm. Stiffening her spine, she pulled herself back into her role of employee. She ran over the list of the four remaining candidates he was to spend time with, then briefed him on each of their backgrounds. Together, they looked for the women in the crowded ballroom as the orchestra hidden in the far corner switched from chamber music to the first waltz.

"The flaming pink gown," Nicole nodded toward the woman. "That's Lady Marla Johannsen. You have her for the first dance." Nicole had already slated him for dances with the women. Caldonia followed many nineteenth-century traditions, and a man was expected to claim dances well ahead of time to ensure he had a chance with the more popular ladies.

"Yes, I've met her before. A comely woman," Rand mused, his speculative eyes on Lady Marla. "The tall Nordic type. She's caught the attention of more than one man here."

"Uh-huh," Nicole said. But his words hit her like a punch in the stomach, and a burning jealousy she'd never felt before flared in her heart. She fought valiantly to pretend it didn't exist. "You'd better go claim her— Oh, she's coming over here."

Indeed, Lady Marla sailed gracefully across the ballroom floor as if she owned it. A paragon of assurance and sophistication, she held out her hands and Prince Rand clasped them, bowing low over them. "Lady Marla," he said. "It's been years since we've spoken."

"Yes, Your Highness. Far too long."

"I believe this is my dance," he said.

The woman met his smile as if she'd stumbled on the biggest treasure in the world. She hooked her arm in his and he escorted her onto the floor. He cast Nicole a final glance, his lips turned up slightly, and she forced herself to smile in response.

She watched the two of them begin to swirl across the floor in perfect synchronicity. Her gaze followed the flowing movement of the couple, noticing small things—the way her pink gown slapped against his shins, the way she never took her gaze from his face, the way he clasped her hand in his and held her firmly in his grasp. They looked perfect together.

Nicole swallowed down a sudden thickness in her throat, furious with herself for her entirely female and completely unprofessional reaction. She'd known at the outset why she was here. There was no excuse or reason to feel jealous.

She sighed and tried to douse her emotions. Thank

goodness she didn't have to pretend for anyone but Rand. Groups of people were engaged in conversation on either side of her, leaving her an island in their midst.

The king and queen were stationed on the other side of the room, relaxing in a pair of thrones, surrounded by attendants and courtiers. The width of the vast room separated her from them. Perhaps they wouldn't even notice she was here.

She gazed out over the glittering ballroom, hardly believing she *was* here. High above, huge chandeliers hung, dripping with crystals. The mahogany ballroom floor had been waxed so smoothly, she could see her reflection in it. Gold-flocked wallpaper and intricate molding decorated the ceilings and walls, while a row of mirrors along one wall gave the impression of the room receding endlessly into the distance. On the opposite wall, French doors opened onto the terrace, and a gentle summer breeze wafted in, carrying the scent of jasmine.

A shadow fell over her, and she glanced up to find a tall, sandy-haired man beside her. "You know the prince? I saw him greeting you. I don't believe we've met."

Nicole smiled politely. "No, but I know who you are, Lord Taybourne, the Earl of Haverington. Didn't you go to school with Ra—with His Highness?"

"That I did. We were on the same polo squad. And you are . . . ?"

"Miss Nicole Aldridge. I'm one of the prince's employees."

"An employee? Oh!" He arched an eyebrow, then glanced out over the crowd. "Well. I believe I have a dance partner somewhere about. Good to meet you." Then he left.

So that was that. Nicole soon realized that whenever someone came over, curious about the woman the prince kept speaking with, they would lose interest once they learned she was only an employee.

Rand danced past, the Nordic beauty in his arms. He kept their bodies a respectable distance apart, Nicole noted with a tingle of satisfaction. Then, he directed Lady Marla toward the outside of the ballroom, passing within a few feet of Nicole on the next turn. He caught Nicole's eye as they moved past, lifting his brows significantly as if asking what she thought.

Nicole raised her own brows, bouncing the question right back at him. The next time he swept past, he gave a barely imperceptible shake of his head, apparently having found his partner unsatisfactory. Nicole sighed. Two down, three to go. And she was no closer to succeeding in her task. Perhaps he would still find her tonight, in one of the remaining three ladies. The woman to share his life and dreams with. His bed. Nicole bit her lip, hard.

The dance ended. Rand handed the countess to her next partner and joined her again. "Unacceptable."

The word sounded like music to Nicole's ears. But she refused to let the prince get off so easily. She hated to think the entire evening would be yet another failure in her effort to find him a wife. No doubt he was being far too picky. "But why? She—"

"She . . . kept trying to . . . to come on to me, as you Americans would put it. I disliked her forward manner. Entirely unsuitable for a royal princess."

"I see." If he'd found the woman at all attractive, would that have been so bad? Physical intimacy could lead to love perhaps. Though it hurt to even talk about it, Nicole began to point this out. "But if you liked her even a little—"

Sighing in exasperation, Rand turned his back and strode away, seeking out candidate number three. Nicole stared at her gold sandals. Why was he being so difficult? He was only making it harder for her to do her job. His snap judgments would get them nowhere.

With the next two women, he made an effort to dance past Nicole on each turn around the ballroom floor. Nicole found herself watching for him, enjoying the way he would seek her out each time, unable to deny the pleasure she felt in receiving his attention even as he held another woman in his arms.

He scowled over the head of candidate number three and shook his head over candidate number four. Though he never said a word about them, Nicole understood what he was silently telling her. Again he had found them unacceptable.

At each rejection, her mood lifted, and she hated herself for it. When Rand returned to her side, she made an effort to stand up for the women in question—and fulfill her duty. "You don't seem to be giving any of the ladies a chance, Rand," she said softly. "How can you tell with one dance whether any of the women would make you a good wife?"

"Of course I can tell!" he shot back. "I'm excellent at reading people."

"You told me you wanted to select a wife logically, with forms and papers and rating scales!" His turnabout stunned and exhilarated her at the same time it frustrated her attempts to find his princess. "Now you're talking about gut instincts."

He scowled. "Either it clicks or it doesn't."

His lack of logic suddenly irritated her. Why had he changed his stance now when more than anything she wanted this over and done with so she could stop longing for something that would never be? "And it didn't click with any of the four women so far?"

"That's right. You have me dancing with them more than once. That should be sufficient for second chances."

"Yes, but—"

His dark eyes flared with an emotion she couldn't decipher. "Nicole, the woman will be my *wife*. I believe I'm the one to say whether or not I could stand the woman's face across my breakfast table every morning."

Nicole had no desire to picture such domestic scenes between him and his future wife. She had managed not to think of such disturbing intimacies for days, and she didn't intend to start now. "All right," she finally said. "At least try to give Lady Julia a try. She's accomplished, pretty—"

"She walks like a duck."

"Rand!" she admonished.

"Sorry, but she does. Just look at her."

Nicole followed his gaze to the lady in question, who was being escorted by her latest partner, Lord Taybourne, over to the prince's side. She *did* walk a little like a duck—or perhaps a tad bowlegged. "That's because she's such an excellent horsewoman, Your Highness," Nicole shot back quickly before the couple arrived. "I believe proficiency with horseback riding was one of your preferences," she said dryly.

"Hang horses," Rand muttered, his eyes sparking. "I wouldn't care if she . . . had trouble keeping her seat." Before Nicole could react, he greeted his friend Lord Taybourne and Lady Julia, then escorted the lady to the dance floor.

Nicole couldn't help pondering his remark. Since when had his standards, his preferences, changed so drastically? A slow flush suffused her skin as she thought about the way he'd looked at her just then. As if he were speaking about *her.*

"Miss Aldridge?" Lord Taybourne said, smiling down at her. "It seems we both lack partners for this dance. Shall we?"

Nicole opened her mouth to refuse the man who had been so rude to her earlier. Why had he decided Rand's employee was worth his time after all?

Her gaze skimmed to Rand and Lady Julia, just in time to catch Rand glancing in her direction. Perhaps it would be best for Lady Julia's chances if she wasn't standing here. Then Rand could focus his whole attention on his dance partner instead of trying to share the dance with her. She nodded, and before she knew it, she was in Lord Taybourne's arms, being waltzed around the dance floor.

Unprepared, Nicole stepped on his foot. "Excuse me, sir. I'm a little out of practice." As a girl growing up in Caldonia, she'd been taught the traditional dances, but since she'd moved to America, she'd only danced in nightclubs. Still, the Viennese waltz steps soon came back to her.

After a few quick turns around the floor, her partner directed them toward the slower, outer ring of the ballroom so he could chat as they danced.

"I find it hard to believe you aren't frequently swept off your feet, a lady as pretty as you," he said, a suggestive tone to his voice that made Nicole uncomfortable. "Hasn't that scoundrel Rand given you a turn yet tonight? He just propped you by the side of the room like a piece of furniture.

"No, it's not like that," she defended him. Then again, wasn't it? Despite that warm light in his eyes when he'd first seen her in her gown, he hadn't really considered her more than an employee all evening. He shouldn't, of course. He couldn't.

"Never fear, Clarence is here," the earl singsonged. They fell into a comfortable rhythm and quickened their pace, moving into the colorful flow of other dancers. More than once Nicole spotted Rand and Lady Julia, but she couldn't read the prince's expression.

"Miss Aldridge?"

At Clarence's quizzical tone, Nicole pulled her gaze back to him. She discovered Clarence had again led her to the slower outer ring of dancers. They slowed enough to talk.

"You know, Miss Aldridge. You must see an awful lot of the prince. As his employee, I mean. I've been wondering what's up with Rand. He hasn't been hanging around with the usual crowd for months."

"He's—He's been busy working," Nicole said, tearing her gaze from the man in question. *Every day, with me,* she added silently, unable to deny her pleasure in the thought. A surge of guilt struck her at having so much of Rand's time—time he could be spending with titled women.

"So I understand. Still, a man needs to take his—recreation—somewhere. I have a hunch I've discovered where." A speculative glint sparked in his eyes, and he pulled Nicole closer. She tensed, wishing the dance would end soon. She felt trapped.

"Rand used to have certain . . . friends . . . he was quite

close to," Clarence said. "And I often patched up their broken hearts when he moved on. Or even before. He didn't usually mind." He lowered his face into her neck and inhaled deeply. "You smell exquisite, Nicole. I can call you Nicole, can't I?" he murmured in her ear.

Nicole felt his hand trail down her back, perilously close to her bottom. Her eyes widened in shock. She leaned back, trying to put more distance between them; then she noticed Clarence looking over her head, a wicked smile on his lips. "Amazing. I believe this time he minds. Here he comes now."

"What—"

Then Rand was beside them, his hand on Clarence's shoulder, forcing them to stop dancing. "Let her go."

Clarence's smile never wavered. "Not very sporting of you, Rand. Can't you see I have this dance?"

Rand's expression turned stony. "No, Clarence. *I* do." Under that flinty gaze, Clarence released Nicole with a resigned sigh and backed away.

Turning his back on Clarence, Rand pulled Nicole into his arms and set off with her across the floor. She caught a victorious expression on the earl's face before Rand spun her away.

"Rand, why—"

"You don't want to let that man get close to you," he replied through stiff lips, hardly looking at her. "He can't be trusted around beautiful women."

His words sent Nicole's pulse into overdrive, but she refused to let him see how his compliment affected her. "How do you know he's the one who can't be trusted?"

"What?" Rand actually stopped dancing, she had managed to surprise him so completely. Thank goodness they were near the edge of the floor, where older couples were slowly circling, or someone would have run into them. "What do you mean by that? You aren't *interested* in him, are you?"

The dismay on Rand's face set off fireworks in Nicole.

He cared! She forced herself to sound composed. "Well he *is* an earl—"

"That never mattered to you before," he said quickly. "You want people to be treated as equals, remember? You've said it often enough."

Nicole cocked her head, feeling victorious. An undeniable urge filled her to make him feel what she'd been suffering this evening, watching him dance with numerous lovely women. "Clarence is suave and debonair. Very sophisticated. Women like that in a man."

Rand's brows furrowed. "Wait a minute. Not you. You're not that shallow."

She shrugged, knowing the gesture emphasized her smooth, bare shoulder. "You have to admit he's quite handsome. That soft blond hair, those blue eyes . . ."

Rand snorted, and she felt his hand stiffen on her back. "Clarence is a shallow, ill-mannered boy, and you'd be a fool to get anywhere near him, Nicole."

She merely shrugged and smiled, reveling in this amazing evidence of jealousy.

Rand's face darkened, his eyes glinting with anger. He said fiercely, "Damn it, Nicole. This isn't funny. He's not the right man for you."

*The right man* . . . Nicole knew they were moving perilously close to things that were best left unsaid. But she couldn't keep herself from asking, "How would you know, Rand?"

"I know you—that's why," he said, his tone dropping to a murmur. "I know *you.*" Before she could say another word, he yanked her into his arms and began waltzing with her. He was no longer communicating with words, but Nicole grew aware of his body's heat so close to her, the electricity that enfolded her as surely as his arms. Where he cradled her hand in his own, his touch felt like fire. His hand on her back burned through her silk gown straight to her heart. Thank goodness no one could see how he affected her. Even Rand.

*Especially* Rand. He was dancing with her as he would

with any woman, keeping a discreet distance between their
bodies as they circled the ballroom. She lifted her gaze to
find him watching her. He smiled down at her with such
intimacy, she stopped breathing. For an endless time, she
could think of nothing but him—she forgot where they
were and why they were there. The music and chatter faded
with the rhythmic movement of their bodies. This moment
was hers and hers alone—her one chance to experience
something she'd only dreamed about.

*It's a complete fantasy, Nicole. You're no Cinderella.* She didn't
care. Her heart filled with joy, she smiled up at him.

Instantly, his gaze sparked in response. His arms tightened a fraction, bringing his mouth close to her ear. "You
like this," he said softly. "So do I."

"Mm-hmm," Nicole said, not trusting herself to speak.
*He enjoyed dancing with her.* Nicole squeezed her eyes shut,
closing out reality to concentrate on the details of him: his
masculine scent, the strength of his body so close to hers.

Somehow, she found herself even closer to Rand, the
length of their steps diminishing, their movement concentrated into a small circle only they shared. Nicole leaned
her forehead against his shoulder as he swayed with her,
and her eyes drifted closed. Someday she would tell her
children how she danced with the prince at the ball. She
would always recall how perfect it was with this unattainable
man, once upon a time. . . .

The music ended, shattering her dream. The noise, the
lights, the crowd spun back into full, sharp reality.

Mortified, Nicole realized she was practically cuddled up
against Prince Rand. She shook herself and stepped back
firmly, but her knees threatened to give out beneath her.

This time as she looked at him, she forced her expression
to remain cool, her voice to sound professional. "Lady
Julia—you left her without a partner."

He gave her a crooked smile, but whether secretly laughing at her distress or merely happy to be with her, she
couldn't say. "I had to rescue you, Nicole."

"But the only reason I'm here is to find you a wife!"

His smile vanished. "Stop reminding me," he said sharply. "I'm well aware of why I hired you."

"Then go talk to her right now," Nicole said, swallowing hard in a suddenly thick throat. Her body still burned where he'd touched her, and she had the crazy urge to press herself hard against him, to feel his heat against every part of her skin. What was she thinking? Why had he let her dance so close to him? Just because he enjoyed seeing women throw themselves at him?

"Nicole," he said gently.

Nicole jerked her chin up. "Make it up to Lady Julia. I insist."

Rand's eyes narrowed and a muscle in his jaw tensed. "Very well. Nothing like a little gentle persuasion." He turned and strode off, seeking the bowlegged Lady Julia.

Nicole sighed and returned to her spot by the potted palm. What had gotten into her? She should never have forgotten she was in the midst of a curious crowd, here to help the prince find his princess. This was how she demonstrated loyalty to her country? And what could Rand have possibly been thinking, allowing her to make such a fool of herself?

She glanced toward where the king and queen sat, and she saw to her relief that they were no longer in attendance. Rand had apparently decided he could do as he pleased. But the photographers—

Only a few of those remained, as well. Many photographers had probably left to file their photos for the morning editions. Thank God. So no one except perhaps a few curious nearby dancers had witnessed her wearing her heart on her sleeve.

Before she could chastise herself further, a uniformed butler appeared before her. "Your presence is requested. Come this way."

Nicole glanced at the man, confusion tightening her stomach. She looked toward Rand, but doubted the request had come from him. He had indeed obeyed her and was even now smiling as Lady Julia said something marvelously witty, no doubt, her hand on his arm, her eyes alight with interest and unabashed attraction.

It had meant nothing, she realized, a swift bolt of pain streaking through her heart. Their dance had meant absolutely nothing. Even now, he was holding out his hand to the titled lady and leading her onto the dance floor, his arms settling comfortably around her.

"Miss Aldridge? Did you not hear me?" the butler said.

"Oh, yes." Who would want to talk to her? She couldn't imagine.

When she learned the answer, she wanted to run straight back to America.

The butler escorted her down a short hall leading from the dance floor to a small sitting room. Inside waited Queen Eurydice. She didn't wait for the butler to close the door before she began. "You, young lady, have gone too far."

"Excuse me, Your Majesty?" Nicole said, forcing her chin up a notch. She refused to lose face before the queen—what little face she had left to preserve.

"Your little display of affection toward my son has not gone unnoticed," she said, standing rigidly before Nicole.

"We only danced," Nicole tried to say, but the queen immediately cut her off.

"Your lack of judgment is appalling. What gives you the right to waste his time as his dance partner? My son tells me you are here only because you are to help match him with suitable women, which does not include you."

A wave of embarrassment engulfed Nicole, but she couldn't help trying to defend herself. "I know that, Your Majesty. I wasn't—"

"Do not interrupt me, girl. I see exactly what you're doing, but I won't allow it. Not for my son, not for his future wife. The travesty perpetuated by the Hollingsworth men is going to end here!"

Nicole fought to grasp what she meant, tried to puzzle it out at the same time a hot knot of guilt and embarrassment constricted her chest.

"I will not allow you to jeopardize his future," the queen said. "You are nothing but an opportunity-seeking hussy, and I'll not have you sniffing around my son. Do you hear me?" She appeared so angry her lips quivered. "Now get out of my sight!"

Stunned at the sheer magnitude of the queen's charges against her, Nicole stumbled back as if slapped. A wash of pain and humiliation swept through her. The queen stood rigid and imperious, waiting for her lowly subject to remove herself from her presence.

Nicole took another step back, turned, and forced her feet to carry her from the room. She found herself once again in the colorful, brightly lit ballroom, surrounded by glittering nobles and aristocrats. A place she had no business being.

She hurried toward the closest exit, which led to the south terrace. Her back stiff, she could imagine a hundred pairs of eyes boring into her, seeing, knowing, condemning.

*They know. They know what I've done.*

The queen had berated her in private—because of what she'd seen in public. Nicole felt as if the stern woman had torn open her chest and exposed her secret passion to the world—a passion she had no business feeling because it called into question her every intention to help her country. A passion that filled her so completely it would be part of her forever.

Outside, Nicole found she still wasn't alone. Several couples had stepped out for fresh air. She strode past them, down the terrace steps, and into the garden.

When she finally found herself alone in the shadows deep in the garden, the full force of the queen's chastisement struck her. She doubled over, a well of tears forcing their way into her throat. She swallowed hard, forcing them down. She wouldn't cry. She refused.

The queen somehow thought she posed a threat to Rand. A threat! She had come to Caldonia to help her country, not tear it apart.

She shook her head hard, trying desperately to pull herself together, *to escape.* She broke into a run, away from the palace, away from the people with their prying eyes. High on a plateau in the distance, moonlight reflected off the roof of Rand's temple. Automatically, her feet turned in that direction.

Struggling up the steep part of the path, she removed her elegant heels and clambered up, heedless of her gown. The moon and stars shone down, mute witness to her misery.

She hurried into the silent depths of the temple and sucked in a breath. Her exertion had helped her battle back the tears that threatened, and the calm, stoic structure served to soothe her, make her feel safe. Here, with the night sounds for company, the music of the ball barely perceptible, she could almost pretend she'd traveled thousands of miles from the scene of her mortification. She leaned against a pillar, pressed her hot forehead into the icy marble, tried to gather back her sense of self-worth, and repair her shattered pride. It was impossible.

"Nicole?" Rand's voice floated across the evening breeze toward her as soft and seductive as a caress.

Oh, God, she couldn't face him. Not now. He had to know the truth now—her secret burning passion for him. She couldn't stand to see him pity her.

She didn't trust herself to answer him, but she didn't have to. He crossed the marble floor and paused beside her. "I heard something about you being summoned," he said, his voice tense. "Who summoned you?"

"I don't want to talk—"

"Who?" he demanded.

His intensity threatened to destroy the little composure she had left. The words fell from her lips before she could prevent them. "The queen."

"Christ!" Nicole felt Rand stiffen beside her. She caught sight of his hand balling into a tight fist. "What did she say to you?"

"Nothing." Nicole turned her back to him. "Please. I

just came out for some air—that's all. I'll go back in a moment, and we can get to work again."

"Like hell! Tell me what happened."

She stiffened at his angry tone. Several seconds passed, during which she could hear nothing but the sound of his breathing. Then he settled his hand on her shoulder. His thumb swept across her exposed skin, the gentle caress nearly causing her to tears to flow.

"Tell me, Nicole. I need you to talk to me."

"She—" Nicole pulled in a breath, desperately fighting the quaver in her voice. "She didn't like us dancing."

A heartbeat of silence. "That's it?"

She wasn't being fair, Nicole realized. The queen's concerns had gone much deeper, even if she didn't completely understand them. "She thinks I'm—I'm after you."

His hand squeezed her shoulder, and she felt his touch in every part of her body, echoing along her nerves. "You did absolutely nothing wrong," he said firmly.

"She thinks I have. She thinks that I'm—I'm trying to seduce you to have power over you."

He muttered to himself. His words sounded almost like, "God knows, it's not intentional." His hand released her shoulder, swept along her bare skin—warm, strong, and inviting.

Nicole trembled under his touch. A wicked tendril of heat unfurled in her stomach and blended with sharp, painful longing. This was Rand, her friend, the man she had shared more with in the past months than anyone. "God, it was so embarrassing. I wanted to die."

"Nicole, I'm so sorry. I should have kept my head when we— That is . . ." He hesitated, then changed direction. "She's done this before," he said heavily. "Accused people of things they were innocent of. I believe she's trying to demonstrate that she has power."

"That should make me feel better, but it doesn't," she said honestly.

"I know."

Two simple words, filled with understanding and tenderness. Their conversation while they danced returned to her. *I know you.* God, how she needed him! His compassion defeated her best efforts, shattering her already shaky wall of composure. She gasped sharply, her breath catching in her throat as the tears came.

Strong arms surrounded her, pressing her to a solid chest. She clung to Rand as the tears flowed, as he murmured in her ear soothing words that meant nothing—and everything.

His warm lips grazed her temple. He pulled back enough to look into her face, to wipe her tears away with his thumbs. "Do you know how beautiful you look tonight?" he asked, his tender smile the most magnificent sight Nicole had ever seen. "The goddess Athena would be sick with jealousy if she set eyes on you. You're my boyhood fantasy come to life."

Though she knew he was only trying to cheer her up, Nicole wanted to lose herself in his sweet words and never surface again. But her common sense fought those wayward feelings. She dropped her eyes, found herself gazing at the royal crest on his emerald sash, a blatant reminder of his status. "I shouldn't have attended the ball. It was a mistake."

"Nicole, I wanted you there." His husky voice instantly turned her pain into desire. He was only touching her shoulders, resting his hands there gently. Yet she could feel the heat of his well-muscled body through the thin fabric of her gown, and her skin flamed with awareness. She couldn't look in his face, thinking of him like this, *wanting* him like this. He would read her desire in her eyes.

But he refused to let her avoid him. He ran his knuckles down her cheek soothingly. Nicole had never felt such a tantalizing touch. Then, with gentle, persuasive fingers, he tilted her face up to his. The moonlight caught in his dark eyes, and Nicole pulled in a ragged breath. Her heart pounded, anticipation—*need*—singing through her blood. She craved more than his touch. She craved an outlet for the intense emotions he stirred in her.

"Nicole," he said, his voice breaking on her name, turning it into a confession, a revelation, a promise.

Despite her resolve, Nicole felt herself disappearing into his gaze. Unable to move, unable to think, she merely waited for it to happen. Amazement, delight—words couldn't describe how she felt as he lowered his lips and finally, achingly, slid them across hers.

# ELEVEN

The wall they had both cultivated so carefully between them shattered at the intimate touch. A thousand sparks of pleasure burst through her, and Nicole knew suddenly, completely, that she'd lost her heart to him. Before she was aware of it, she had closed the imperceptible distance between them and pressed her tender, aching breasts to his chest with a sigh of sheer delight.

Her small acquiescence seemed to break something in Rand, for his touch grew far less tentative. He clamped his strong hand around her waist and dragged her tight against him, pressing her soft curves against his steel-hard body, his wonderful, sensual mouth claiming hers in no uncertain terms.

*He wants me. He burns for me, too.* At the heady realization, Nicole arched her head back, opening herself to him completely. Through parted lips, the tips of their tongues touched. At first, each thoroughly savored the feeling, the flavor of the other. With increasing urgency, they explored each other, and the kiss grew hot, possessive, unleashing the heat of pure desire, a desperate, raging need.

Clasping her hips, Rand turned and braced his back against the pillar. He spread his legs and pulled her between them. He shifted his hips provocatively, and Nicole felt the strength of his desire press hard against her womanhood, sending a shock of liquid heat through her. Instinctively, she arched into the forbidden embrace, craving an even more intimate touch. His palm curved around her bottom, snugged her hard up against him. Their groans mingled through the kiss.

"Oh, yes," Rand moaned, trailing kisses along her cheek and chin. "Yes, yes, yes!" With small nipping kisses, he slid his lips down her neck and along her bare shoulder, his teeth, his tongue, sending brilliant shocks of pleasure through her sexually awakened body.

Her eyes closed, Nicole began to lose all sense of her surroundings, her knees so weak she relied on his intimate grip to keep from falling. She sighed deeply as he ravaged her tender skin. She relished his lovemaking, craved it. How long had she wanted this? From the first day she'd met him? Met him . . . When he'd hired her to find him a titled wife. And she was behaving exactly as the queen expected her to.

Nicole stiffened as shame coursed through her. She forced herself to push away, forced herself to ignore the hunger eating her up inside. "Rand, stop—"

"Nicole—"

"I can't. I have to— I have to go now." She stumbled backward out of his grasp, toward the exit. Rand's hands tried to keep hold of her, reached out toward her.

"Back to the ball?" he rasped out. Nicole forced herself to ignore the confused look on his face.

"No, to my room." So that he wouldn't assume that was an invitation, she added harshly, "Through the servant's entrance." She spun on her heel and ran down the steps, across the grassy plateau, and onto the shadowy path back to the garden.

The insistent knocking refused to stop.

Nicole forced her eyes open. Her emotions raw, she had tossed and turned long into the night, wanting, craving what she couldn't have, reliving her brief yet rapturous moments in Rand's arms over and over again. Sometime toward dawn, she had fallen asleep.

Unable to ignore the noise, she pulled herself out of bed and slipped on a robe. She shoved her tangled hair out of her face and cracked open the door. Gerald stood uncertainly, his arms full of newspapers. "Yes, Gerald?"

"The prince asked me to deliver these."

"Newspapers?" Confused, Nicole opened the door wider and took the papers from him, at least half a dozen heavy Sunday morning news sections.

"He wanted you to see these before . . . before learning of it elsewhere."

Nicole hardly heard him. With unsteady hands, she stared transfixed at the front page of the *Caldonian Times* on top of the pile. A huge photo of herself in Rand's arms stared back at her, the headline above screaming out:

## MYSTERY WOMAN REVEALED!

The photo had been cropped so close it looked less like they were dancing than engaged in a passionate embrace. For the first time, she saw Rand's expression as he danced with her, as if he also had been oblivious to the people who had surrounded them, his desire-filled eyes gazing down at her as she snuggled into his shoulder.

After the way he'd kissed her, she accepted that he was attracted to her. But to have such evidence of his desire laid out for all the world to see—

Nicole's knees gave out and she sank onto the chaise longue before the fireplace. She pressed her hand to her mouth, a sick swell of regret, of dread, forcing its way into her chest. "Oh, no."

"I'm sorry, Nicole." Gerald hesitated. "You know how the press can be."

Nicole made herself flip through the other newspapers. More headlines:

RAND'S NEW EMPLOYEE—HAS SHE
STOLEN HIS HEART?

PRINCE RAND TAKES NEW MISTRESS,
INSIDERS SAY

And from the stodgy conservative press:

PRINCE FLAUNTS MISTRESS BEFORE PEERAGE

More photos—endless photos. Most were variations on the first photo, taken when they danced together. One photo of them dancing captured Rand's cheek pressed against her hair, his eyes closed. Another, a closeup of her with a dreamy smile on her face.

And the copy: sidebars on her; editorial speculation; a shot of her uncle, Lord Phillip Aldridge, escaping photographers outside his home late last night.

Worst of all, a late edition with interviews from old schoolmates who knew her. One girl said:

*She was always out to find a rich guy, grab a title. Wanted to be the most popular girl at school.*

Nicole could hardly remember the girl being quoted, but what she remembered wasn't pleasant.

"Why?" Nicole rasped out. She scanned an article questioning Rand's suitability to serve his country after his string of flagrant affairs. "Why would they take pictures of Rand with me and not with any of the other women he danced with?"

Gerald appeared vastly uncomfortable, and Nicole realized he might believe what had been printed. With sick certainty, she understood that he'd been trying to warn

her last night. Warn her that the prince also was in danger
of losing his sense. And she'd helped it happen.

"Perhaps you would be interested in page three of the
*Times*, Nicole," Gerald said softly. With that, he politely
bowed out.

Nicole barely noticed the door closing behind him as
she frantically sought the page in question. "Oh, my God."
She stared at the photos—a montage of at least ten of them.
Almost every one featured her and Rand together, illustrating their evening together.

The moment he stepped forward and escorted her down
the steps, a broad smile on his face. Their heads bent close
in a private discussion as they stood by the wall. The moment he cut in on Lord Taybourne, his face revealing jealous irritation.

The only photos she didn't appear in showed a glowering
queen, and Rand waltzing with one of the princess candidates, appearing bored, glancing away. Probably looking
at her. The caption read:

> *Despite dancing with numerous beauties at the ball,*
> *none of them sparked a fire in the prince's eyes like his*
> *own employee, the commoner Nicole Aldridge.*

Damage control. They would have to do something to
stop the rumors.

She grabbed the papers and was at the door before realizing she was still in her nightclothes. She couldn't appear
like this in front of the prince. Not now. She prayed she
could face him at all and maintain her distance, her professional demeanor. She had no choice. It was the only way
to salvage this mess and restore a remnant of her tattered
pride.

As she dressed in her most conservative suit, she forced
memory of their kiss out of her mind. It hadn't meant
anything. She couldn't allow it to mean anything.

* * *

Ignoring the breakfast set out on the terrace, Rand stared at the photo. The look on his face—he looked like a lovesick schoolboy. He'd been such a fool the night before. He'd had no idea he could be so transparent. All his life he'd learned to hide his emotions in public, but last night he'd forgotten everything but the joy of holding Nicole.

He'd been so heedless of prying photographers, so ready to believe the feelings he'd kept hidden until now would remain hidden. So certain no one would ever know.

No one would know . . . what?

His gaze fell on the picture of himself, crossing the floor to shove Clarence's filthy paws off Nicole—*his* Nicole. His competitive college buddy had danced with her for just this purpose, Rand now realized. Rand had always prided himself on keeping hold of his heart, of never falling prey to a woman's charms, of maintaining control at all times.

Clarence had wanted to tweak Rand's nose, to rub his face in it, to bring out the truth, which was so clearly written all over Rand's face. The truth . . .

*Christ, I'm in love with her.* The truth hit him like a punch in the stomach. He lurched to his feet, knocking over his wrought-iron chair. He stumbled to the banister and gripped it, staring out unseeing at the crisp green lawn and neatly tended flower beds.

When had he lost his heart to Nicole? How could he have allowed this to happen?

Swearing, he jabbed his fingers in his hair. How in the hell could he have prevented it? He couldn't have made Nicole be less than perfect for him, and now it was far too late.

Sweeping the paper up, he paced back inside and around the room, restless energy gnawing at him. He flipped through the pages, staring at the photos, reading their truth.

Tossing that paper aside, he picked up another from the couch. Even now, knowing what a fool he'd been, he couldn't help finding enjoyment in gazing at her. She had completely entranced him the night before. Was that all it was—a temporary magic?

No. Not at all. She could have shown up in a sack and worn those silly glasses of hers and it would have made no difference. She'd lit up the ballroom with such intensity, he hadn't been able to see any other woman. His body still hungered for her; his soul craved hers. He longed to share his secrets, his dreams with her. As he'd been doing for the past months.

Yet what he could never share was his heart.

*Make her your mistress.* . . . His father's words came back to him, taunting him. No, he refused to demean her like that. She may be a commoner, but she was far too good for a halfway relationship, even if he was the prince.

The truth crushed down on him like a lead weight. The energy left his body and he sagged on the couch. He would have to find some other woman—some *noblewoman*—and marry her. A woman he would never love as he did Nicole. The best he could hope for was to find a comfortable companion. He'd once told Nicole that was all he expected in a wife. God, that was ages ago. To think he'd actually believed he needed nothing else! To think Nicole herself had shown him how wrong he was.

*Nicole* . . . He could never have her. He could never again hold her, comfort her, feel her lips under his. Unless . . .

The dangerous thought leaped into his mind, tantalizing him. His body reacted with ferocity. Instantly his stomach burned with acid, more fiercely than it had since Nicole came into his life. He struggled to his feet and headed for the bathroom. Once there, he found the antacid bottle and shook out two tablets, swallowing them dry.

He stared at his face in the mirror above the sink. His hair was mussed, he hadn't shaved, and shadows accented his deep-set eyes. Never in all his years fulfilling the role he'd been born to had he ever considered something so drastic. That he considered it now shocked him as much as it proved to him how deep his feelings were for Nicole.

But how did she feel about him? Oh, he knew she was

attracted to him. He'd known that for months. Was it
merely an infatuation? No. His heart told him her feelings
ran as deep as his own. But he couldn't trust his own heart
anymore, after it had pulled such a dastardly trick on him.
He was at the mercy of his feelings, and it scared the life
out of him. He would have to be very careful, or he might
become the world's biggest fool. He'd been a dreamer all
his life. This time, he couldn't allow his heart to rule his
head.

Perhaps, if he knew for certain she returned his feelings . . . If he knew, he might—

Might what? He didn't want to define it further. He
didn't even want to consider it; he felt like such a disloyal
bastard. All his plans for the country hung in the balance.
The full implication of what he was considering flooded
his brain and he sagged on the sink.

A crisp knock cut through the blurred pain in his mind
and he jerked up. He tightened his midnight blue robe
and crossed to the door. Was it Nicole? He'd sent the papers
to her room, wanting to prepare her, wanting her to know.

Wanting her to recognize the passion that lay between
them so they could begin to deal with it—together.

He yanked open the door. Nicole swept past him, hardly
giving him a glance. She looked about the room, taking in
the papers tossed on the furniture and floor—papers he'd
riffled through in his haste to see what had been done to
them. She was already neatly dressed, wearing a brown suit
that Rand thought was her ugliest. The double-breasted
thing appeared designed to mask all her curves and softness. Curves that had been so hotly pressed to him the
night before. She'd pulled her hair back into a severely
tight roll. And sure enough, the oversize glasses again sat
on her nose.

Her gaze swept over him, no doubt seeing evidence of
his own ravaged emotions on his face. He tensed, waiting
for her to say something revealing. Something he needed
to hear. Far too much was at stake to be wrong about where
her heart lay.

But her eyes remained cool, her voice composed. "Thank you for alerting me to the situation. It's apparent we have to do something immediately."

"Yes," he said slowly, not certain what he was agreeing to.

He wasn't sure he recognized this woman. He'd expected concern, perhaps tears. A distraught Nicole—one he could pull into his arms and comfort in painful acknowledgment of their love for each other.

But the passionate, *feeling* woman of the night before had disappeared. This morning, everything seemed different. The air between them vibrated with a strange tension.

"We have to explain that they're wrong," she said.

"Wrong?" The word hit him like a slap in the face. His heart chilled. She didn't see what everyone else saw. She didn't see how much he loved her. My God, did this mean she didn't feel the same?

She shifted her feet, but her spine remained stiff as steel. "About us."

"Set them straight, Miss Aldridge?" he said, forcing the words out past a tight throat. "Is that your plan?"

Nicole seemed to stiffen even further at his use of the formal address. Always before it had irritated her. Now, her composure was remarkable, as if their brush with passion the night before meant nothing to her.

"Yes," she said primly. "We have to erase the mistake."

"Erase the mistake," he repeated woodenly.

"Yes." She nodded emphatically. "I thought perhaps we could issue a statement. Tell the truth, I mean—that there's nothing . . ." Her expression seemed to tense and she flicked her gaze away. But when she once again met his eyes, he could see no evidence that she had been affected, that memory of their kiss assailed her as it did him.

She lifted her chin and continued. "No facts to support these erroneous reports."

Rand turned from her, afraid if he didn't put distance between them he might grab her and shake her hard. He tossed over his shoulder, "A statement won't do it, Miss

Aldridge." No, only one thing would draw press attention from the two of them—something that any woman—if she loved the man involved—would find horribly painful to witness.

He spun to face her. "I see only one way out of this fiasco, and that's for me to marry."

She shrugged as if it didn't even matter. "Of course, that would help, but—"

"But nothing!" he snarled. "I hired you to find me a wife!" Rand's patience snapped. This woman had waltzed into his life and stolen his heart, and she didn't even care what she'd done! From the coffee table, he swept up a folded newspaper splashed with a huge photo of the two of them, their heads together in intimate conversation. "It's been months now, and there's not a decent prospect on the horizon!"

"I'm well aware of that," Nicole shot back. "But you haven't exactly been enthusiastic about the women—"

My God, couldn't she see *why?* "Damn it all! Can't you find me a single acceptable female in the whole of this planet? I gave you my preferences. I even selected candidates, but your method must be royally screwed up because it's not working!" Rand slammed the folded newspaper against the back of a nearby chair.

Nicole jerked at his show of anger, but maintained a perfectly businesslike demeanor, as if she'd been trained all her life to work as a servant to a man like him.

"I apologize, Your Highness," she said with icy calmness, "but your own attitude is critical in such an enterprise, and you have been less than enthusiastic toward virtually every candidate. You hardly give any of them a chance."

"Now you listen to me," Rand said, pointing at her. "You find me a woman I can marry within the next month or—" He faltered, unsure of his next words.

She arched one eyebrow. "Or?"

God, she was so cold! He had the sudden urge to strike her where apparently it mattered most—in her profession. He gritted out, "Or you're fired."

The woman before him remained completely still for several heartbeats. Rand waited, hardly able to breathe. If she allowed that professional mask to slip, allowed a flicker of her feelings through—

"Very well. One month," she said, her voice devoid of emotion. "If I don't find you a wife in that time, I'll gladly quit. Now, if you'll excuse me, I'll get to work."

In painful silence, Rand watched as she turned on her heel and walked from the room, taking his heart and his hope with her.

As soon as she'd closed the door behind her, Nicole sagged against it, her hand pressed to her face in an effort to contain a sob. The bastard! He would fire her, after all the effort she'd put in on his projects? After he'd offered her permanent employment? *After he'd practically made love to her the night before?*

She suddenly longed to leave here, to pack her bags and go straight to the airport. She'd done more than enough for her country, including sacrificing her heart.

But she couldn't leave now, not without seeing it through. Not without attempting to salvage something from this mess. Not her heart—that was already broken into a thousand pieces. But perhaps she could walk away with a tattered remnant of her pride as a Caldonian, as her parents' daughter and her uncle's niece.

In defiance of her own heart, she would accomplish what she'd been hired to do.

As soon as the limousine pulled into the palace's curving drive, Nicole stepped outside to meet it. Within, behind the black glass, was perhaps Caldonia's last best hope for a princess—and Nicole's last chance to repair the mess she'd made.

Nicole had almost given her notice a dozen times in the past two weeks and returned to New York. Inevitably, her pride stopped her. She had never been a quitter. She hated to fail at any job, and she vowed to see this one through, despite her own foolish heart. Even stronger was her need to prove to everyone—the public, her uncle, Gerald, even the king and queen—that she did not have designs on the prince, that she truly cared about her country.

And she cared about what was right for the prince.

Only late at night, when she was alone, she found she couldn't deny another, darker motive—the need to be near the man she loved, even though he didn't return her feelings.

A palace footman opened the rear door of the limousine, and assisted the woman to alight. Draped in ivory silk, Princess Zara of Omat wore a matching scarf wrapped about her head, concealing her features. A swarthy, gray-haired man exited from the other side, along with a plump matronly woman. Both were dressed far less exquisitely. Nicole guessed they were personal attendants to the princess.

After speaking with Zara's personal secretary, Nicole had determined that like tradition-bound Caldonia, Omat faced similar challenges of modernization. She thought this might give Rand a place to start as he became acquainted with Princess Zara. Furthermore, Zara had been invited for a lengthy stay—not a one-night date that Rand could shrug off as unacceptable. He would actually have an opportunity to get to know this woman.

Nicole strode down the steps and bowed before the princess—the traditional sign of respect on meeting a member of the royal family of Omat.

"Princess Zara, I'm so glad you could accept the royal family's invitation. I'm Nicole Aldridge, assistant to Prince Rand."

"Where is the prince? He is not here to greet me?" Zara asked, her accent bearing the exotic stamp of her home country, a tiny yet progressive Middle Eastern nation.

"The prince and his family await you inside. He thought you might wish to freshen up first," Nicole explained. In truth, she had no idea what Rand thought. Whenever they spoke—which was seldom these days—their conversations were short, brisk, and painfully businesslike. Not only had the wall between them been erected once again, but this time it was built so solidly, she could hardly see the man on the other side.

She had told him of the princess. He had said she sounded satisfactory and agreed to invite her for a visit. Gerald had helped with the arrangements. Since the ball two weeks ago, and the terrible morning after, that summed up the contact they had shared. And only two weeks remained before she would be let go, unless Princess Zara turned out to be the one.

*The one* . . . Pain grabbed Nicole's heart and gave it a sharp twist. She had thought her emotions under control, but now that Princess Zara stood before her, all the agony of her hopeless love flooded back to her.

Turning away from her guest, she blinked hard at the moisture threatening to build behind her eyes. She refused to let her feelings conquer her. She refused.

Lifting her chin, she pasted on a smile and led Princess Zara inside. She took her and her female servant upstairs to her guest suite while a palace butler showed her male servant to a nearby room and others carried her luggage.

The princess's suite was one door down from her own, even closer to Rand's.

Inside, Zara unwound the silken scarf from her head with long, graceful fingers. She held the scarf out and instantly her servant was there to take it.

Daughter of the Caucasian wife of an Arabic king, the young woman was even more attractive than her photographs. Wing-shaped eyebrows emphasized her deep-set ebony eyes and long Arabic nose. Yet her skin was creamy rather than swarthy—a heritage from her blond mother, no doubt. With her dramatic coloring and svelte figure, she appeared exotic and serene, while exuding sensuality. Beautiful by anyone's definition.

As she gazed at the princess, Nicole grew light-headed,

seeing her worst nightmare coming to life. No man could resist this woman. She was a perfect wife for a prince.

With the help of her servant, Princess Zara also removed her full-body ivory wrap, revealing an ornate silken two-piece pantsuit. She cast Nicole a warm smile. "Since emerald is your country's color, I selected this outfit as a special courtesy. It will suit, will it not?"

"You look lovely, Princess," Nicole replied, forcing her voice to sound composed and professional, to battle back the jealous demon raging inside her. She could stand this. She had to stand it.

*Rand may not even like this woman,* she thought, instantly hating herself for her petty thought. Still, she imagined him comparing the two of them and knew she'd come up short. She'd never been a knockout, not like this woman, who was checking her reflection and touching up makeup she didn't even need.

Nicole escorted the princess downstairs to a private sitting room, where the royal family waited. The butler had gone ahead to let them know of Princess Zara's arrival.

Nicole glanced at the lovely woman gliding so gracefully at her side. Zara bore herself with regal flair. Clearly, she had been born to royalty, to expect those beneath her to treat her with the respect due her station. Yet she did not seem overbearing; she merely assumed that respect from others was her right.

As Nicole neared the door, her stomach twisted sharply. This was it; in a few moments, Rand would meet the princess, and Nicole would know whether she had finally failed or succeeded. She had no idea which was which anymore; she knew nothing but the desperate need to continue on despite the agony, pretending nothing had happened between her and Rand, pretending she felt nothing for him.

A pair of green-garbed guards swung open the double doors at their approach, while a butler slipped inside to announce their arrival. Nicole had never been inside the Blue Receiving Room before, but she barely noticed her surroundings.

Instead, her gaze went to where Prince Rand stood beside his father. His gaze followed Princess Zara; his expression was impassive and unreadable. For an instant, his eyes slid toward Nicole, then returned to the princess. Nicole trembled inside, wondering what he was thinking. He had never seemed so distant to her, as if an impossible gulf separated them.

Nicole brought the princess to the king first and made the introductions; then as protocol demanded, she turned to the queen, who remained seated.

She braced herself mentally before finally turning to Rand. "Your Highness, may I present Princess Zara Al-Talla Al-Umbaraq, first daughter of the King and Queen of Omat." She turned to the princess. "Your Highness, this is Prince Randall Hollingsworth, first son of the King and Queen of Caldonia."

Nicole watched Rand's face as he bowed low over Zara's hand, then met her gaze. He smiled warmly, and Nicole saw an answering smile on Princess Zara's face. Clearly, their first impressions were mutually positive. Nicole congratulated herself on her success, but she could not control a painful tightening in her chest. She chastised herself for her weakness, fiercely reminded herself that her work was all that mattered, all that *could* matter.

"Please sit here," King Edbert said, gesturing to a nearby chair. "You must be fatigued after such a long journey."

"My, that's a lovely costume," Queen Eurydice said, "so elegant." Nicole had never seen the queen smile so warmly. It seemed Zara was finding favor with her as well.

"It suits her," Rand said quietly, his voice appreciative. "Most definitely." He gave Zara one of his famous smiles, and she responded with a gracious smile and a regal bow of her head, as if to say, "I accept your compliment."

Yet Nicole saw beyond her manners to the sparkle in her eyes. She definitely liked what she saw in Prince Rand. Nicole saw the answering glimmer in Rand's eyes and quickly excused herself. Not one of them looked up. All of their eyes were fastened on Princess Zara.

Safely outside, Nicole dragged in a quaking breath. In the time she'd been in the room, Rand hadn't once focused on her. He'd only had eyes for the princess. *That's the way it should be,* she told herself sternly. *The way you want it to be. The way it* had *to be.*

Rand watched Nicole leave the room, anguish twisting his gut. She hadn't once looked him in the eyes. She really wanted this. The realization settled like lead in his chest. So many times over the past two weeks he had expected her to say something, anything. To lose her temper. To cry. To look at him with feeling in her eyes. Even to quit, thereby revealing how she truly felt.

But she was like a rock from the Caldonian Mountains, unshakable and impossible to read. More of a stranger than this princess she'd brought him.

His gaze skimmed over Princess Zara's svelte figure. Nicole had actually done it—she'd delivered another woman to him. She hadn't skimped on the woman's looks or her breeding or any other quality he'd once outlined on his goddamned forms. He had expected Nicole wouldn't be able to handle such a painful chore. Had hoped that would be the case. How *could* any woman stand it if she was truly in love? Such a huge *if* . . .

My God, did her career mean more to her than whatever she felt for him? True, he had violated the employee-employer relationship. He had dragged her hard against him and kissed her and tasted heaven.

But how did she feel about their encounter? Was this why she'd grown so cold toward him? Had his inability to control his passion disgusted her that much? Or was she afraid of revealing how she really felt? Hope flared in his chest, but only briefly. For if she did return his love, what could he possibly do about it? The uncertainty was eating him up inside.

"Rand." His father's voice jerked his attention back to the present, to his parents and the woman Nicole had handpicked for him. She was indeed beautiful, refined, *noble*.

The word made his stomach churn. Nicole had personally selected Princess Zara to meet his needs. She *wanted*
her choice to please him. Drawing on years of royal train-
ing, he forced a smile to his lips and turned to the princess.

"You have done yourself proud."

At the sound of Rand's voice in her room, Nicole stiffened. Her hands stilled on the pile of papers she was sort-
ing on her desk.

Since the ball, she had moved her work back to her own
suite, and Rand had moved back to his office. Though they
had continued working in the library even after she no
longer needed crutches, they pretended her healed leg was
the reason for separating their work.

Nicole pulled in a breath and gathered her poise. She
turned to face him and forced herself to remain calm as
she gazed at the man she loved. "I'm glad I've pleased you,
Your Highness. I assume then that Princess Zara meets with
your approval?"

"Most definitely. She has managed to charm both the
queen and the king."

Was he trying to remind her of her own failure in that
arena? But the prince's opinion mattered the most. She
forced herself to ask the question. "And yourself?"

"Of course," Rand replied, the corners of his mouth
turning up in a small smile. "I find her charming, intelligent, and an excellent conversationalist."

"No . . . annoying habits then," she asked softly.

"Absolutely not." He spoke crisply, yet Nicole detected
an underlying edge to his voice. In defense of Princess
Zara? "In fact, she would make an excellent princess for
Caldonia, providing a badly needed infusion of new culture. I assume you thought of that. You *think* of everything."

"Well, yes, it had occurred to me." Nicole's heart ached

and she longed to fidget, to react in some way. His presence filled the room, filled her senses with secret, unattainable longings that took all her power to ignore. With fierce determination, she forced herself to remain perfectly still, perfectly poised. "Thank you, sir."

"In fact, I want you to work with Gerald to plan a special outing for the two of us to my country estate. I'd like to spend some time alone with her . . . in private." His voice took on a slightly hesitant tone, as if he were unwilling to reveal the secret desires behind his request.

The image of the two of them alone together cut into Nicole. She saw him sitting beside Zara before a fire, giving her that special smile of shared intimacy that had so entranced her. She saw him kissing Zara, knowing from experience how exalted his lover's touch could feel, knowing how Zara would naturally melt in his arms. She imagined him giving Zara something greater, something she could never have, the bond between lovers—

She dropped her gaze to the desktop. She couldn't allow him to see it, allow anyone to see the pain stabbing her heart. She'd brought this hopeless love on herself. She'd been hired to do a job, to help her country. She had expected to make Uncle Phillip proud and instead she'd embarrassed him, made him a laughingstock among the peerage. She had hoped to live up to her parents' expectations and her own. Instead, she'd done the unthinkable.

"Nicole?"

The husky, hesitant voice slid into her heart, nearly costing her her composure. The memory of how he'd spoken to her that night in the temple poured over her and her knees grew weak. She stiffened her legs and battled back with fierce determination. Desperate for a distraction, she grasped a notebook from her desk, flipped it open, and scrawled an unnecessary note to herself.

"Anything else?" she said without looking up, sounding coolly brisk and businesslike to her own ears. "Special dinners perhaps? I imagine the princess would enjoy seeing Caldonian culture since she might become a citizen of this

country. Have you considered taking her on a tour around
town? Or to concerts—perhaps the National Art Gallery,
that sort of thing? I'm certain she would find it fascinating,
and it would enable you to . . ." She glanced up at Rand
then and faltered. His face appeared chiseled from stone.

Nicole plowed ahead. She had given up trying to read
him since he'd changed so drastically toward her. "To get
to know her better," she finally finished.

"All excellent suggestions," he said coolly. "You are as-
tonishingly professional."

Was that a compliment? Nicole decided to take it as such.
"Thank you, Your Highness."

"No need to thank me. That's why I'm paying you."

He stressed the word *paying,* and Nicole felt it like a slap
in the face. *He didn't mean it as an insult,* she told herself.
It was only the truth.

Silence descended, and Nicole felt his presence like an
electric current. Why was he still standing there, watching
her? He said finally, "You really want this, don't you? For
Zara and me to—"

*"Yes."* The word shoved up from somewhere inside her,
some well of strength she didn't know she possessed. It
reverberated on the air between them. A sense of dead
calm came over Nicole, born of hopelessness and despair.
Only the calm transmitted itself in her voice. "Yes, very
much."

His gaze attempted to connect with hers, but Nicole kept
her gaze on his jaw, noticed the muscles tensing under his
tan skin. "Our union would make you happy then?"

"Yes," she smoothly lied.

"I see," he said, his voice as unreadable as his face.
"Then please carry out the arrangements for all of it. I
want to spend as much time with Princess Zara as possible."

"Yes, sir."

"I have no desire to drag out this courtship. I plan to be
married before year's end, and it's already late July."

"Yes, sir."

He stood there a moment longer, his face impassive. Nicole waited, her pen poised for any further instructions. Then he turned and left, closing the door solidly behind him.

Nicole sagged against the desk. At least arranging his series of dates would keep her busy, keep her from thinking too much, feeling too much.

Impossible. How could she not think about what he and the princess might be saying, doing, feeling for each other on these outings? How could she keep her heart from aching as she saw him dote on another woman?

She would have to pretend to be as stonelike as the statues in the garden temple—that was all there was to it.

Nicole sat beside the chauffeur and stared impassively out at the serene rolling hills along the country highway. In the seat behind her, Rand and Zara carried on a lively discussion of their childhoods as royals. In a second limousine behind them, Zara's servants rode with Gerald.

How had she ended up here? Why had Rand forced her to accompany them to his country estate?

A trip to hell—that was what it promised to be. Four long, endless days—and even longer nights—under one roof. Sure, technically, they had slept under one roof in the palace. But the palace was so huge, it never mattered. The country estate would feel far more intimate.

If only she could have gotten a seat in the other car. The two-hour trip was already pure torture, and it was only half over. Rand had insisted she attend since she had personally selected Zara and Zara considered Nicole her personal escort in her new land.

As if she'd spent more than a handful of hours entertaining the princess, Nicole thought ruefully. Rand had been her real escort, spending every minute he could in her company during the days past. Only when he had to attend to business had Nicole stepped in to ensure that Zara was not left wanting for attention. Nicole knew in any other circumstances she would have enjoyed Zara's company. She was certainly pleasant, if a bit expectant of having her royal needs met. In other words, perfectly trained for the role of princess.

When Nicole had attempted to beg off accompanying them on this outing, Rand had insisted he needed her there to entertain Zara in case he was called back to Fortinbleaux on business. *Not bloody likely,* Nicole thought, fuming. He'd made Gerald block out the entire four days for nothing but this vacation.

"You must have been a precocious child," Zara said to Rand, her voice almost a purr. "You have much fire in you."

"I sense fire in you as well, Princess," he replied, his voice slightly suggestive.

"Perhaps so. Perhaps not. I would not show merely anyone my true nature."

He chuckled. "No?"

"My husband—when I wed—he will know my true nature. And experience the heat of my fire." Now Zara's voice had turned suggestive.

"He'll be a lucky man, Zara." Rand's voice was an intimate rumble.

"This I know. As will the woman who captures you for her husband."

Nicole closed her eyes and willed herself away, thousands of miles away. Their teasing banter continued for a solid hour. It made her physically sick. Not only was it disgustingly transparent, but she hated that Rand was subjecting her to it. Did he think she was made of stone? Did he think their kiss had meant nothing? As it had meant nothing to him.

The two royals could have each other. She didn't care. She didn't care, except that it would prove her a success, would prove to the entire country that she did not have designs on the prince. And to herself.

Already, the world's fascination with Rand's employee had faded in the wake of speculation about Princess Zara. Now the tabloids were filled with predictions about a future

match between them. The Palace Press Office even provided photos of Rand and Zara on their many dates, pic-
turing him as the attentive escort to his exotic foreign
guest.

Naturally, the palace denied any official engagement,
saying it was premature, but the signs certainly pointed in
that direction. The press endlessly discussed what it might
mean for the two countries to link their royal houses. Nicole did her damnedest to find satisfaction in her success.
Somewhere.

Blended male and female laughter carried to her from
the backseat. Why couldn't Rand have the courtesy to roll
up the window between the front and back? Fury and pain
roared through her. He was completely despicable.

By midmorning, deep in the pine-covered mountains,
Nicole's immediate suffering finally ended as the pair of
limousines pulled into a winding drive and stopped under
the portico of an ancestral hunting lodge.

Gerald gave Nicole a kind look as they trailed in the wake
of the prince and princess. They'd been left to their own
devices as the servants and staff of royals often were.

"This lodge was built by King Edbert the Second in the
mid-1700s," he told her. "The only addition to the original
structure is a large garage. Its roof is actually the deck, out
there." He gestured toward French doors off the living
room.

"That's interesting," Nicole lied, hoping Gerald would
think she cared. Instead, she found his sympathetic gaze
on her. She glanced away, hating that he might know her
heart. Only when Rand wasn't in her presence could she
relax even a little, but she didn't want Gerald to know how
badly she ached every moment of every day.

Even now, she couldn't help watching Rand escort Zara
down the hall to her guest room. And Rand's bedroom as
well? A bitter twinge shot through her heart.

She forced her attention back to the living room and

dully glanced over the heavy oaken beams, elaborately carved wood-paneled walls and the massive stone fireplace that Gerald pointed out. "They're lovely," she said, her voice barely above a whisper.

"Are you . . . well?" Gerald asked.

Nicole nodded, then smiled gamely, determined not to let him see how miserable she felt. "Just a little headache. Could you show me to my room please? I'd like to freshen up."

Their small party occupied only half of the bedrooms. Nicole was placed at the opposite end of the hall from Rand's double-doored master suite. She couldn't help noticing that Princess Zara—as befit her station—was given the second most elegant suite only one door down the hall from Rand's. For all Nicole knew, an adjoining door connected the suites.

She would just have to avoid the both of them as best she could for the next four days. Unfortunately, in such a small group, she had a hunch that would be impossible.

# TWELVE

Rand crossed to the sofa and handed Zara the glass of wine he'd poured. He had dismissed the house servant so that they could be alone.

He had dismissed *all* the servants, Gerald and Nicole included.

Over the past days, he'd taken Zara sailing, hiking, and picnicking—all outings Nicole had planned. During all of them he had pretended to be the interested suitor. He had to *be* the interested suitor. He had to court this woman until she agreed to be his wife.

It was the most difficult thing he'd ever done.

He'd insisted Nicole accompany them on this trip in the vain hope that he might rattle her composure, that he might see evidence of her feeling for him if she witnessed him with another woman. Yet if anyone's composure had suffered, it was his.

Dinner had been sheer hell. Nicole had practically shoved Zara down his throat, reminding him of her good points anytime the conversation lagged. And he'd played the role of fascinated suitor to the hilt, watching for any crack in Nicole's armor. Finding none.

He longed to be alone, to dream impossible dreams. Instead he had to romance his guest as was expected of him.

Zara accepted the glass and smiled up at him, patting the sofa beside her. He pulled in a breath and sat down, propping an ankle on his knee. He stared into the fire, his memory taking him back to the time before the ball when

he could have shared his concerns, his heart, with a special
friend.

"You seem distant. What are you thinking of?" Zara
asked.

"Smoke."

"Smoke?"

His gaze on the curling smoke in the fireplace, he recalled Nicole's impassioned expression, and her words, telling him in no uncertain terms that his wife shouldn't be
willing to sit passively by and let him rot his lungs out.
"Would you care if I smoked?" he found himself asking.

"Not now. In general." He swung his gaze to her. "Would
it bother you?"

Zara shrugged, clearly perplexed. "Of course not. You
would be free to pursue your pleasures, as I'm sure you do
now. I imagine you are quite used to satisfying your desires.
You *are* a royal prince, after all." A small smile teased her
lips.

He sipped his wine. "You can't mean that. Not completely."

She arched a delicate eyebrow. "Why ever not?"

"What if—" He hesitated, knowing asking might offend
her, might kill his chances with her. Still, he burned to
know, a tiny hope remaining unextinguished in his heart.

"What is your view of . . . the domestic side of royal marriage?"

A smile widened her lips. "I would enjoy it if I were married to the right man."

"No." Rand put down his wineglass. "No, I mean—fidelity."

"Fidelity? Are you . . . saying you would have mistresses?"

Rand didn't answer. He just waited to hear what she
might say.

After a moment, Zara shrugged. "My country is more
progressive than yours, Rand. We recognize the different
needs of men and women and our culture allows for it. My
grandfather had four wives and a dozen concubines. But

my grandmother—she was the queen. No one could take that from her. She was very powerful and highly honored."

She was giving him permission to have a mistress! Rand stared at her in shock for a minute, trying to shuffle the information into place in his mind. How could he keep from imagining Nicole in that role? Why in the hell wasn't he happier to hear this woman say this?

"You wouldn't mind?" he asked again, not certain he'd fully understood her answer.

"Being a queen is a great honor, one I will not have in my own country, for my brother will rule with his wife. Why would I complain over something that means so little?"

That was the problem, Rand thought, desperation searing his gut all over again. Being with Nicole would not mean little. It would mean everything, his whole heart and soul. He stared into the fire, remembering the evenings he'd gone to her suite to relax. If he'd known his taste of heaven would be so short, would he have relished it even more?

"Something is on your mind."

Rand realized he'd been lost in thought, probably for several minutes. He fought to respond. How in the hell was he supposed to pretend he hadn't been thinking of another woman? He forced his gaze back to Zara. "It's nothing," he lied smoothly, praying Nicole would forgive him—if she even cared. He'd lost the ability to know her heart.

He studied Zara's face, analyzing each feature, the parts that made up the glorious whole. Her eyes—while brilliant ebony pools—were too dark. Her nose was too narrow, and her face too long. He knew he wasn't really seeing her. He was seeing another face superimposed over hers—a face with a wonderful blend of beauty and individuality that he'd completely fallen in love with. No other woman could compare.

He realized Zara was leaning closer, her eyes warming at his intense inspection, no doubt believing something else prompted it. "I'm glad you sent the others away." Her hand slipped over his thigh, one long fingernail trailing toward his knee and back up again.

Rand pasted a pleasant smile on his face and tried to feel aroused by this woman, tried to focus on her. She was pleasant, she was intelligent, she had impeccable breeding.

Breeding. He felt like a goddamned dog—one that could only be mated to a female dog with a purebred pedigree.

Zara apparently sensed his lack of response, for she slid her hand away and leaned back. "Are you unhappy?"

"Unhappy? No. No, I'm not unhappy." Unhappy was such a mundane word for the tumult of pain and regret and despair that tore him up night and day. At the complete irony of it, a scalding laugh broke from his throat.

Zara jerked at the sound, but she rallied gamely. A tentative smile formed on her perfect lips, and she laughed softly. "I almost find I'm sorry. I'm quite good at cheering people up." Again she leaned toward him. "I think you might like it if I cheered you up."

Rand stilled his body, not welcoming or withdrawing from her. Allowing her to close the distance between them. His gaze skimmed her svelte body, and he tried to imagine undressing her. Laying her down here on this couch and making her his. Despite the erotic image forming in his mind, his groin didn't even stir. He could hardly believe his body could be so unresponsive. He'd slept with numerous beautiful women. Now, when the future of his country hung in the balance, he didn't feel even the smallest tingle of desire.

Zara pressed her hand against his chest, drawing even closer. Her half-shuttered eyes and relaxed lips told him she wanted his kiss. He slid his arm along the back of the sofa, then around her shoulders, drawing her closer. She really was a beautiful woman. He was a fool to be so particular, especially when the woman he loved demanded he court this one.

He bent his head and settled his mouth over Zara's.

A bang sounded behind them. Rand jerked around, guilt piercing his heart as his gaze settled on Nicole. She was just coming to her feet, her purse in her hand. Apparently she'd dropped it. She stood in the entrance to the hall, her brown eyes wide.

"Excuse me," she said quickly. "I left my bag out here on the table. I—I forgot to get it earlier. I'm sorry. Don't let me interrupt. Go ahead with whatever you were doing." She spun on her heel and disappeared down the hallway.

Rand retrieved his arm from behind Zara, feeling sick inside. He rested his elbows on his knees, his hands tightening into fists, a blend of rage and frustration swelling within him. Nicole—so calm, so professional, so damned unaffected! Suddenly, he not only needed to be alone, but he needed a drink a hell of a lot stronger than wine.

"She should have kept better track of her things," Zara was saying, her casual voice so out of place with his raging emotions he found it hard to comprehend her. "That's what makes servants valuable: keeping track of details. Don't you agree? When I manage a household, I will be certain the servants understand their roles." She ran her fingers along his neck and into his hair. "My husband will not have to deal with such mundane tasks."

She sounded as if she was at a job interview. My God, it was the truth. Rand stiffened and forced his voice to sound calm when his emotions were storming inside. "Perhaps we'd better call it a night, Zara. I'm more tired from our sail today than I thought I would be." He rose and helped her to her feet.

Zara sighed, and Rand knew he'd disappointed her. She allowed her fingers to trail along his shoulders as she said a soft good night.

Rand knew he couldn't put her off forever. He would have to give up any hope of discovering what lay within Nicole's heart. His country depended on it.

Only one more night in this purgatory, and they would return to the palace.

Nicole knew that, but still she couldn't sleep. For the

past four days, she had cultivated a cool, professional demeanor. She congratulated herself on her composure. She
had allowed nothing to rattle it—not Rand and Zara's at-
tentions to each other, not the way he requested everyone
but Zara to leave them after dinner.

Not that intimate kiss she had interrupted.

A sharp pain cut into her heart. Why had she forgotten
her purse? She hadn't needed to see that. But she'd needed
her contact lens case and she'd thought she could grab
her purse from the small table with neither of them being
the wiser. Until she'd seen him lean close to kiss her . . .

Had it gone farther than a mere kiss? No. She refused
to wonder. She was a professional. She was being *paid* to
see this romance succeed. No one could say she hadn't
done her part for her country. After Nicole returned to
America, Zara might even continue the work in helping
Caldonia grow more progressive. That was what mattered.
That was all that ever mattered.

Still, in the past four days, Nicole had noticed that Rand
had ceased laughing so freely, had become almost moody.
Perhaps he was merely fatigued from his efforts to show
the princess a good time. Unless he was feeling sexually
frustrated because the princess hadn't allowed him into
her bed. Or had she?

Restless, eaten up with doubts and questions, Nicole
pulled herself out of bed and slipped on her satin robe.
The old wooden house was blissfully silent, without the
echoing sound of Zara's bright laughter responding to one
of Rand's dry observations. For once, she was alone.

She stepped into the hall, not certain where she was going, but needing fresh air. She looked down the hall toward
Rand's room. His door was open. The door to the princess's
room remained firmly closed. Were they in her room together?

Nicole squeezed her eyes shut, forcing back her private
pain with self-recriminations. Why did she even dwell on
such thoughts? It was none of her business.

Her thoughts in turmoil, Nicole wandered out to the

silent deck. A cool breeze from the lake slid over her too
warm skin. She stopped at the railing and ran her hands
over its moss-touched surface. Cocking her head, she lis-
tened to the night sounds: the lake lapping against the
shore below, a chorus of frogs and crickets somewhere in
the dark.

She looked up at the sky and wished she could get lost
in the stars. Memory of another starry night flooded back
to her, a magical meeting in a Grecian temple. She must
have dreamed it. The man who'd kissed her so passionately
was not the same man who'd dragged her here, deep into
the country, to witness his seduction of another woman.

"You're restless."

The deep voice, thick with irony, shocked Nicole and
she froze. *She wasn't alone.*

She schooled herself to keep her back ramrod straight,
her quivering emotions under tight leash. She pulled in a
deep breath and slowly turned to face him.

Rand sat at a table in the corner of the deck, his face
obscured by shadow, his hand wrapped around a shot glass.
A decanter of whiskey rested at his elbow. Despite her better sense, Nicole found her gaze roving over his body. He
wore his pajama bottoms and a silk monogrammed robe,
which lay open, revealing the lightly furred, hard planes
of his chest.

"I've been sitting here thinking," he said slowly, rotating
the shot glass this way and that, as if studying the color of
the liquid in the dim security light attached to the eaves.
"You were right about that evaluation form of mine. I don't
need it."

Nicole kept her voice carefully modulated, revealing absolutely nothing of her inner pain, her unfulfilled longings.
"Zara is exceptional, isn't she?"

His expression appeared carved from stone, except for
his eyes glittering in the starlight. He didn't look at her.
"Exceptional. Indeed." He knocked back another swallow,
then dropped the glass to the table. In breathless fascina-

tion, Nicole watched as his lean fingers toyed with the glass, tilting and rolling it back and forth on its base.

"Things are going well, aren't they?" she said hesitantly. He didn't respond, so she felt compelled to explain, to fill the strained silence between them. "You seem happy with her. As if you click. Perhaps the search is over."

Nicole hated to say the words aloud, but certainly they were nothing he hadn't thought himself. Indeed, his every action and word demonstrated his delight with the princess. And soon, Nicole's role in the process would be concluded successfully. Surely she could find a nugget of satisfaction in there somewhere, something to sustain her aching heart.

"Things are going very well," he acknowledged. "Unfortunately, I find myself unable to seduce her—in case you were wondering."

That was what had driven him out here in the dead of night. His burning, unquenched desire for Princess Zara. The thought caused a sick lurch in Nicole's stomach. She fought for a light tone to cover her pain. "Perhaps your reputation has preceded you."

"As the randy prince?" He smiled ruefully. "No doubt. Still, I don't think the princess is put off by my past affairs. A royal title excuses a multitude of sins."

"It's not just your title, I'm sure. None of that matters if she cares for you." Her words sounded far too heartfelt, and Nicole feared she was revealing her own feelings. She quickly added, "And I know Zara cares for you."

Nicole had to remember that she wasn't part of the equation, it was Princess Zara who would have him in her bed every night, should she so wish it. And what woman wouldn't wish it? All that dark magnetism, that passion, that sensual smile, that way he could kiss a woman and transport her to another plane of existence, one of pure pleasure and delight.

Setting his tumbler on the table, Rand rose with a sigh. Nicole expected him to cross to the door and return inside.

Instead, he headed straight for her with slow, measured steps.

Afraid he would read her thoughts in her eyes, Nicole looked toward the night sky. Still, she sensed him closing in on her and felt the heat of his body, his audible breaths, as if his presence vibrated the very air around her. So close. Right behind her now.

His strong, lean-fingered hands appeared beside hers on the railing, his arms and body trapping her. "She is built like a goddess," he rumbled slowly, his words vibrating in her own chest. "Those shapely legs, that svelte body. Yet I don't think she realizes how entrancing she is. If she understood, she would be shocked at the lengths I would go to satisfy her." He sighed deeply, and Nicole felt his whiskey-tinged breath tease the hair against her neck.

She squeezed her eyes shut, her heart pounding hard. *God, let him stop!* Hearing his praise for another woman cut into the heart of her. Yet she found herself enduring the torture, craving his nearness, his attention, his touch. She couldn't move an inch; she could hardly breathe as his sensuous tone wove an erotic spell around her.

"She is indeed grace personified," he continued, relentless, cruel. "The perfect match for a royal prince."

*He's speaking of another woman,* Nicole's mind insisted. Still, she couldn't help imagining he was speaking of her. Nor could she help an answering desire in her own body at his nearness, an unquenchable longing to experience the heat of his desire. She bit her lip, fought not to visibly tremble against him. His hands disappeared from beside hers, and for a moment, she thought he'd granted her a reprieve.

Instead, his heated palms branded her thighs and began sliding upward. The outrageous touch sent prickles of pleasure straight to her sex. His lips drew so close, Nicole felt their soft whisper along her cheek as he spoke. Her own lips trembled in response.

"A prince should hunger for the woman he marries,

wouldn't you agree?" he whispered in her ear. "For the sake of the royal line."

Confused by his words, by his seductive intent, Nicole stiffened in his arms. "You forget yourself, Your Highness," she said coldly.

He ignored her tone, his hands sliding up the curve of her hips to grasp her waist, turning her body into one throbbing, heated coil of desire. Her breathing sounded ragged in her own ears; her stomach muscles quivered as his fingers slid over her abdomen.

"Tiny, but adequate to carry the future princes of Caldonia. An important consideration. I should have included it on my goddamned form."

Nicole wished like the devil he would remove his hands from around her waist. *He is the devil,* she thought, for she seemed unable to push his hands away despite her better sense. Only a thin layer of silk separated his hands from her naked flesh, yet she craved more, hungered to feel his unhindered caress on her body.

"You're trembling, Nicole," he said hoarsely in her ear, his whiskey-scented breath promising wicked delights. She fiercely reminded herself that she was merely a substitute for the woman he truly wanted.

The reminder did no good as his hands slid the last few, agonizing inches upward and settled over her aching breasts. Delicious spirals of pleasure wound through her as his palms rasped her nipples, transforming her body to molten fire. She felt his chest shudder against her back. She squeezed her eyes shut and began to lose her sense of everything but the tantalizingly sweet heat of his touch.

"These may be merely a commoner's breasts, yet they are the perfect size and shape."

"Stop it, Your Highness," she said, her voice alarmingly weak. He still desired her. Despite the allure of Princess Zara, he desired *her.* She forced the betraying thought back to its small corner, forced her body and voice to go rigid. "You're drunk."

His palms roved over her breasts, molding them, shaping

them. Nicole had never found anything more difficult than not reacting to his sinfully delicious treatment of her body. Every fiber of her being cried out for her to turn around, press her body against his, and succumb to his misdirected lust.

"The perfect fit for my royal palms. Full. Firm. No doubt sweet to the taste. And these—" His fingertips flicked her nipples and sent bolts of pleasure straight to her sensitized sex. "You stand here stiff and unyielding, but these betray you. Swollen and hard, begging for attention."

His raspy voice was thick with irony, with heated lust. It slid along her raw nerves and made her want to scream with frustration. Why was he torturing her like this, shaming her like this? Why couldn't she fight the hunger he'd unleashed?

"I would wager," he said as one hand traveled down again, across her stomach, heading even lower, "that, should I strip your panties from you, I would find you ready and willing to accommodate the royal lust."

She reacted fiercely, desperately, like the cornered animal he'd turned her into. She slammed her elbow into his diaphragm, then spun around and slapped him hard across the face. He bent over with a grunt.

The shock of what she'd done—actually striking a member of the royal family—barely registered before she felt his viselike grip on her forearm.

He straightened and hovered over her, his glittering eyes boring into hers. His lips drew into thin lines over tightly clenched teeth. "Go straight to bed, Miss Aldridge. That's a command." He shoved her back against the railing and released her arm.

Nicole stumbled in her haste to retreat. She hurried toward the inside door. Before she passed through, she heard her name once more on his lips. She glanced over her shoulder. He stood frozen against the star-filled night, his face set in an unreadable mask.

"Close your bedroom door," he said ominously. "And lock it."

Nicole didn't reply, but hurried to do his bidding.

Rand stared after her, appalled at what he'd just done. His stomach burned; his face stung from her slap. And still his body shook from unquenched desire at finally, blissfully sliding his hands along that alluring body of hers. He knew he'd terrified her. He'd wanted to terrify her, to punish her for what she was doing to him, unwitting though it might be.

For he could find no reason not to make Princess Zara his wife. Except one.

How could he have let this happen? How? This *mistake* as Nicole had termed it when referring to the news articles. Photos that told nothing but the truth, yet only hinted at the powerful, all-consuming hunger that tore him up inside every minute of every day. A hunger he could never satisfy, yet couldn't subdue, despite his frantic attempts to romance a more suitable woman.

Until tonight, they had both successfully maintained the pretense of a professional relationship. Nicole did it with ease. She remained cold and distant, hid her brightness from him, punished him for loving her by encouraging him to want Zara. His Nicole, so honest in every way, found it so easy to pretend she felt nothing for him. Unless she never had.

*We have to erase the mistake.*

A harsh laugh caught in his throat. That morning after the ball, he had imagined holding her, soothing her, finally tearing down the last barrier between them and acknowledging their true feelings. Nicole hadn't needed soothing. She had instead wanted to wipe out all evidence of their attraction, pretend it never happened. Erase the mistake.

*Mistake.* No truer words . . .

Was it purely his mistake, or did Nicole suffer as he did? My God, he should hope not. He had nothing to offer her but a life filled with even more deception. For a woman of Nicole's sensibilities and old-fashioned values, such a life would also be filled with pain as she watched him marry another woman and father her children. He could see no way out.

That goddamned ancient law. What did it say? He tried to focus, to recall specific words, but his drink-fogged mind made it impossible. He couldn't remember ever knowing the words, but then, he wasn't in the best state to puzzle it out right now.

Still, a tingle of hope slid through his heart. He frowned and tried to concentrate, but the source of the hope wouldn't come. He shook his head. He didn't have the strength to struggle with it, not knowing her heart. And after tonight's painful, frustrating encounter, he had the horrible, sick feeling that nothing would rattle her careful composure.

Nicole was no doubt already lost to him. The clock was ticking, and his father's threat to withdraw his allowance continued to hang over his head. More than ever, his funds were critically needed to launch his plans for the country's future. He had to make a decision, had to carry out that decision.

*Had to start dying inside.*

He crossed on unsteady feet to the table and lifted the whiskey decanter. The neck rattled loudly against the edge of the tumbler as he poured out another shot. He held the glass up to the light. As he stared into it, he knew he'd find no answers in its heady forgetfulness.

Frustration and swift, raw fury gripped him. He hurled the glass toward the wall of the house and it blasted into a thousand pieces.

Nicole was turning the doorknob of her room when she heard the glass shattering. She knew it came from the deck outside. She forced herself to ignore the sound and slipped once more into her room, closing and locking the door behind her.

Weak, unable to stand a moment longer, she collapsed onto her bed, buried her face in the pillow, and cried herself to sleep.

# THIRTEEN

"I have not yet thanked you," Zara said to Nicole the next morning at breakfast. "If not for you, I would not have met Rand. I have never met a man quite as intriguing. At times, I sense an underlying melancholy in his spirit, but I am determined to push past that."

Melancholy? Rand? Nicole hadn't seen anything of the sort. "You don't have to thank me, Princess," she said.

Though Rand hadn't yet appeared to take over playing host, Nicole soon escaped to her room to pack. She wondered what the princess would say if she knew how her Prince Charming had transformed into a drunken beast the previous night. She paused in her packing and stared into her suitcase as the memory of the night before returned in full force.

Rand's hands roving over her body, lifting and cradling her breasts, making her feel deep, primal yearnings that threatened to destroy her common sense.

Furious at her weakness, Nicole slammed the suitcase closed and carried it outside, where the chauffeurs were loading everyone else's luggage—except for Rand's. She stood beside Gerald on the stone steps. Below, next to the first limo, Zara spoke loudly in her native dialect to her two servants, making sharp, emphatic motions with her hands. Nicole guessed the princess wasn't used to being kept waiting.

"Your Highness." Gerald caught sight of Rand before Nicole did. "Good morning."

The prince had stepped through the heavy oaken doors and stopped briefly on Gerald's other side. "Let's get this caravan moving. We're wasting time."

Nicole had dreaded facing him this morning, hadn't wanted to look in his eyes after the appalling way she'd let him embarrass her the night before.

She needn't have worried. He wore dark glasses, which obscured his eyes, and never once looked in her direction. *Probably hungover,* she thought with grim satisfaction. She hoped he had a thundering, brain-splitting headache.

He wore jeans, tennis shoes, and a tan sportscoat over a sinfully body-hugging black T-shirt. He hadn't shaved, so a dark shadow colored his cheeks and jaw. His hair was mussed as if he had pulled his comb through it only once before coming outside. To her dismay, his rugged appearance enhanced his dark good looks and gave him a dangerous, uncivilized air.

She swallowed hard, knowing she was really reacting to how he'd tried to seduce her last night. She'd have to put it completely out of her mind.

"This outing has put me far behind in my work," he muttered to Gerald. He called to the chauffeur of his limo, "Get my suitcase from the top of the stairs and get us out of here."

"Yes, Your Highness." The chauffeur inclined his head and hurried to fetch it.

Rand didn't give Gerald a second glance—or Nicole even a first glance—before he hurried down the steps.

Gerald passed the case to the chauffeur, then glanced at Nicole. "It seems he's a little out of sorts this morning," he said softly.

"He's acting like a spoiled movie star," Nicole muttered.

Gerald cocked his eyebrow at her, his brown eyes sparkling. "An interesting comparison, Miss Aldridge, considering he's even more of a celebrity than most of them."

Nicole wanted to kick herself. Again, she had completely forgotten who Rand really was. *Prince of the Royal Family, Heir to the Throne, Future King of Caldonia, Sole Hope to carry*

*on the royal line, which stretched unbroken back to the Cru-
sades . . .*

*He's just a man,* she thought in irritation. *Fallible, irritating, unpredictable . . .* She knew it was true, knew him far
too well to believe otherwise. True, his role in life was to
serve his people as their prince and future king. His obligations meant more to him than anything. As they should.
*But does he have to treat you like dirt?* an inner voice taunted.

Without waiting for the chauffeur to return with his bag,
Rand yanked open the passenger door of the limo. "Get
in, Princess," he said to Zara, who stared at him with wide
eyes. But she complied quickly enough. Without looking
up, Rand called out, "Gerald, you're riding with me." Then
he slid in beside Zara and slammed the door closed.

Nicole got into the other limousine and spent the two-
hour ride listening to the musical native language of Zara's
servants riding in the backseat. At least she didn't have to
hear the flirtatious banter of Zara and Rand. That was
something to be thankful for.

"Miss Aldridge, the prince commands your presence in
his chambers."

Rand's valet stood outside her door, his pale face appearing even more washed out than usual in contrast to his
black pencil-thin mustache.

"I said the prince commands your presence—"

"I heard. In his chambers," Nicole said briskly. "Why?"

The valet clasped and unclasped his gloved hands. "I
am not at liberty to say."

"Very well." Nicole dropped the draft report and pushed
away from the desk. Rand had sent her a message demanding she review and check all the facts in the two-hundred-
page report supporting his proposal for the Grand
Assembly—by first thing Monday.

She had no plans for the weekend—no personal time at
all since she had to be available to entertain Princess Zara

at a moment's notice. Still, she couldn't help resenting how casually he had yanked away her free time.

His demands came in a never-ending stream but—since their visit to the country estate—usually through a third party. With his attitude so changed toward her, Nicole knew she wouldn't stay in his employ even if he begged her. Which, of course, he never would.

She checked her French roll and makeup in the mirror over her dresser, adjusted her glasses on her nose, and followed the valet into the hall. Her steps slowed as she approached Rand's royal suite. The last time she'd been here had been the morning after the ball when she had lost her friend and a new, cold version of the prince had taken his place. A uniformed butler standing outside swung the door open for them.

Glimpses of Rand's personal life jumped out at her— framed pictures of him and his friends, not stuffy portraits but casual photographs, showing him enjoying the pastimes of the very rich: polo, yachting, horseback riding. A stack of books lay on the coffee table before the sofa— mostly modern titles on economics. And a lovely painting above the marble fireplace portrayed nymphs frolicking in the Grecian countryside.

Horatio led her through a massive pair of white carved doors into Rand's personal chambers. Nicole's steps grew unsteady as she caught sight of a huge circular bed. Hangings draped from the ceiling at its head, giving it a highly sensual feel.

A bed for more than sleeping certainly. A bed fit for a royal couple to spend a lot of time in, engaged in the vital work of carrying on the royal line.

Nicole's steps slowed as she caught sight of the portrait hanging on the wall opposite the bed. This one depicted another Greek myth: the kidnapping of Persephone by the dark lord Hades. The god bent his swarthy face to the maiden's creamy bosom, which swelled over her Empire-waist gown. The look on her face: Was it fear or ecstasy?

A shiver slid along Nicole's spine, and her body suddenly

remembered the feel of Rand's strong, insistent hands on her body, forcing her to burn for him. Did Rand lie here alone at night and stare at this portrait? Imagine what the couple was feeling—the longing, the desperate passions? Did he think of—

"Miss Aldridge?" the valet asked hesitantly. "It's this way."

Nicole shook herself, pushing the ridiculous thoughts away. The valet led her into a dressing room the size of a living room in any regular house.

Rand stood in the middle of the room before a pair of full-length gold-framed mirrors. He was dressed in a fine tuxedo—except for a jacket. His eyes flicked up to her; then he returned to adjusting his braces. "What took you so long to attend me, Miss Aldridge?"

Nicole looked at him and his twin reflections, the two reflected pairs of eyes staring right at her. "I was working on your economic report—"

"When my servant summons you, I expect you to obey. You are my employee, Miss Aldridge." Without looking at the valet, he said, "You may leave us."

"But, sir, I haven't finished dressing y—"

*"Now,"* Rand said sharply.

Looking hurt, the valet bowed his way out and closed the door behind him. *So, he's beastly to everyone, not just me,* Nicole thought, wishing she could find satisfaction in the thought. *As beastly as the King of the Underworld stealing an innocent maiden from the life she knew to make her his queen.*

"What did you *need* to see me for?" Nicole had a strong suspicion he hadn't needed to summon her at all.

Perhaps because of that odd light in his eyes . . . Goose bumps broke out on her arms as she recalled yet again how it had felt to have his body pressed tight and hot against hers. Lord, if only she could forget!

"I assume you're aware of the plans for tonight," he said briskly.

Certainly *he* had forgotten his drunken ardor. "Yes," Nicole nodded. "The King and Queen of Omat have arrived and you will be dining with them and your parents."

"Very good, Miss Aldridge. Perhaps what you don't know is that, once our dinner is through, I will be escorting Princess Zara on a more personal outing." He strode to the dressing table and retrieved a gold-and-emerald cuff link, then inserted it into his cuff. "A walk in the moonlit garden seems like the right approach. In fact, I plan to take her to my temple. It's quite a romantic setting, a fitting place for me to propose to her." Fastening the second cuff link, he turned to her. "What do you think of that, Miss Aldridge?"

The temple . . . Did he even remember kissing her there? Or had he taken so many women to his temple over the years that their encounter had been completely meaningless to him? She felt her face lose its color, but battled back valiantly to show her approval of the match she herself had arranged. "That's wonderful, Your Highness."

"Wonderful." He propped his hands on his slim hips. "Indeed, you're quite the success, aren't you, Miss Aldridge? The consummate professional in every way."

Nicole felt he was taunting her, but couldn't think why. She felt more edgy than ever.

Without waiting for her response, he continued. "Perhaps, then, since you are such a success, you can help with my current dilemma." He strode to a brass rack and removed two jackets on hangers. He lifted a hanger in each hand, one a traditional black woolen suit coat that matched the slacks he wore, the other jacket a rich burgundy suede. Nicole itched to run her hands over the material to see if it felt as butter soft as it looked.

"Which one do you think is more suitable for a romantic proposal to a princess?"

Nicole hesitated. Despite herself, she recalled a day from another lifetime, the day of their picnic. On that morning, she had given him fashion advice, encouraged him to wear casual clothes to show he could relate to the people.

Her idea had worked better than she could ever have

predicted. Commentators had remarked on the prince's new, more approachable image; editorials had raved when Rand followed up the superficial change with more substantial reforms. The small change had helped him tap into public support he might not have received otherwise.

All because he had trusted her opinion. Was he thinking of that morning as well? From his impassive expression, she couldn't tell. Nor did she care to give him any more advice, especially of such a personal nature. It wouldn't matter to the country what he wore when proposing to Princess Zara in private.

She kept her voice carefully even. "You should ask your valet about the appropriate jacket."

"I know damned well I should ask my valet," he snapped, a tense muscle marring the smooth plane of his cheek. "But he isn't acquainted with Zara. You're a woman. You know Zara. So I'm asking you which you think she'll prefer."

Nicole imagined Zara sitting beside Rand in the temple, running her hands over his arms, over his shoulders, burying her hands in his ebony hair as he pressed his mouth on hers. And he—no longer the man of ice who stood before her, but the hot, passionate lover who had stolen her breath with his embrace in that very same temple— made her feel like the most desirable woman in the world, *like his goddess come to life* . . .

The memory stabbed her like a knife in the chest. With tremendous effort she managed to shove her painful emotions into a corner of her heart and lock them away tight. Keeping her tone neutral, she said, "I really don't think it matters."

Rand tossed the jackets over the back of a sofa, heedless of how they landed. "Like hell it doesn't matter! You of all people know how much a successful match *matters.*"

"That isn't what I meant." Nicole fought to remain composed. "I think Zara will be pleased with either choice. I'm certain she'll . . . be happy, whatever you're wearing."

His hands flexed at his sides. "She'd damn well better be happy after all I've gone through to find her."

Nicole lifted her chin a notch. "You don't have to swear."

He swung a hand toward the jackets. "Well, pick one! Then you can leave and stop listening to me swear!"

"All right! That one." She flung out her finger toward the plain black jacket, hating herself for her pettiness in selecting it.

"This one?" He yanked the black jacket from the sofa, held it up, and considered it. His eyes gleaming, he stared at Nicole for a heart-stopping second.

Then he tossed the jacket back on the sofa and retrieved the burgundy one. His eyes never leaving Nicole's, he slid the jacket off the hanger and slipped into it.

Nicole gasped at the blatant insult. What was wrong with him? Why had he called her in here just to embarrass and belittle her? She narrowed her lips as she watched him pull on the jacket, yank down the hem, and shoot his shirt cuffs.

"As I said," she said coldly, "I believe she will find either jacket acceptable."

He turned away, dismissing her. "That's what I'm counting on. You may go."


Nicole spent the evening in her room, trying unsuccessfully to read a book. She threw the volume aside and picked at her dinner, then rang for the maid to take it away. She couldn't take her mind off what Rand was doing with Zara. The dinner was still in progress, no doubt. He probably hadn't yet spirited her off to the garden. But soon. Very soon.

*Nicole stop it,* she chastised herself. *Let him. It's exactly what you want. And you know she'll say yes. Your work will be done, and you can leave here with a clear conscience.*

She wandered into the bathroom and turned on the faucet, letting hot water fill the claw-footed tub. After stripping off her clothes, she slid into the bath and closed her eyes.

Despite the relaxing warmth of the water, images formed

behind her eyes of Rand kissing Princess Zara. Nicole fidgeted in the water, and a moment later, the woman in his arms transformed into herself. A sharp spasm of desire swept through her as she recalled the sweet heat of his mouth commanding her own, his passionate words. They were once more as close as that night in the temple before he became a man of ice.

It had only been the romantic setting, her own silly tears that caused it. If he'd been a true gentleman, she might have expected an apology afterward. At the very least, he should have allowed them to carry on as if nothing had happened, to work together to solve the problems created by the media's outlandish speculations about the two of them. But he'd taken even his friendship from her, punishing her for her weakness that night.

Then at his country estate, he had turned worse than cold, using her appalling weakness for him against her, shaming her—and mercilessly enflaming her.

*Think of something else, anything else but him.* She tried to remember life before Rand had invaded her heart. She tried and failed. Ever since coming here, meeting him, working with him, her life seemed connected to his, despite her efforts to keep their relationship on a purely professional basis, despite how he'd changed.

She recalled with a shaft of pain the wonder of that first night he'd arrived at her room unannounced, to see her computer. He'd startled her with his lack of ceremony, his casual, friendly air, his expectation that she would treat him like a regular man. She should never have allowed him in that first time. Not into her room, and certainly not into her heart.

As if her memory had come to life, she heard a sharp rap on her door. Nicole jerked in surprise, then pulled herself out of the water and grabbed a towel. "Coming!" she called as she quickly dried off. "Just a minute!"

The knock came again, harder, so loud Nicole feared it would alarm everyone in that wing of the palace. *Rand.* He was the only one who had ever visited her at night. It couldn't be him. Not anymore. "I said I'm coming!"

Entering her bedroom, she slid on her peach-colored satin gown. Forgoing the matching robe on the bed, she crossed to the door.

She'd barely cracked the door open before the prince shoved his way into her room, just as he had all those months ago following his first miserable date. He closed the door behind him and locked it. Shock swept through Nicole at seeing him here, once again in the intimate confines of her suite.

A thrill of fear—and anticipation—worked its way up her spine. What could possibly have drawn him here? Was he planning to report his success in securing his future wife? My God, why did he have to subject her to such torture?

"Aren't you supposed to be entertaining your royal guests?" she asked, trying to sound composed while her pulse raced. She stiffened, fighting to hide her nervousness.

"I'm through with my royal duties," he said tightly. He turned and stared at her, his eyes sliding down her barely clad form.

Nicole crossed her arms over her breasts, regretting that she hadn't slipped on her robe. Where she hadn't completely dried her body, the satin clung to her like a second skin. The last thing she wanted was to be revealed before him, physically or emotionally.

She stepped near the fireplace and hid partly behind the chaise longue there.

Rand's eyes continued to bore into her, as if seeking something. His handsome face appeared tense and unyielding in the firelight, chiseled from stone. When he spoke, his voice sounded impersonal. "I just thought I'd stop by before I successfully concluded the project I hired you for. You'll be pleased to know that all signals are go from both our families. The dinner conversation was filled with plans for the union of our royal houses."

Nicole ran her hand along the back of the wine-colored

velvet chaise, imagining instead the suede of his burgundy jacket, which pulled so snugly across his broad shoulders. "So . . . you have proposed to her?" She forced the words out.

"Not officially, no," Rand said, taking a few steps closer to her. "The dinner conversation had the pretense of being hypothetical, but everyone there knew what we were really discussing. It's a perfect arrangement, Miss Aldridge," he said coolly. "I know you take great pride in seeing all your hard work come to such a satisfactory conclusion."

She swallowed past a lump in her throat, searching desperately for the pride she should be feeling—patriotic pride that would make her private pain mean something. "Thank you, Your Highness."

He reached into his jacket pocket and pulled out a small velvet box. "Here's the ring I intend to give her." He snapped open the box and held it out to her. Nicole had no choice but to take it. Her hand shook slightly as he placed it in her palm.

Inside, on black velvet, nestled the hugest solitaire she had ever seen. Tiny rubies and emeralds in a swirling pattern accented the gold band.

"Lovely, isn't it?" Rand said almost wryly. "A ring fit for a princess."

A ring . . . This was real. He would finally select his princess tonight. "It's exquisite," Nicole said while her soul shriveled and her heart surely stopped beating. *You want this,* she reminded herself fiercely. *You have to want this.* "I'm sure she'll be pleased."

"It's a bit gaudy, but we have those Caldonian traditions to uphold, you know." His voice lowered. "It was my grandmother's."

"Queen Esmerelda," Nicole said automatically. "The outspoken, popular lady from the northland—the one who rallied the country during World War II. This was hers?"

"Yes."

Nicole couldn't resist running her fingers along the jewels, imagining this ring worn by such a dynamic woman. If the country had more women like her, it wouldn't be in the backward state it was today. "She was amazing," she murmured.

She glanced up and caught Rand's intense gaze on her. She thought she detected warmth there, just before shutters seemed to fall behind his eyes.

She continued. "Knowing it was hers, Zara will no doubt treasure it all the more." She wondered if Zara had ever heard of Queen Esmerelda, if she would even care about inheriting her ring. She held the box out to Rand and he took it.

"I damn well hope so." He studied the ring for a moment, and silence descended like a leaden blanket over the room. The sounds of the fire crackling and of their breathing seemed unnaturally loud. Watching his dark, closed expression, as he bent his head over the ring, Nicole felt her nerves stretched so taut she feared they would break.

Why had he come? His presence once again in the privacy of her suite filled her with sharp, painful nostalgia. She wanted to touch him, to feel the heat of his body and the texture of his hair under her hands. At the same time, she never wanted to see him again.

Finally, Rand spoke, his deep voice musing. "Maybe tonight, after I slide this ring on Princess Zara's royal finger, I'll take her to my bed."

The words slammed into her, forced her to recognize the truth of what marriage would mean. He planned to make love to Zara—here in the palace, under the same roof, just down the hall. Nicole's stomach rolled and she feared she would be sick.

His dark eyes snapped up and caught hers, as if watching to see if he'd scored a direct hit, the bastard. "To seal the bargain, you might say. I suspect she'll be more than willing."

Nicole couldn't contain a gasp. A warm flush slid over her skin at his audacity, at his rudeness, at his coldness in talking to her about such intimate matters. "You needn't share that with me," she said tersely.

"Oh?" He raised his eyebrows. "Excuse me for offending you. You did, after all, find her for me. I thought you'd be interested to know exactly how successful you've been."

He stared hard at her, and Nicole fought down the urge to look away. She met his gaze with an equally cold one of her own.

"Very well," he said. "On a more prosaic topic, what do you think: Will Zara make a good mother for my children?"

Nicole gripped the back of the chaise longue, her fingertips digging into the plush velvet. "I expect so. She seems of good character."

He cocked his eyebrow. "And . . . do you think she'll be a pleasing wife?"

Nicole swallowed. Feeling suddenly as if she were in a weak position hiding behind the furniture, she stepped before the chaise longue. She gave a chill edge to her reply. "Of course. I had thought it well established that she had many virtues to recommend her."

He snapped the ring box closed and slid it back into his jacket pocket, then propped his hands on his hips. "Certainly in all the outward aspects. I was thinking more of the . . . intimate aspect of marriage." A tight, dangerous smile slid over his sensuous lips. "Do you think she'll please me in bed?"

Nicole stared at him, unable to answer. How dared he ask her that?

He decreased the distance between them from a comfortable six feet to a distinctly too close three feet. "She has an alluring figure, don't you think?" His voice turned suggestive. "It isn't hard to imagine her wrapping those long legs around a man's waist, is it?" His tone turned even more suggestive. "Around *my* waist."

"Stop it." A sick painful feeling clawed at her insides. An image of them together burst into her mind, then stabbed into her heart. His hard, sexy body lying on Zara's own naked figure in the twisted silken sheets of his massive bed. Her face in ecstasy as he strained against her, murmuring her name . . .

She finally lost the battle to remain poised and dropped her gaze to the floor. She prayed this devil would leave, prayed she would never again have to look at his seductive face, hear his wickedly silken voice.

He refused to let her off so easily. He stood before her and yanked up her chin. His steellike fingers burned into her flesh. "You found her for me. You should be happy with the thought she'll satisfy me in bed," he said, a muscle knotting in his jaw.

Nicole wrenched her chin from his fingers, but he grasped it again, forced her tortured gaze to his. "Every night, we'll be together, Nicole, in the same damned bed, and I'll be doing a hell of a lot more with her than kissing her."

Moisture sprang to her eyes and she blinked fiercely, desperate to keep him from seeing her weakness. But her voice cracked when she spoke. "You make me sick."

"Sick? Why should the idea that Zara and I will enjoy a passionate sex life make you sick?" His words turned hot, the ice man vanishing. His coal-colored eyes took flame. "Or is it just the idea of men and women giving in to their desires that you can't handle?"

"Go to hell!"

He released her chin, only to grasp her shoulders, his fingers digging into her bare skin. "Goddamn it, woman! You'd rather die than reveal how you feel!"

His frontal attack threatened to crush her careful defenses, which were already shaky from his brutally suggestive words. Nicole shoved at his chest, desperate to get away from him. He grasped both her wrists in one strong hand, imprisoning them against his silk-clad chest. Nicole tried to yank free, but he merely pulled her closer. She thought she would faint from terror, from the potent, unwanted desire that swept through her at being so near him once again. She turned her tortured gaze up to his. "Why are you doing this to me?"

"Damn it. Tell me the truth!" He shook her hard, his expression exposing a dangerous determination she had never seen before. His hands felt like iron bands around her wrists. "You're in love with me, aren't you?"

Nicole gasped in shock. He wanted her to confess her secret? To shame her before making Zara his wife? How could he be so heartless? How could she love such a devil? But God forgive her, she did. She still did despite his coldness, his brutal treatment of her. With every fiber of her being.

He shook her once more, fiercely. "Admit it!"

"Yes!" At the admission, the fight bled out of Nicole and she began to sag. "Yes, I love you. I love you so much that I'm sick with it!" Rand's hold on her loosened, and Nicole pressed her fists against her mouth, desperately trying to contain a sob and failing. She bit out raggedly, "Are you satisfied now?"

He released her and stepped back. Through tear-filled eyes, Nicole watched him sag forward, his knees buckling as if the wind had been knocked from him. He squeezed his eyes shut, his expression transforming to one of such emotional intensity, she couldn't believe he wasn't suffering physical pain. "Oh, God, thank you," he murmured. "Thank you."

Nicole gasped, understanding breaking through her anguish. He wasn't experiencing pain, but the overwhelming relief of a prisoner granted a reprieve from a life sentence.

He sucked in a breath and straightened up, his gaze lifting to hers, locking on. He said nothing, but she knew. The man she loved had returned.

For one long, breathless moment, time stood still while the earth shook under her feet. Without knowing who moved first, she found herself in his arms, his hands pressing her hard and fast against him as if his life depended on keeping her close.

"Oh, God, Nicole!" He rained kisses along her temple, her neck, her face. "I never thought you'd say it. God, how I've missed you!"

The stress of the past weeks, of trying to hide her feelings and pretend she didn't love him suddenly caught up with her. She pressed her face into his satin lapel, a ragged sob tearing from her throat. "Rand? Why?" she cried, too overwhelmed to explain her confusion.

"Shh. Don't cry, darling," he said, stroking her hair with a lover's tender touch. "So much is at stake, I couldn't risk revealing the truth in case I was blinded by it, blinded by the fact that I'm desperately, passionately, helplessly in love with you."

Nicole couldn't think past his heated declaration to decipher his reasoning, and after a moment, it no longer mattered. Nothing mattered but the incredible, blissful truth: He loved her, too. He loved her.

The realization blended into sweet sensation as his palms skidded along her flesh, learning her shape through her thin satin gown. She admitted that she'd answered the door hoping against hope it was him. She hadn't donned her robe wanting it to be him. Wanting him.

"So perfect," he cried in her ear, his palms shaping her waist, her hips, her bottom as his lips continued to work blissful magic on the bare skin of her neck and shoulders. "So perfect. A goddess."

"You seemed so pleased with Zara—"

"I don't want Zara," he stated emphatically as if the very idea was ludicrous. "I don't care about her one way or the other." Brushing her hair back, he cradled her face between his hands. "You're the only woman I love—the only woman I've *ever* loved." An emotion-filled laugh burst from his throat. "You slipped inside me when I wasn't looking. You've become such a part of my life and my heart, I can't imagine going on without you."

"Rand," Nicole gasped, just before his mouth found hers, searing her lips, sealing their new bond with pure, heartfelt passion. Delirious, she kissed him back with everything in her heart, over and over again, touching his face, his hair. She grasped the fine fabric of his lapels in a crushing grip, but that kept her too far from him, so she locked her arms around his neck and felt the muscles of his back tense under her palms as he anchored her against him.

Their kiss was exquisitely familiar territory, even more overpowering than when he kissed her in the temple. This time, it communicated a blissful, shared understanding that swept away the last speck of doubt in her heart. *He loved her.*

He swept his palm up her bare thigh beneath her nightgown, then cried out against her mouth when he discovered she wore no panties. Hiking up her gown, he cupped her bare bottom in his callused palms, massaged, and lifted her hips hard against his. Grasping her thigh, he pulled it up until she instinctively locked it around his waist.

Never breaking the kiss, he dragged her to eye level, trapping her against him in his strong embrace. Now that she was exposed to his touch, his fingers slid along her soft, naked folds, flooding her body with languid heat so fierce she shook with it. Unable to support herself, she gave herself up to his strength, knowing she would fall if he let go, knowing he never would.

The next thing she knew, he sat with her on the chaise, pulling her spread kneed onto his lap facing him, the hot center of her need meeting his own hard maleness. Nicole had occasionally brushed close to lovemaking, but she had always pulled back, because some inner force insisted the time or the man wasn't right. Now that voice was silent.

She arched into him, wriggling her pelvis against his, abandoning all pretense of demureness in her suddenly insatiable desire for Rand. Her Rand.

Gripping her hips, he bucked under her, his fullness sliding along her most sensitive flesh. "Sweet, beautiful Nicole. I'm lost for wanting you."

His impassioned murmur vibrated along her flushed skin as he kissed her neck. She buried her face in his tanned neck, inhaling his wonderful male scent. Lord, how she loved him! "I can't believe you're really here with me."

"Oh, God, woman. I want you so badly." He tugged down

the top of her nightgown, freeing first one breast, then the other, leaving the fabric in a tangle about her waist, baring her to his sight, touch, and taste.

So fast. This was happening so fast. A niggle of doubt tickled at Nicole's mind, but then his hot mouth sucked hard on her exposed nipple and waves of sensation obliterated rational thought. An explosion went off inside her— a conflagration that consumed her with pure need. She became passion, enflamed with the need to touch Rand, to feel him, to express the powerful emotions she had so long held in check.

She'd shoved off his jacket, unknotted his tie, and unbuttoned half his shirt before fully realizing her actions, desperate to explore the heat of him. She stroked his tanned chest, provoking another ragged groan from him.

"Yes, darling," he said against her lips, his own hands lifting and shaping her breasts, his thumbs flicking her nipples, sending pulses of fire through her body to pool between her legs. "I knew we would be like this."

She moaned assent, suddenly unable to imagine them any other way since this felt so right.

Before she managed to work his shirt off his shoulders, he pressed her back against the chaise. She arched her back and found herself trapped between plush velvet and the vastly more sensuous heat of his teeth trapping her nipple while his tongue teased it mercilessly.

She dragged her fingers through his hair, pulled his face to hers, his mouth to hers. He moved his bare chest, stroked his fine hairs against her sensitized breasts. "I dreamed of this so many times," he murmured. "No matter how hard I fought it, I couldn't stop wanting you."

She fought with his shirt fabric, trying to work it over his thick biceps, but the cloth knotted. "Please," she panted softly. He wriggled the shirt down his arms, but the sleeves hung up on his wrists.

"My cuff links," he gasped, trying to yank his hands free. "We have to undo them."

"Cuff links?" *Just take it off,* Nicole silently begged.

"Let me—" He sat up and tried to maneuver his sleeves away from his shirt cuffs so he could get at the gold links. "Damn it! I'm all tangled up."

Her frustration matched his until her passion subsided enough for her to find the situation humorous. There could be worse things than having Prince Rand tied up and at her mercy. He also smiled, but he still worked at the shirt with grim intensity.

She almost reached out to help him, but since she was no longer in his potent embrace, her desire cooled enough for her head to clear. The magnitude of what they were about to do struck her like an electric shock. Had she lost her mind? She slid her nightgown back over her breasts and tugged it over her hips.

Rand finally managed to yank off his shirt. He balled up the expensive silk, tossed it aside, and turned toward her. His body was so magnificent, a fresh surge of desire swept through Nicole, warring with her sense, intensifying her confusion. He began to gather her close once more, but she forced herself to press her palms against his chest. "Rand, no."

"Nicole—"

"You left them."

"Left . . ." He nuzzled her neck and again slipped her straps off her shoulders.

Nicole fought the sensation and managed to push back enough to capture his gaze with her own. "You left her to come here. Zara, I mean. Your family—they're going to miss you."

His eyes sparked like twin flames, reflecting the fireplace beyond. "They've had me for years, Nicole. Tonight is for us."

When she opened her mouth to protest, he silenced her, his fingers on her lips. "Shh. Don't you understand? They don't exist—nothing exists outside this room."

Indeed, it felt as if the world had shrunk, had become a circle of firelight surrounding only the two of them. But it was dangerous to pretend. "Your duty—"

He laid her back on the chaise and encompassed her head in the protective cocoon of his bent arms, filling her vision with only him. His gaze explored hers. "Don't question *us*, Nicole. Never question the importance of us."

"But—"

"Don't withhold yourself from me anymore, Nicole. I can't bear it. I'm only a man." His voice shook with emotion. "A man who needs you desperately."

She stroked his angled cheeks and firm jaw as she explored the dark beauty of him, thinking of how much she wanted to give to him, how badly she wanted him to know her love for him. The heat of his chest burned through her palms straight to her heart.

His entire life he'd been pressed and pushed into a mold, forced to act the proper way, expected to fulfill duties and obligations that threatened to strangle the heart out of him. Faced the overwhelming task of changing a country completely alone without the support of his family. Expected to sacrifice his own happiness by marrying a woman he didn't want.

She had no answers for him. But she could give him what he wanted tonight. For tonight, she would keep guilt at bay, submerge all thought in the joy and beauty of loving him.

She tightened her arms around his neck and kissed him, a passionate expression of her own need. At her final acquiescence, he groaned, his body trembling in her arms like a leaf in a storm. Then his power seemed to return, and he stripped her nightgown from her, defeating that barrier once and for all. His hand claimed the moist, hot center of her need.

His fingers stroked her, sending sharp bursts of pleasure through her. "My goddess," he murmured. "I want to give you heaven."

And he did. At his sensitive yet insistent touch, the potent sensations swept through her, turning her entire body liquid, taking her to the edge. She dug her fingers into his back, heedless of hurting him as the heat and tension grew unbearable. Suddenly, she exploded. Shuddering against him, she melted in his arms, crying his name on a ragged breath.

"Show me how you feel," he cried, urging her to lose control again and yet again. "No more barriers, my love."

Nicole was sure she couldn't stand any more. She begged him to stop, but he refused until her entire body glowed in the firelight with a thin sheen of perspiration.

He leaned over her, his fingers exploring her deeper than before, feeling her readiness for him. "I have to be in you, Nicole, or I swear I'm going to die," he groaned.

Nodding, Nicole cradled the long, hard outline of his sex through his slacks. She popped the inner clasp of his waistband and slid the zipper down. "No more barriers."

At her bold touch, fire ignited in his eyes. He stood and stripped off his slacks and his shoes. Nicole's gaze traveled over his well-toned body, the muscles bunching under his honeyed skin, his broad shoulders, flat stomach, sleek thighs—and his arousal, huge and ready. She held her arms out to him, and he came into them, his skin hot against hers.

His gaze locked on hers, he thrust into her. She felt a single burst of pain, followed by the amazing sensation of being filled by him.

His face was a blend of agony and ecstasy. "Nicole, I—I'm broken into nothing and remade."

"Oh, God, Rand. I can't believe you're inside me." She bit down a sob, her heart feeling as if it would burst.

"I love you, woman. God, I love you." He shifted his hips, slid deeper inside her, then slowly withdrew. Nicole arched her hips, seeking him, needing him.

His eyes sparked with victory as he gazed down at her. "You want me this way."

"Every way," she whispered raggedly.

He moved faster within her, his own desires taking hold of hers, sweeping her with him. Nicole hadn't thought herself capable of any more passion. She'd been wrong. Brilliant ecstasy pulsed through her, echoing his. She melted into nonbeing, losing herself, burning away under the sheer heat of him.

An eternity passed, or had it only been a handful of minutes? Nicole had no idea.

She lay cradled in her lover's arms, facing him on her bed. He'd somehow carried her here, but she could scarcely remember when. After the first time? Before the third? He'd been insatiable, and her own passion seemed never to end.

His head propped on his hand, he tenderly stroked her cheeks with the backs of his fingers. "I can hardly believe you're finally mine," he said softly, his voice tinged with awe. "You were made to be my lover."

His words continued to amaze Nicole, at the same time she acknowledged how right they felt. Completely right. She had never felt closer to a living soul than to this man.

He swept his thumb over her lips, down her throat. "Heaven knows how you put up with me the past few weeks. I've been a demon from hell toward you."

"I think I understand that a little better now." She hesitated, lowered her eyelids, and tried to prevent the outside world from intruding. But she didn't succeed, and a sick feeling twisted her stomach, threatening to ruin the cocoon of perfection she'd found with Rand. She lifted her gaze to his, noting the worry lines forming on his brow, knowing with a lover's certain knowledge that he was reading her mind. "I know that you can't marry—"

"Shh." His brow smoothed, and leaning down, he began kissing her shoulders, her chest. "Let's not talk about that now. Not tonight."

As the silken heat of his mouth caressed her swollen nipple, Nicole allowed his delicious touch to distract her yet again. She also wanted to pretend nothing could possibly separate them. Both knew it was a lie. Spending this one night with him was the most selfish thing she had ever done, and she would never be able to repeat it and face herself.

"I was a fool to try to choose a wife with papers and forms," he murmured against her flushed skin. "I'd completely discounted love since I'd never experienced it."

A wife . . . Awash in the heady discovery of their love, in the wickedly delicious sensation of having him nuzzle at her breasts, Nicole barely managed to realize that his words made little sense. He still needed to marry a noble lady. Though he'd never revealed why it was so urgent, only a handful of months remained in the year.

She pushed up on his shoulders. Reluctantly, he lifted his gaze to hers. "You—You have to become engaged by the end of the year, you said. Yet you never explained why."

"Later."

"No, now."

With a heavy sigh, he gave up trying to distract her and propped his head on his hand. "My father threatened to yank my budget if I don't marry. I need that money for our projects, for my mission to help Caldonia."

"Then—" My God, had he sacrificed the country just for a night of passion?

Wait. She was thinking like a commoner. Would his father care that he was sleeping with her? Would Zara? Perhaps not. Nothing had really changed, not for Rand. Only for her . . .

"You're doing it again," he said, his deep voice resonating along her nerves, drawing her focus back to his nude presence beside her, the evidence of his renewed desire rapidly growing apparent against her thigh. Locking his leg over both of hers, he began kissing her again, her lips, her face, whispering in her ear. "Nicole, don't think about it. Not now. I suppose that's a difficult request for a woman who thinks all the time. But do it for me."

Unable to fight such persuasion, Nicole nodded, began to tremble as Rand once again lowered his lips to her breasts.

"I wanted so badly to make love to you the night of the

ball," he said. "You chose your gown just to tantalize me, didn't you?"

Nicole admitted to herself that she had. "I wanted you to notice, yes. But I wasn't intentionally trying to steal you—I don't think." God, had she? Had she all along tried to become his lover?

He lifted himself over her and his gaze clung to hers. "No," he said firmly, reading her mind yet again. "No woman who meant this to happen would have behaved as you have these past weeks. My God, I couldn't take a step without tripping over Zara." He stroked her cheeks and smiled tenderly at her. "You're too damned noble for your own good."

*Noble?* Not her. Not born to nobility, certainly. And not noble enough to deny her love for this man, who happened to be the prince of her country. Even though loving him could destroy everything they had worked so hard to achieve.

As if determined to distract her, he locked his hand behind her head and kissed her explosively, hungrily. She couldn't resist such a command. Desire burst like a conflagration in her blood and she moaned against his mouth.

He rolled to his back, bringing her with him so she lay on top of him. Nicole felt his insistent need against her pelvis, already seeking her again. With the same sure understanding that longtime lovers shared, she guided him deep inside her and found a new and exquisite rhythm that put him at her command.

She had a single clear thought before passion burned logic away. She would have to make it right to atone for her sin of loving this man. And with her limited resources, she could think of only one way to do that.

As she loved Rand with her entire being, she clung tightly to him, never wanting to let go. This time, when she felt him climax deep inside her, she had tears on her face.

# FOURTEEN

Nicole became aware that an unfamiliar heat warmed her back. Heat. From a human body. Sliding up from sleep, she gradually realized exactly why she should be feeling the body of another person in bed. Last night's events came back to her as if out of a romantic fantasy. If it weren't for the brawny arm draped over her waist, and the slight soreness between her legs, she might have thought she'd dreamed it.

She wriggled onto her back and found herself gazing at a Prince Rand, asleep. He looked younger, she thought at first, as if he had no worries at all. Then she realized the tension had vanished. The lines that had crossed his brow, the taut muscles of his jaw—they had relaxed. There was even a small smile on his lips.

Had she done this for him? A sense of wonder filled her at her own power, to be able to alleviate the stress that often seemed to eat away at him. The effect was only temporary, she thought with a catch in her heart. It could never be anything else, not with her.

A soft tapping came at her door, and Nicole realized it had awakened her. She began to reach for her glasses on her nightstand; then she blinked hard and realized she'd slept in her contacts. The little bit she'd slept. She slid out of his sleeping embrace and threw on her robe. Gerald stood outside the door, looking uncharacteristically embarrassed. "Gerald, good morning," she said, pulling her robe more firmly closed.

"I was wondering if perhaps . . . That is to say, I . . ."

Nicole finally realized he was trying to peek over her shoulder into the room. She glanced over her shoulder, opening the door wider in the process, and realized Prince Rand's evening clothes were spread all over the carpet.

Suddenly, the real world came crashing in on her—no longer something to be shoved aside until the bright light of morning. She'd slept with the prince. They'd become lovers.

"Nicole?" Gerald asked, drawing her attention back to him. She stood stiff as a board before the neatly garbed gentleman, unable to think what to say, how to act, what excuse to give. What excuse could there be for so horribly violating the very purpose for which she'd been hired?

Mortification worked its sinuous way up her body, making her feel weak and ill. She wanted to melt into the floor.

"If you wouldn't mind," Gerald said, "could you let the prince know that the king and queen are anxious to speak to him? About his sudden disappearance last night."

Sudden disappearance . . . He had been about to take Zara for a romantic walk in the moonlight to propose to her. They had sat there, wondering where he was, while he'd been here in her suite making passionate love to her.

Gerald continued, avoiding looking at her. "You might also let him know that his parents are rather . . . disturbed, as is the Royal Family of Omat."

The thought of the five royals sitting in another part of the castle discussing Rand's abhorrent behavior filled her with shame. She was the cause. She had brought the prince to this low, made him forget his obligations. "They don't—don't know where he is, do they?"

"Let's just say there has been speculation," Gerald said.

Nicole admired his honesty. So they undoubtedly knew exactly what had happened last night. She'd proven them right. All of them. The queen would never believe her innocent of coldheartedly maneuvering her way into the prince's life. Worse, she had most likely ruined Rand's chance with Princess Zara. What had she been thinking?

She hadn't been thinking—she'd only been feeling the strongest, most powerful emotions she'd ever felt.

Gerald turned to go; then he paused and cast her a kind look. "Historically, it's a high honor to serve the nation as the king's confidante. Or the future king's, as the case may be."

His confidante . . . A polite term for mistress. Nicole could hardly believe the word applied to her, but that was exactly what she'd become. During the night, she'd realized she had to take action to end this now. She had to find the strength.

How much strength would it take to give up the man she loved?

With unsteady hands, she closed and relocked the door, then returned to the bedroom. She stood in the doorway of the bedroom and simply looked at him, imprinting his image in her memory. She memorized every part of him, from his tousled midnight-dark hair to his longish nose to his strong jaw. And that smile of sleep. She bit her lip and forced herself to turn away, hating to think she would soon be causing that smile to disappear.

As silently as possible, she slid her suitcase from the closet, opened it on a chair, and began to pack. More than anything, she wanted to disappear and never come back to this place, to this country. She never should have returned. She'd been a fool to think she could contribute anything. All she'd done was compound the problems a hundred times over.

She forced herself to continue packing and not look at him, praying he wouldn't wake, wouldn't have the chance to persuade her right back into bed. She emptied one drawer and slowly slid out the second.


Rand drifted awake, heated recollections of the previous evening filling him with a contentment he'd never felt before. Contentment and boundless joy. He wanted to run for miles. He wanted to stand on the roof of the palace and shout to the world how much he loved Miss Nicole Aldridge. He wanted to pull her right back into bed and show her how much he loved her.

Everything about her intoxicated him: the soft, sexy scent of her skin; the little sounds she made when she climaxed; the way she looked at him as if he held the secrets of the universe in his hands. She made him feel as if he did.

He reached for her but the space beside him was empty. Cracking open his eyes, he focused on Nicole's back clad in a peach-colored satin robe, her sleep-tousled hair brushing her shoulders. For a moment, he was satisfied to watch her graceful movements—until he realized she was packing her suitcase. Trepidation shot through him. "Darling?"

At the sound of his sleep-husky voice, Nicole stiffened, but she continued to pack.

"What are you doing?" Ignoring him, she continued transferring sweaters and underthings to her suitcase in steady, determined movements. "Nicole," he said, more sharply. "Tell me what you're up to."

"I believe it's called packing," she said, her attempt at a carefree tone failing completely to alleviate his concern.

Driven by irritation—and more than a little fear—Rand threw off the covers and slid his legs over the side of the bed. "It looks like you're going somewhere."

"I am."

A shaft of pain jolted his heart. "Mind telling me where? Or were you planning to leave without telling me?"

She stilled her motions and finally turned to face him. "I'm going home."

Her response only added to his confusion. "What? You live here—" Realization struck him like a punch in the gut. "You mean America."

"Yes." She turned her back on him and stuffed another sweater in her case. She was packing sloppily, as if she couldn't get done fast enough.

"Like hell you are." He stood and clasped her wrist in one fast motion. Her gaze shot up to meet his, her eyes wide with distress. God, just looking at her made his heart turn over. Last night, he'd laid that heart at her feet. "What's going on here? After last night—"

"When you made me your mistress—"

The word pierced his armor like nothing could. It turned their love into a joke, a travesty. Did she really think him capable of lowering her to such a level? "Is that what you think?"

"It's the truth. Now please let go of me." She wrenched her arm from his grasp and tossed her last sweater into the suitcase. She crossed to the closet, removed her garment bag, threw it on the very slept-in bed, and began placing her suits inside.

That was when it struck him. She had no idea. She didn't understand what had really happened last night. She didn't believe he could offer her anything more.

Could he? He had imagined possibilities once: wild speculations, hypothetical ideas to explore if and when he learned that she loved him in return. They hadn't been real.

He would have to make them real. Yet he could do nothing if she left. He wouldn't have the strength or the heart without her by his side.

Stepping behind her, he settled his hands on her shoulders, felt her tremble beneath his touch. "You can't leave. You have to stay here."

"I have to?" she said, her back stiff.

"I order you to stay." The words escaped before he realized how wrong they were.

She yanked away from him, her eyes sparking with anger. "How dare you. You may be my future king, but you don't rule my heart. I refuse to be your mistress."

"Quit saying that word! This isn't about that. It's about *us.*" He sucked in a steadying breath, tried to catch her gaze with his own and hold it. "Nicole, last night you said you love me. Has something changed since then?" *God, don't let her say yes.*

"No! I . . . no," she said, her voice communicating her misery.

He met her gaze and knew with a lover's certainty that she was remembering all the ways they had expressed their love: all the words, all the unspoken gestures that said what words never could. Tears began to fill her eyes. How could he have doubted her even for a moment? He reached for her, but she hurried into the bathroom to collect her things.

He sagged on the bed. He hated to see her cry. He wanted more than anything to make her happy. But he knew she would never be happy if he sacrificed his duty, if he failed to marry and give the country what it needed. He rubbed his face, the worry and tension that loving her had alleviated coming back in full force. The quandary tore at him. He had to find a way out, or he would be no good for the country at all. No good for her or himself.

She reentered the room and dumped a handful of brushes and bottles in her suitcase. She headed back to the bathroom, but he caught her hand and pulled her between his knees. Clasping her hands he waited until she met his eyes. "Listen to me. I know you love me. And I happen to love you, even more than I did last night if that's possible. You've become such a part of my life, I can't imagine not having you by my side, whatever I'm doing."

Nicole's gaze clung to his for a long heartbeat. Then she extracted her hands from his and stepped away, her arms crossing over her chest protectively. "What you should be doing is thinking about your country. Rand, I'm not good for you. Last night, you completely forgot your duty when we . . ." She swallowed hard, then glanced up at him. "Gerald came by. It seems your parents are furious with you, and so are Zara and her parents, and I can't say that I blame them. Neither of us gave them any thought."

"Why in the hell should we?" he shot back. He owed them no explanations. Last night when he'd left them, he hadn't promised he would return. He'd expected he would, of course. He hadn't dared hope he would discover the glory of Nicole's love for him. For the thousandth time since meeting this exceptional woman, he felt the strait-jacket of duty tightening around his chest, squeezing his heart. "If I was just any man, this would be no one's business but ours. I'm not married. I'm not even engaged."

"But you're *not* just any man." She zipped her bag closed. "And we both know it."

Rand opened his mouth to explain his spark of an idea, their slim possibility. But he thought better of it. If he failed, he might be hurting her more. Worse, if she knew, she would do everything she could to prevent him, her loyalty to her country ran that deep.

He rose and stood beside her. He slid his hand under her chin, forcing her to look him in the eye. "Assume I was a commoner, just for a moment."

She laughed unsteadily. "You'd never be common."

He smiled at her compliment, but refused to be distracted. He had to hear her say it to give him strength. "Well, pretend anyway. Would you marry me?"

*"What?"* Her eyes grew huge, and a tortured expression came to her face. He knew she had no idea why he would ask about such an impossible thing. "Rand, please—"

"Would you marry me?" he insisted.

"Yes, of course, I would. In a heartbeat. But—"

*Yes.* Her admission filled him with joy. He'd known that would be her answer, known her love for him had nothing to do with his title. She loved him as a man, not as a prince.

He cradled her face in his hands, then ran his thumbs along the smooth, elegant contours of her face. "Give me a week, Nicole. Don't leave for a week. Please."

"Nothing will change in a week, Rand, and we both know it."

Her insistence struck him hard. Perhaps he *was* deluding himself. Centuries of law and custom hung over them, weighing down on their chests like a ton of rocks. Never had Caldonian tradition felt so smothering. Still, he had to try. "Nothing will change how we feel either. Stay one week, darling."

She seemed to consider, yet her gaze darted to her suitcase. Panic clutched at Rand's chest. He had to keep her from leaving. His voice trembled as he spoke. "I'm begging you, Nicole, and I never beg."

Nibbling worriedly at her lush lower lip, she demurely lowered her gaze. "They may not want me around that long."

*They* . . . His parents. One had deemed her suitable only to be his mistress. The other had deemed her unsuitable in every way. Raw anger tore at him on Nicole's behalf. "This has nothing to do with them. Now promise me."

Slowly, she nodded her head, her eyes lifting to his. "All right, Rand, if it matters that much to you. One week can't make any difference, but I promise to stay that long. For you."

Relief flooded through Rand. He smiled at her. "Now kiss me."

"I don't think—" Rand cut off her protest by pulling her into his arms and claiming her mouth with his, reminding her of the love and passion that lay between them.

She moaned at the heat between them, encircling his neck with her arms. Her body fit so perfectly to his. Amazement filled him and threatened to bring tears to his eyes.

She broke the kiss and pulled in a breath. "They're waiting for you. You'd better go."

He squeezed her shoulders. "One week."

"A week." Her voice was hardly more than a whisper.

He turned away and began gathering his clothes from the floor and slipping into them, keeping his back to her. Now that he'd gotten her assurance that she wouldn't bolt, he had to put distance between them. He was afraid if he looked at her or said anything more to her, he'd say too much and reveal his plans.

Carrying his jacket and shoes, he stepped to the door and began to open it. He paused then, unable to help himself. He turned and looked back at her.

She was watching him, her robe barely covering her slim

body, her heart revealed in her eyes. She smiled tremulously. Bravely. Her lips formed the words *I love you*.

Rand felt his heart fill with strength. He swore to himself he would find a way. He gave her a last, reassuring look before leaving her.


Seven days. Seven days of knowing nothing except that she should stay in her room.

Nicole hadn't been able to refuse Rand's request for a week's grace. For what reason, she had no idea. But he had actually begged her—something she knew the proud prince had never done to another living soul. Put in such a way, she could hardly have refused him.

In that long week, not only hadn't they slept together, she had hardly seen him. Private audiences with the queen, the king, and even an angry Princess Zara had taken their toll on Nicole, not at all helped by the sideways glances being cast her way by the palace staff.

When Rand showed up at her door the morning of the seventh day, Nicole was already packed and ready to leave, her plane reservation made.

He entered the room and closed the door. His eyes met hers, and Nicole felt her heart start to break. He looked battle weary, small lines radiating from his eyes, his sculpted cheeks unnaturally shadowed. Her heart ached for him. Unable to help herself, needing only to hold him, she stepped forward and into his arms.

For several long moments, they clung to each other. Finally, reluctantly, she slid from his grasp. "I'm ready to go back to New York, Rand," she said softly, trying desperately to ignore the emotion in his gaze.

His jaw tightened. "I would prefer you stayed."

Her words came out a broken whisper. "I can't."

"You gave me seven days, Nicole," he said harshly. "This is the seventh day, and it's not over yet. I'm going into town to take care of something. We'll settle this when I return."

"There's nothing to settle. I won't be your mistress." Her voice trembled. "It's not right."

He cradled her face in his hands. "Have I asked you to, darling?"

He hadn't. At least not in so many words. He'd only begged her to stay when there was no chance of a future for them.

"I know this past week has been hard on you," he said. "I know my mother tried to make you feel ashamed, and my father tried to talk you into becoming my mistress."

The audiences with both royals had been beyond awful. She'd had nothing to say in her defense, except that she loved Rand with all her heart. Which simply wasn't good enough.

He brushed back a strand of her hair. "And I'm aware that Princess Zara scolded you for playing her for a fool, as she so neatly put it."

"She did have a few choice words to say to me before she left with her family."

Supporting her chin in his fingers, he ran his thumb along her lower lip. "None of that will matter, Nicole. Not after today."

Trepidation shot through her. Rand was planning something—something he refused to share with her. "Why?" She clutched his arm. "Rand, what are you going to do?"

"Caldonians have been living in the Dark Ages far too long. I'm going to force them to decide whether they intend to stay there or join the real world. If you want to watch the fireworks, I suggest you use the television in my suite. It's the only color set in the palace." He smiled at her ruefully, then kissed her gently, almost chastely, on the lips. Then he left her, his determined strides echoing down the marble corridor.

Nicole entered the hall with every intention of following him. But Gerald and three other retainers had already slipped into place behind Rand. The entourage soon disappeared down the marble staircase at the end of the hall.

Dispirited, yet filled with uneasy energy from Rand's odd

pronouncement, Nicole finally took his advice. She entered his suite and turned on his television.

The Caldonian network was continuing its coverage of the royal crisis. The broadcast cut to the main hall in the Grand Assembly Building in downtown Fortinbleaux, where the legislators and lords had assembled for an announcement from the palace. The dark, immense hall appeared designed for the stern-looking lords on the floor wearing stodgy suits. A massive domed ceiling emphasized the historic importance of the place.

This must be where Rand had gone. Why? Nicole wondered. Slowly, she sat on his couch, her hands tight in her lap.

It couldn't have anything to do with this situation involving her. She certainly wasn't so self-centered to consider that a possibility.

True, the country had been able to talk about little else but Rand's personal life all week. Word had gotten out—as word always does—that Rand had stood up Princess Zara and that there would be no engagement, the family having returned to Omat distinctly displeased.

Worse, commentators and so-called palace-watch experts had filled the airwaves with speculation about the cause of Zara's departure—considered the best hope in years for a serious match. The experts hadn't needed to look far to find a scapegoat—the commoner, Miss Nicole Aldridge, who had ruined the Prince's future.

Not every reporter painted her negatively. Some speculated on her role in the prince's life. Others made her the star of a Caldonian Cinderella story. Gerald told her he had fielded no less than two dozen requests for interviews from the press, and her fashion editor friend at *Aristocrats* reported that the designer of her gown was ecstatic over the publicity.

Even now, commentators were discussing her as if they knew her, speculating on her character and background as if she were a celebrity. Which she'd somehow become.

Her very lack of noble status had raised the debate about

the requirement that a prince marry a noblewoman. Nicole suspected Rand's own press secretary had been using his contacts to raise that question. But to what end? There was no getting around Caldonian law and seven centuries of revered tradition. Besides, the idea of actually becoming the prince's wife was ludicrous, and Nicole knew it. It simply would never happen. Unless—

Unless he were no longer the prince.

Nicole sat frozen as Rand began to speak, the shock of such an outrageous possibility sinking in deeper the longer he spoke. He began discussing his reform policies, and Nicole assumed she'd been wrong—hoped, prayed she was wrong. Until he said that his inspiration for change was a special individual.

"As most of our citizens know, I have taken a strong stand on the need to modernize our country," Rand said calmly, his voice carrying across the crowd. "For years I have made plans. Discussed ideas. Even spoken about the need for change.

"Still, I did little to make change happen. It took a commoner—a commoner like most of you—to make me understand how desperately we need to change to survive in the twenty-first century. To be a strong nation, proud of our traditions, yet not held back by them."

Nicole stared at the screen, hardly able to breathe. He was talking about her to his entire nation, talking about her influence on his life! What did he hope to gain by this?

Rand continued. "Not only did she make me see what we'd become. She inspired me to seek change *now*. Here, today. And every day. Until we become the nation I know we can become."

His tone changed, grew emphatic. "In many ways, our country is so mired in tradition, it will never be able to hold its own in the world. I plan to change that. One tradition is even now being debated in the media—one that affects me personally. Over the past centuries, it has become so ingrained in our culture, it has taken on the status of law of the land."

A poignant smile crossed his lips. "Sometimes, to quote a phrase, laws are made to be broken. I and my staff have conducted a careful research of existing law. And what we have discovered is that no law exists—*none*—that requires the heir to the throne to marry a noblewoman."

Nicole sat dumbfounded. He thought he could rewrite centuries of tradition just like that? "No," she whispered in shock. "He can't do it. They'll never let him do it!"

She gripped the neck of her blouse. He was hanging out too far on a limb, one that would surely snap under him. To think he would try so hard to be with her— Tears sprang to her eyes, the responding love in her heart a physical pain. She would never have asked him to do this. Never! He knew her too well. He hadn't told her of his plans, knowing she would try to prevent him. If only she had!

His voice slid into her consciousness. Realizing she'd missed a few of his words, she refocused on his speech. "I have introduced several popular changes into our country in the past months—to improve our health, to increase the chances for jobs for young people, to equalize the status of men and women. None of these—not one—would have been successful without Miss Nicole Aldridge by my side."

The fact he actually mentioned his mistress's name in an official speech caused a wave of shock to pass through the distinguished assemblage. Heads bobbed, feet shifted, a rising murmur filled the hall.

Rand paused, his eyes revealing nothing as he looked out over them. He leaned forward slightly and spoke clearly into the microphone. "I will marry her—and only her. I ask you, the people of Caldonia, to stand behind my choice."

Nicole gasped, unable to comprehend at first that she'd heard right. Yet she had. He was demanding permission to marry her. He would never succeed!

The Grand Assembly dome filled with the outraged voices of two hundred distinguished men on the main floor and hundreds more shocked spectators in the gallery. The camera zoomed in on a few of the lords' faces. They looked stunned, furious, appalled.

"Oh, God," Nicole groaned and pressed her hands to her face. "Dear, sweet man, what have you done?" A ruler needed his people's respect. Rand was tossing his chance for respect away with both hands.

After a moment, Rand continued to speak, and the assemblage quieted just enough to enable his words to be heard. "This, then, is where it stands," he said, his strong words booming through the hall. "Either I marry her as your prince, and you accept her as your princess. Or I relinquish my claim as the heir to the throne of Caldonia. Thank you."

He stepped from the podium and disappeared through a door behind the podium. Guards took up posts beside the door he'd gone through, and the broadcast cut to the newscaster's stunned face.

Nicole sat in a daze, only vaguely aware of the newscaster scrambling to react to the prince's astonishing statement. The camera cut to the gathering. Most of the people were on their feet, arguing furiously among themselves. She couldn't stand to listen to another word. She clicked the remote's power button and the screen went blessedly dark.

Her fault. This was all her fault. Guilt and shame crushed down on her, threatening to smother her. She sucked in a painful breath. She should never had allowed him into her room that night, never have fallen so completely into his arms. Oh, God, what had she done to Rand, to her country?

She rose on shaky legs, took two steps, and stumbled. Grabbing the back of the sofa, she forced her legs to support her. She had to go. She had to go *now*.

She should never have stayed this past week, despite Rand's request. Because of her foolish weakness, her misguided love for him, the country might turn against its future king. The royal line that had endured for hundreds of years might end. All because of her.

# FIFTEEN

In the Fortinbleaux International Airport, the sound of ongoing coverage of the prince's speech on a television monitor reached Nicole, despite her efforts to sit well away from it. Worse, everyone around her was discussing the prince's ultimatum.

"He's off his rocker, is what he is," said a sturdy woman with graying hair seated behind Nicole.

"He's in love," a blond teenager with her replied. "I think it's sweet. Why does he have to marry a blue blood, especially a foreign one? What are they to us?"

"It's tradition!" the older woman said scornfully. "It's the way it's done, and it's not his place to change it."

"Why not? He is the prince, after all."

"It's all because of *that woman,*" the elder lady said.

Nicole tightened the scarf around her head and adjusted her large-framed sunglasses. She prayed no one would recognize her. After leaving a farewell note in Rand's apartment, she'd called a taxi and left the palace. The taxi driver, a congenial middle-aged man, had stared at her in shock. Then he grinned wryly. "You got him to do it, didn't you?"

"What?" Nicole had asked, guilt stabbing her.

"Give up smokes! Once the prince did it, my wife did, too. No more cigarettes after thirty years! Thirty years! I gotta thank you for that." Nicole didn't know what to say.

When she'd finally entered the airport, she thought she might be able to hide. But the ticket clerk, a young woman, had also recognized her. "He got me this job, you know," she confided, leaning over the counter.

Distracted, Nicole couldn't determine what she meant at first.

She laid her hand on Nicole's wrist. "You know, your boyfriend. The prince! He made the national airport change its policy, and now they hire women like me." She actually winked. "Sure you want to leave? I bet he's going to miss you. Or is he joining you later?"

"No, I—" Nicole held out her hand, but the agent didn't relinquish the ticket.

"A lot of us like having you around to stir things up," the young woman said. "I used to think the prince was just a playboy—you know, a party guy. A typical nose-in-the-air aristocrat out to have fun at our expense. But not anymore. He cares about people like me."

"Oh. Well, yes. He does. Very much."

The agent finally gave her the ticket. Nicole thanked her, then hurried toward the gate, her head aching from the confusing reactions of regular Caldonians. She had expected to be publicly vilified. Then it struck her. The ticket agent and the taxi driver had been working and hadn't heard Rand's speech. They didn't know she'd almost cost them their prince.

She had been out of the palace so rarely in the past weeks, she had forgotten how Prince Rand's new policies had affected the average person. Now she remembered the hundreds of supportive letters that had poured in each day. Perhaps not everyone felt she deserved their scorn.

Still, in less than an hour, she would be in the air, on her way back to New York. With her out of the picture, Rand would have to listen to his people, his advisers, his parents. He would learn to forget her. Even if she never managed to forget him.

An attendant opened the door to the gate and began the boarding process. Knowing she was taking an irrevocable step, her stomach tightened. Once she fled, no one would want her back, not even Rand. Not after he risked so much for her, so publicly. She heard her seat row called and rose to head to the gate.

Just then, a murmur of excited conversation rose behind her accompanied by a flurry of activity of some kind. She heard running feet pounding along the wide corridor.

"Nicole!"

*Rand.* He'd followed her. Why couldn't he have been slower? She refused to look up. He couldn't recognize her from the back, not in this heavy coat and scarf. In front of her, people were gaping, stretching their necks to look past her, slowly rising to their feet.

"Nicole." A hand landed on her shoulder and spun her around. Nicole found herself gazing up into Rand's distraught face. He was winded, tense, and more handsome than she had believed possible.

He slid the sunglasses from her face and shoved the scarf from her head. Desperate, she reached for her disguise, but he pocketed the glasses. "You can't leave."

She had wanted to avoid seeing the agony on his face when she left him. Certainly she had never imagined confronting him in such a public place. Their love had been secret, only between the two of them.

Knowing dozens of pairs of eyes were now on them, she realized that had been a foolish belief on their part. Neither one of them had been able to hide their feelings, and the world had known the truth before they had themselves.

She met his intense gaze, hardly able to speak through her constricted throat. "Rand, I have to go. If you think about it with a clear head, you'll know it's true."

Rand glanced around at the growing crowd surrounding them and led Nicole to a slightly more private corner. He turned his back on the crowd and spoke low. "All I know is, I cannot serve this country well if you're not by my side. You said you would marry me if—"

"If you were a commoner. Of course I would! If you were anyone else, I'd marry you in a second!"

He smiled grimly. Slipping his hand behind her neck,

he pressed his lips to hers, as if to confirm her declaration. Despite being in public, despite the crowd of people straining to watch them, Nicole gasped at the surge of desire that swept through her at even this simple kiss. Cradling his hand in hers, she pressed her lips to his fingers. "I love you so much," she whispered. "But I never meant—I never wanted you to sacrifice the throne. All I've done is cause trouble for you."

"That's not true. You made me come alive, Nicole." He caressed her cheek. "More truly alive, more excited about our country and its possibilities, than I have ever been. Before you came, I was in my own little world. You gave me the world, Nicole. Please marry me."

"It's not possible. They'll never accept me." She swallowed past a thick lump in her throat and blinked back a sting of tears. "I never meant to fall in love with you. If I leave now, it might not be too late for you to make amends with your family and your people."

"They're your people, too."

She shook her head vehemently. "I'm just a commoner, Rand. They will never accept me as their princess."

His voice grew gruff. "They should. They will. They're smart people, Nicole. They'll see that you're a finer woman than any of those candidates you found for me. You truly care about your country, Nicole. You love it as much as I do! What better princess could I possibly have, could *they* possibly hope for? You're perfect for me *and* for the country."

"Please, Rand!" His wishful talk only intensified her agony. It could never be, nor did she even imagine it could be. "I never wanted to be the princess," she said. She laid her hand on the face she loved so much, knowing she would have to leave him forever. "When I fell in love with you, I forgot everything but who you were to me: my dearest friend. I didn't fall in love with a prince— I fell in love with *you.*" She fought down bitter tears. "A man who happens to be a prince. Oh, Rand, I feel like

I'm on a precipice, and either way I fall, I'll be hurt or I'll hurt someone else."

He pulled her into his arms as he would a child. "Shh, darling. I'm here to catch you."

Nicole shuddered as he caressed her back, wanting to melt against him and forget everything else. "Oh, Rand, you're the one I'm afraid I've hurt the most!"

He pulled back, his eyes alight with a determination that Nicole could not ignore. "Come back with me, darling. Whatever happens, we'll face it together."

She swallowed hard and found herself drowning in his gaze, unsure if she should risk it.

"Please?" he said again, once more pleading with her. "I need you more than I've ever needed anything or anyone."

Finally, Nicole understood. Rand needed her there to catch him if he fell. She found herself nodding. She would stick by him until the furor passed, perhaps manage to convince him not to forsake the throne for her. And if she could not, or if the people already had rejected him, he would need a friend by his side. He would need her there when he stepped down from the role he'd been raised for and faced the anger of the people.

She nodded, still shaky and unsure, knowing she would be the primary target of people's outrage. Yet she wouldn't run from what she'd caused. Rand deserved better.

"Good. Now, come." Rand turned her and steered her down the terminal toward a patiently waiting Gerald, who had accompanied him. A few feet down the terminal, they ran smack into a crush of photographers and reporters coming the other way. They must have followed the prince to the airport. Rand shielded Nicole on his way out to the parking lot, saying only that he would have a further statement later that day.

But nothing stopped the photographers from snapping shot after shot. Rand whispered into her ear, "You'll have to get used to this if you marry me. Regardless of the throne."

She nodded. "That's the least of our concerns, Rand."


On the way back into town, Gerald told Rand that the royal family waited for him at the Grand Assembly Building, so he directed the limousine to downtown Fortinbleaux. Nicole almost asked to be returned to the palace, but she knew she would have to face the music sometime.

It took them more than an hour to drive from the airport to the Grand Assembly Building. The traffic was unusually heavy, as if something had brought the people outside into the streets. They were forced to stop twice, then to take an alternate route to avoid the most tangled intersections.

As the limousine pulled into the private royals' entrance behind the building, Nicole noticed crowds of people in the side streets. She couldn't see the front of the building, and she wondered what event was taking place today—a festival of some sort? She thought she heard chanting and singing.

Rand kept her close to him as they entered the building through the highly guarded side entrance and took an elevator to the third floor. They entered a wide parlor, and Nicole's trepidation grew tenfold. The king, queen, and various advisers rose when they entered, their eyes all on the wayward couple.

Nicole's eyes met those of her uncle, Lord Phillip, who sat stiffly in a wingback chair, looking distinctly shell-shocked. She sent him an apologetic look. How could she ever make it up to him for humiliating him like this?

Another one of those innocuous television sets sat against one wall with continuing coverage of the royal crisis.

"Well?" the king said in exasperation. "Is she going to stay or go?"

Nicole's feet felt like lead, but Rand propelled her forward, his arm locked around her waist. "Stay," he said firmly, challenging his father with a narrow-eyed look. "As my wife."

"Rand, you can't—" Nicole began once again.

"I see," the king said. "What do you think of that, Eurydice?" he asked the queen, his tone surprisingly mild.

The queen rose regally from the sofa and approached her. "You say you love my son."

Nicole's mouth went dry. They had already had this conversation, but before, it had been distinctly one-sided. "Yes, I do," she said, her voice sounding firm from her conviction. "More than anything."

"Enough? Do you love him enough to handle the pressure of a royal spouse? You are hardly bred to it, after all. Even if you felt you could, you would not understand what you were facing. No woman does, even those of us born with the responsibility of a title."

Nicole wished she'd get to the point. Start reaming her out and get it over with. "I imagine not," she finally said.

"It's apparent some things must change in our country, or we will lose the support of the people." She looked down her nose at Nicole, despite her shorter height. "And it appears that I may have been hasty in my judgment of you. I have decided to accept you."

Nicole stared in shock at the queen. Rand's arm slid from around her waist, and Nicole realized that he was as shocked as she. The queen was not a woman to admit she'd made a mistake. As the queen moved aside, Nicole saw the television set over her shoulder, and her breath stopped. On the screen she saw herself and Rand, deep in intimate conversation at the airport, every word they had shared being broadcast to millions of people.

Shock and mortification flooded through Nicole. Someone had caught it on film. She hadn't noticed a cameraman about—but then, she'd been a little preoccupied. "Oh," she murmured. "Where . . . How did—"

"A reporter must have followed you, Miss Aldridge," Gerald said softly. "When you left in the taxi from the pal-

ace. The broadcasts have been filled with it for the past
half hour."

Stunned, Nicole heard again her own heartfelt words,
that she never wanted to be princess, had never meant to
hurt Rand. Her admission that she would love him regardless of his role, and Rand's own declaration of love and
how much he needed her. Emotion threatened to engulf
her once again, and she blinked back the moisture in her
eyes.

"It seems the people have decided to accept you, Miss
Aldridge," the king said. "There have been so many calls
to the palace in your support that the telephone system
cannot support it. Another system that it seems needs to
be modernized."

Nicole looked at Rand. He appeared no less shocked
than she.

"I'm afraid you've caused a real stir this time, Rand,"
the king said. "The people are about to riot in the streets.
Thousands have gathered outside. Security reports that
they're clogging the streets, demanding your appearance."
His gaze flicked to Nicole. "Both of you."

As if the king's words set the world back into motion,
the royal advisers stepped forward and surrounded Nicole.
"Have you ever been arrested?" asked a man Nicole recognized as the chief security adviser.

"Can you have children?"

"She'll need a full physical," a third commented.

Still not recovered from shock, Nicole gathered herself
together and managed to answer their questions. "No. As
far as I know. And later," she told each of them, earning
her a smile from the king at her rapid responses.

"Who were your previous lovers?" a fourth man asked.

Rand's angry voice cut through the room. "She had
none," he said, a challenging glint in his eye as he slipped
his arm around Nicole. The adviser shut his mouth and
stepped back.

"Come, girl. We have work to do. You look a state!" The
queen ushered her toward another room off the main

room. "That beige suit—it would not have been my first choice, but I suppose it will have to do. We haven't time to find something more suitable."

Nicole let herself be led away, still trying to accustom herself to all that had happened and was even now happening. Rand's eyes met hers before she slipped through the door, an encouraging grin on his face.

In the privacy of a nearby parlor, the queen turned to Nicole. Nicole tensed, expecting now that she would learn the truth about where she stood with this cold woman.

"I admit I have been unkind to you over the past months. I would like to explain."

Nicole was too stunned to answer, almost afraid she'd heard wrong.

The queen looked toward a window, but didn't appear to see the view. "When I was younger than you, I came here to marry the king. I was an earl's daughter, but I had been raised in the country. The palace, the court amazed me. The king also amazed me. He was so strong, so commanding. I—" Her voice dropped. "I failed to prepare myself for the truth."

Nicole read between the lines, understood that the young queen had loved her husband. She tried to grasp the idea of the queen as a young girl in love. For the first time, she saw her as a woman and not as a figurehead.

The queen squared her shoulders. "When I became pregnant, I learned the truth. My marriage was based on nothing more than expediency, nothing more than my title and my ability to produce an heir. The king made no secret of the fact that he loved another woman. I did not handle it well."

Her confession stunned Nicole; at the same time it explained so much about the queen's coldness, her lack of motherly devotion to Rand. Brokenhearted, the young queen must have found it hard not to blame her son for causing her husband to desert her.

"The king has taken a series of mistresses over the years, and he has never once—never once—seen anything wrong

in such a practice," Eurydice said. Her voice dropped, her
gaze returning to Nicole. "When I saw how devoted my
son was to you, I feared he would be following in his father's
footsteps."

Nicole couldn't think what to say. That the queen might
have suffered all these years had never occurred to her.
She'd been too wrapped up in Rand to think about what
might be driving the woman's intense dislike of her. *No,
the queen's fear of her.* Now it made perfect sense. "I'm sorry.
I wish I'd understood better."

"No." The queen looked at her, a small smile on her
lips, a warmth in her eyes Nicole had never seen before.
"Now is not the time for apologies. You have a prince who
loves you enough to give up everything for you. And he's
waiting, no doubt quite impatiently."

The queen's composure returned and her gaze moved
over Nicole with fresh interest. "Your hair has gotten quite
mussed. I believe that style where you wear it behind your
head might suit. It gives you a regal air. You have fine skin
and a pretty neck. You should show it off." She yanked a
bellpull and a maid appeared, accompanied by the palace
hairstylist.

Nicole found herself glad of the queen's attention. She
would need her guidance in this complicated world she
was being thrust into. She was determined not to let Rand
down.

A short while later, after having a royal makeover and
her hair dressed in a sophisticated French roll with tendrils
curling around her face, Nicole emerged from the dressing
room, feeling remarkably calmer.

Rand turned from talking to his father. He crossed to
her and grasped her hands. "The press and the public are
waiting for us to make an appearance, Nicole. You look
beautiful—like a princess. *My* princess. Are you ready?"

Nicole warmed at his compliment, but she knew it
stemmed from his own personal love for her. "As ready as
I'll ever be."

He said softly, "They'll fall in love with you, too, Nicole. Just as I have."

Nicole saw Uncle Phillip standing nearby, still looking overwhelmed. She smiled at him and stretched out her hand.

Phillip grinned and took it. "When I managed to get you back here," he said, patting her hand, "I was rather hoping you'd find a nice Caldonian boy and get married. I just never expected . . ."

Nicole hugged him, and he whispered, "Your parents would be very proud of you."

"Thank you." She wished they could have been here to see her. They wouldn't have believed it. She still wasn't sure she believed it. The sheer size of the role she would be thrust into intimidated her. Her knees suddenly felt as if they might give out.

"He's very lucky," Phillip said as he released her. His eyes sparkled. "He may be a prince, but you're an Aldridge!"

Rand slid his arm around her, lending her his strength. His gaze met hers; his tone was intimate, yet emphatic. "I'm going to be there for you, my darling. There will be stressful times—there's no getting around that. A lot of press attention, of course—not all of it good. I can't make it easier, but I can teach you how to handle it. I swear, I won't let you down."

He wouldn't let *her* down?

Rand seemed to sense her trepidation. "It's not too late to back out, darling. It's a lot to ask of any woman."

As she gazed into his eyes, she knew without a doubt that he would be there for her now and in the coming years. He would break yet one more Caldonian tradition and remain devoted to his wife. Together, they would begin a new tradition of royal marriages filled with love and families with warmth.

She squeezed his hands and smiled up at him. "Yes, it is a lot to ask, Rand. But I happen to remember how fairy tales end."

He grinned at her in understanding. Then, tucking her arm in his, he led her out onto the balcony to meet their people.

# ABOUT THE AUTHOR

Tracy Cozzens has been writing for as long as she can remember. She has been a newspaper reporter and editor, a national magazine editor, and a public relations specialist. Born in California, she grew up in Eugene, OR, where she earned a journalism degree from the University of Oregon. She recently moved from Washington State to upstate New York, where she works in communications for a government contractor. She and her husband Steve, a newspaper editor, are the proud parents of their son Kellen, a middle school honor student.

Tracy has won several writing awards, including the Romance Writers of America's 1998 Golden Heart, the highest honor given to unpublished romance writers. Watch for Tracy's second Zebra Bouquet in May 2000, and her first Zebra historical romance, *Star-Crossed,* to be published next spring.

Tracy would love to hear from readers. Write to her c/o Kensington Books, 850 Third Avenue, New York, NY 10022; and visit her Web site at http://members.aol.com/TCozzens.

# BOOK YOUR PLACE ON OUR WEBSITE AND MAKE THE READING CONNECTION!

We've created a customized website just for our very special readers, where you can get the inside scoop on everything that's going on with Zebra, Pinnacle and Kensington books.

When you come online, you'll have the exciting opportunity to:

- View covers of upcoming books

- Read sample chapters

- Learn about our future publishing schedule (listed by publication month *and author*)

- Find out when your favorite authors will be visiting a city near you

- Search for and order backlist books from our online catalog

- Check out author bios and background information

- Send e-mail to your favorite authors

- Meet the Kensington staff online

- Join us in weekly chats with authors, readers and other guests

- Get writing guidelines

- AND MUCH MORE!

**Visit our website at
http://www.zebrabooks.com**

# Coming October 1999 From Bouquet Romances

**#17 Somewhere In The Night** by Marcia Evanick
__(0-8217-6373-3, $3.99) When detective Chad Barnett finds Bridget McKenzie trembling at his door, the devastating memories of the case they worked on together five years ago come rushing back. While he can't deny the beautiful clairvoyant's plea for help, he knows he must resist the tender feelings she stirs in his heart.

**#18 Unguarded Hearts** by Lynda Sue Cooper
__(0-8217-6374-1, $3.99) Pro-basketball coach Mitch Halloran would have sent the gorgeous blonde bodyguard packing, but death threats were no joke—and Nina Wild didn't take "no" for an answer. But when Nina becomes the target of his stalker, he realizes she's the one woman in the world he isn't willing to lose.

**#19 And Then Came You** by Connie Keenan
__(0-8217-6375-X, $3.99) When attorney Cole Jaeger returns to Montana to sell the ranch he inherited from his uncle, he discovers one big problem—feisty beauty Sarah Keller, who not only lives at the ranch, but has the crazy notion that he's a rugged cowboy with a love of country life and a heart of gold.

**#20 Perfect Fit** by Lynda Simmons
__(0-8217-6376-8, $3.99) Wedding gown designer Rachel Banks creates dresses brides can only dream of, even if her own dreams have nothing to do with matrimony. But when blue-eyed charmer Mark Robinson shows up at his sister's final fitting, sparks fly between the two.

---

Call toll free **1-888-345-BOOK** to order by phone or use this coupon to order by mail.

Name_____

Address_____

City_____State_____Zip_____

Please send me the books I have checked above.

I am enclosing                               $_____

Plus postage and handling*                   $_____

Sales tax (where applicable)                 $_____

Total amount enclosed                        $_____

*Add $2.50 for the first book and $.50 for each additional book.
Send check or Money order (no cash or CODs) to:
**Kensington Publishing Corp., 850 Third Avenue, New York, NY 10022**
Prices and Numbers subject to change without notice. Valid only in the U.S.
**All Books will be available 10/1/99.** All orders subject to availability.
Check out our web site at **www.kensingtonbooks.com**

# Put a Little Romance in Your Life With
# Fern Michaels

| | | |
|---|---|---|
| __Dear Emily | 0-8217-5676-1 | $6.99US/$8.50CAN |
| __Sara's Song | 0-8217-5856-X | $6.99US/$8.50CAN |
| __Wish List | 0-8217-5228-6 | $6.99US/$7.99CAN |
| __Vegas Rich | 0-8217-5594-3 | $6.99US/$8.50CAN |
| __Vegas Heat | 0-8217-5758-X | $6.99US/$8.50CAN |
| __Vegas Sunrise | 1-55817-5983-3 | $6.99US/$8.50CAN |
| __Whitefire | 0-8217-5638-9 | $6.99US/$8.50CAN |